POPULAR AMERICAN FICTION

SETH JONES
Edward S. Ellis

AND

DEADWOOD DICK ON DECK
Edward L. Wheeler

Dime Novels

EDITED BY PHILIP DURHAM
University of California, Los Angeles

THE ODYSSEY PRESS · INC · NEW YORK

INTRODUCTION

In the summer of 1937 in an essay in *The Yale Review,* the American historian Merle Curti wrote of the dime novels that these "fragile, rare, and highly fugitive books will be useful . . . to anyone interested in proletarian literature"; and that they "must be taken into account particularly by those interested in the democratization of culture . . . , in the rise and reinforcement of our traditions of adventure and rugged individualism, in the development of class consciousness, and in the growth of American patriotism and nationalism." Now, after nearly thirty years, we are following the historian's suggestion by reprinting two of the hundreds of those "fugitive books" which were so immensely popular in the nineteenth century.

For too long it was customary to look down on popular fiction; if it was written for the masses and cheaply printed, cultivated people either did not read it or did not confess to having read it. Until recently we have been unwilling to admit that much of the peripheral writing, generally far more widely read than "serious" literature, has had a tremendous influence on our social, cultural, political, and economic life. Now in the United States there is a growing awareness that our popular fiction speaks for us. The popular American novel presents a romantic picture of the hero and his culture, but it is significant in the sense that it continues the traditional legends and myths.

Such were the dime novels which were first printed by the publishing house of Beadle and Adams (originally Irwin P. Beadle & Co.) in the summer of 1860. Dime novels had been anticipated several years earlier by twenty-five cent, paper-covered novelettes, but it was the firm of Beadle and Adams which turned this kind of publication into a million dollar business.

Their first dime novel, *Malaeska, the Indian Wife of the White Hunter,* by Mrs. Ann S. Stephens, had already appeared serially in *The Ladies' Companion.* This first novel, set in the Catskills in early Colonial days, was a great success, and Beadle and Adams sought to fill the demand by publishing two such books each month. When they issued number eight on October 2, 1860, they discovered one of the most popular and prolific writers they were to have during the firm's existence; the writer was Edward S. Ellis and the novel was *Seth Jones; or, The Captives of the Frontier.*

As the demand for dime novels increased—it was reported that they were shipped to the Union troops by the freight car load—Beadle and Adams branched out. When the Dime Novel series reached number 321 on November 17, 1874, the firm began the New Dime Novels. But in 1861 they had already started Beadle's American Sixpenny Library, in 1864 Beadle's Dime Fiction; and throughout the thirty-eight years of the firm's existence such further series as American Tales, Pocket Novels, Fireside Library, Half-Dime Library, and Dime Library: thirty-three series in all.

Beadle and Adams understood the mass audience for which they published and took advantage of the reading public by reprinting novels in different series under the same titles or changed titles, by the same authors or under a variety of pseudonyms. Their entire list included over 5,000 titles, but the actual number of original novels, after eliminating duplicates, was 3,158.

The dime novels of the last half of the nineteenth century attempted to be all things to all readers. Trying for every possible audience, Beadle and Adams began the Half-Dime Library in 1877 by reprinting five well-known works during the first two months: *Gulliver's Travels, Aladdin, Baron Munchhausen, Robinson Crusoe,* and *Sinbad the Sailor.* The boys, however, for whom this series was intended, refused to spend their nickels on classics, so Beadle and Adams quickly changed to stories of the Wild West.

The spread of dime novels reached from *Single Eye, A Story of King Philip's War* by Warren St. John, to *Dandy Jack; or, The Outlaws of The Oregon Trail* by T. C. Harbaugh. A general classification is necessary to indicate the variety. The following classification is of 1,531 novels—48 percent of the total and a fair cross section of the whole. Although the grouping is quite general, often arbitrary, and has obvious overlapping, it at least gives some idea as to the scope of the novels. The figure in parentheses following each classification represents the percentage of the whole.

WEST IN GENERAL (30) These deal with romance, hunters, plainsmen, pony express riders, cowboys, Indians, outlaws, horse thieves, cattle thieves, badmen, "desperadoes," gamblers, tough towns, stage holdups, vengeance, violence, and murder. Western life, with all of its facets, is depicted as an exciting adventure, the way it was supposed and expected to be. The romantic plots are stereotyped. Being introduced late in the dime novel period, the cowboys were used only as characters incidental to the story, for the "Cowboy" or "Western" story as we know it today is a twentieth-century genre.

MINERS, MINING, AND MINING TOWNS (10) This group describes life in the gold diggings of the West. In addition to the typical Western heroes and badmen, there are regulators and vigilantes. Gold robberies are introduced in the novels of the 1880's, preparing the way for the coming to the West of the detective.

TEXAS LIFE (6) Using famous Texas heroes and desperadoes, the action develops around the Alamo, the Mexican War, the Rangers, and buffalo hunts. Pictorially, life in the haciendas and at roundups is also expressed.

CITY LIFE (6) The setting for these novels is generally New York City, but it can also be Philadelphia or San Francisco and occasionally a continental capital. Theme situations develop around "poor but honest" girls, bootblacks, and messenger boys, as they seek "true love" and suffer poverty and misfortune, only to find success and wealth in the end.

SEA (6) These contain the standard situations for sea tales: Tripolitan wars, Arctic exploration, South Sea adventure, whaling expeditions, mutiny, buccaneer fighting, and pirates' escapades.

DETECTIVES OF THE CITY (5) The detectives in these novels work mostly on bank robberies and missing jewels; murder mysteries are included but not frequently. When the detective investigated the Haymarket riot and the McCormick Reaper Works riot in Chicago, the dime novel took on a social and political coloration. In the early 1890's the Pinkerton detective was introduced.

DETECTIVES OF THE WEST (5) When the Eastern detective went west to investigate robberies in mining towns, he stayed to become a regular employee of a Cattlemen's Association, riding the range in search of cattle thieves.

INDIAN TALES (4) These novels are of three types: in the early period the Indians were of the Eastern seaboard, fighting in the King Philip's Wars and the French and Indian Wars and acting like inhuman animals toward their captives; during the middle period the locale moved to the Great Lakes where the Indians were the villains in the Pontiac wars and the Minnesota massacres; later, the Indians covered the whole of the West, where they were constantly on the warpath.

BORDER LIFE BEFORE THE CIVIL WAR (4) The pioneers and settlers participate in covered wagon treks, shooting matches, hunting trips, and friendly and unfriendly fighting.

SCOUTS (3) The dime novel scout begins in the image of Leatherstocking and Nick of the Woods, but as the locale moves westward he becomes Buffalo Bill.

AMERICAN REVOLUTION (3) Divided between land and sea battles, these novels tell of the patriots' struggles against the British and of their involvement in the Stamp Act crisis, where Tories are spies and villains.

FUR TRAPPERS (2) The fur trappers of these books are often fictitious mountain men; however, Jim Bridger, Ewing Young, and Kit Carson are among them. Including the Hudson's Bay Company and the Northwest Fur Company, the localities and background materials are generally authentic.

OVERLAND JOURNEYS (2) By dealing specifically with emigrants moving overland, the authors of these novels had an opportunity to express social and religious attitudes concerning the Mormons.

SOUTHERN MISSISSIPPI RIVER (2) The setting of these novels provides an appropriate scene for ante-bellum romance, but most of the writers who use this locale extoll the virtues and vices of gulf pirates, flatboatmen, gamblers, and highwaymen.

COLONIAL TIMES (2) This classification includes the semi-historical treatments of the settlers at Jamestown, New York, Plymouth, and Massachusetts Bay—with the Mathers and witch-hunters.

MEXICO (1) These recount the American invasion, various aspects of the Mexican War, border scrapes, and the activities of the American adventurer in Mexico.

MISCELLANEOUS (9) Of all the novels included here, only a few types can be listed: stories of slavery, the Civil War, circus life, missionaries among the Indians, race tracks, Europeans in America, logging camps, historical aspects of the border in the eighteenth century, the War of 1812, and reprints of English classics.

INTRODUCTION

Although Beadle and Adams reprinted many English and American authors such as Milton, Byron, Dickens, Cooper, and Twain, one can see from the classification that approximately three-fourths of the dime novels deal with the various forms, problems, and attitudes of life on the frontier, and that more than half are concerned with life in the trans-Mississippi West. The breakdown also shows that there was but little of American life which escaped the pen of the dime novelist. In the pages of these fictional, semihistorical novels there is source material in abundance for the literary and social historian if he wants to add to our understanding of the significance of the settlement and development of America during the nineteenth century.

Almost as soon as the house of Beadle and Adams closed its doors in 1898, Dr. Frank P. O'Brien began collecting the fugitive books which had been published by the firm. By 1920 O'Brien had accumulated more than 3,000 items, including duplicated titles, and on May 10, 1920, he brought his collection to the attention of the public by offering 322 items for auction in the Anderson Galleries of New York City.

Realizing the tendency to look down on cheaply-printed popular literature, Dr. O'Brien was careful not to refer to his books as dime novels; the descriptive title of the catalogue was *American Pioneer Life*. The selection of 322 included only those items which could be described as "relating to American pioneer life, character, conditons, exploits, stories, biography and history." When these little novels of pioneer life sold through a Park Avenue gallery for as much as $62 each, the collector, Dr. O'Brien, no longer hesitated to call them what they were: dime novels from the house of Beadle and Adams. Shortly after the auction, Dr. O'Brien presented approximately forty percent of his collection to the New York Public Library. The remaining sixty percent was purchased *en bloc* from the Anderson Galleries by Henry E. Huntington for his library in San Marino, California.

Although the dime novels had their full share of violence, they were otherwise "pure" and sexless. From the very beginning Beadle took the attitude that he was publishing "high-type" literature, and so instructed his authors. Some of his requirements and regulations were:

> We prohibit all things offensive to good taste in expression and incident.
> We prohibit subjects or characters that carry an *immoral* taint.
> We require unquestioned originality.
> We require pronounced strength of plot and high dramatic interest of story.

We require grace and precision of narrative, and correctness in composition.

Authors must be familiar with characters and places which they introduce and not attempt to write in fields of which they have no intimate knowledge.

Beadle and Adams were quite capable of slighting an occasional requirement if the slight increased sales. But when dime novels began to be thought of as "sensational," Beadle advertised that they were "good, pure, and reliable"; "Exhilarating without being feverishly or morbidly exciting"; "elaborate in drama, discriminating in character, choice in incident, and impressive in denouement"; and adaptable "to all classes, readable at all times, fit for all places."

Jacksonian Democracy, frontier independence and self-reliance, and the confidence in manifest destiny all contributed to the democratization of culture which Beadle and Adams included in their dime novels. Class consciousness was evident in the early novels: the heroes and heroines were well-bred and often the real protagonist was held back because he was only a rugged, common type. But as the locale moved west this distinction was gradually abandoned until finally the hero could be a hardened westerner with an unknown background. There began to develop on the frontier a feeling that if one could prove himself all man, a real man under any circumstance, and capable of holding his own, his cultural heredity was not especially important. The West was developing a new definition of culture: the old class lines became unimportant, the new class needed to be physically and mentally strong and independent, and the rather specialized Western moral code had to be adhered to.

Choosing two from among more than 3,000 dime novels of American life is a bit difficult when they all have so much in common and when none is distinguished by an especially brilliant style. *Seth Jones; or, The Captives of the Frontier* was chosen because it was one of the earliest and consistently most popular. *Deadwood Dick on Deck; or, Calamity Jane, the Heroine of Whoop-Up* was one in a typical series which dealt with the legend and myth of the West.

Edward Sylvester Ellis, the author of *Seth Jones*, was born in Ashtabula County, Ohio, April 11, 1840. The son of a famous frontiersman, Edward at age six was taken by his family to New Jersey. As a young man he began teaching in the public schools, a profession he continued while writing dime novels. Eventually he became superintendent of schools in Trenton, and in 1887 he received an M.A. degree from Princeton.

So prolific was Ellis that a complete checklist of his work will probably never be attempted. Under his own name he wrote 150 novels for Beadle and Adams, but he also wrote other novels for them under fifteen different pseudonyms, using such pen names as James Fenimore Cooper Adams and Frank Faulkner. He also wrote dime novels for many other publishers and under several more pseudonyms. Among his many other kinds of writing were dozens of volumes of history—*Library of American History* in nine volumes with 1,200 illustrations, for example.

So popular was *Seth Jones* that Beadle and Adams issued it nine times in eight different series. It is impossible to guess how many millions read it and to determine its impact on the mass audience.

Seth Jones was set in a remote spot in western New York at the end of the Revolutionary War; the characters had emigrated from the more settled provinces of the East. The novel is romantic and in the Cooper tradition, dealing with "nature's noblemen" and an "eccentric" Yankee. The theme is that a truly "enterprising" American will grow tired of civilization and go West where he will find challenges worthy of him. Ellis's heroes were taken to the frontier because it was the most satisfactory proving ground, for "When the Anglo-Saxon's body is pitted against that of the North American Indian, it sometimes yields; but when his mind takes the place of contestant, it never loses."

Yet it was the stoically trained body which the author gloried in exhibiting, over and over. Seth became truly heroic when he could be indifferent to pain and show absolute coolness in the face of danger or probable death.

When Seth was allowed to marry, Ellis deviated from the Natty Bumppo tradition which insists that frontier or Western heroes remain celibate. The marriage is hardly consistent with the plot, but it is an obvious concession to romanticism.

The language is stilted, and it frequently becomes pathetic as Ellis tries for a "daown-Eastern" accent. The grammar and spelling are careless, although some of the errors may have come from a lack of proofreading; Beadle and Adams were working on a quantity basis, and had but little time for the niceties of book publishing. The point is, however, that the mass audience could easily overlook bad grammar while it was getting high adventure.

Edward Lytton Wheeler, author of the Deadwood Dick novels, was born in Avoca, New York, in the middle 1860's. According to Albert Johannsen, little is known about Wheeler other than his published work. Certain it is, though, that Wheeler did not visit the West about which he wrote, and having Cheyenne lie east of the Black Hills was an example of his geographical carelessness. He referred to himself as a "Sensational Novelist," the author of Deadwood Dick Novels, Rosebud Rob Novels, Sierra Sam Novels, and Denver Doll Novels.

On July 25, 1877, Wheeler began Beadle's Half-Dime Library with the first Deadwood Dick novel: *Deadwood Dick, the Prince of the Road; or, The Black Rider of the Black Hills.* The Black Hills had been opened to the miners only the year before, and any stories about Deadwood were in great demand. Wheeler's lore and legend were far more exciting and acceptable to his audience than any realistic account. Using a topical reference and the fabled rider of the Black Hills, Edward Wheeler wrote thirty-three Deadwood Dick novels during the next nine years.

Deadwood Dick on Deck; or, Calamity Jane, the Heroine of Whoop-Up first appeared on December 17, 1878 as number 73 of Beadle's Half-Dime Library and number eight of Wheeler's Deadwood Dick novels. It is typical of the Western melodrama which used every cliché known to the trade. As long as the author utilized a mythical character such as Deadwood Dick, and a real character such as Calamity Jane who became mythical, and as long as his setting was even near the already legendary town of Deadwood, he could throw in as much fiction as he was capable of creating. A creaky plot was no barrier to success if the readers' ears were kept ringing with gun shots. Impossible disguises were overlooked while the villains continued to meet violent deaths. Hardly anyone mourned the loss of fifteen "good guys" in one fight, for the author arranged for them to be men without families. And who noticed or cared (Chapter XIII) that Sandy "knocked the ashes from his pipe" while "smoking an evening cigar"? That was the way the West was.

Edward Wheeler knew well the sympathies of the mass audience for which he was writing. Using a Danite as a villain to exploit the anti-Mormon feeling of the day was a common trick. Having Joe and Sandy keep out of the capitalistic corporation by selling off small pieces of their mining property to individuals was an appeal to the common man during a period of capitalistic strife. But above all, of course, was the constant elevation of those characters of high courage who acted within and lived by the code of the West.

The dime novels had their day and left their impression on the mass culture. But why did such a popular genre disappear, and why should we be bringing this small bit of it back to life? One of the reasons for its disappearance, according to Albert Johannsen, is that the "deterioration of the 'dime' novel may be said to have begun in the early 1880's, and they degenerated rapidly after the introduction of detective, gamin, and bootblack stories." It is also fairly apparent that by the

end of the century the mass audience had become somewhat more so-
phisticated and was demanding something more challenging than Hor-
atio Alger and Edward Ellis.

One reason for bringing these fugitive books to life again is to re-
mind us that the glorification and idealization of the frontier as a dis-
tinctively American phenomenon have been part of America's heritage, and that heritage has probably never been more enthusiastically
exemplified than in the pages of the dime novel.

I wish to thank the American Council of Learned Societies under
whose auspices, several years ago, I began working on Dime Novels.
I also wish to thank Marjorie Griffin for her patience in typing.

My contribution to this volume is for my father and mother.

PHILIP DURHAM

University of California, Los Angeles

BIBLIOGRAPHICAL NOTE

Although the dime novels produced one of the most popular genres
in American history, they have as yet received scant attention as literary, cultural, or social phenomena. There is, however, one truly monu-
mental work on the dime novels: Albert Johannsen, *The House of
Beadle and Adams,* 2 vols. (Norman: Univeristy of Oklahoma Press,
1950), Supplement (1962). This exhaustive work on the publishing
firm of Beadle and Adams is indispensable to anyone interested in a
study of the dime novel.

One of the early articles on the dime novel, interesting for its time,
is Charles M. Harvey, "The Dime Novel in American Life," *The
Atlantic Monthly,* C (July, 1907). At the turn of the century George
Ade wrote some amusing parodies of the dime novels; an example is
Handsome Cyril; or, The Messenger Boy with the Warm Feet (Phoe-
nix: The Bandar Log Press, 1903). Edmund Pearson, *Dime Novels*
(Boston: Brown, Little, Brown, 1929) is an attempt to recapture the
dime novel days by quoting and by reminiscing.

In more recent times there have been a few serious treatments of
dime novels which indicate their importance. One of the best is Merle

Curti, "Dime Novels in the American Tradition," *The Yale Review,* XXVI (Summer, 1937). In Henry Nash Smith, *Virgin Land* (Cambridge: Harvard University Press, 1950), the dime novel hero is treated as "symbol and myth." Suggesting that Robert Montgomery Bird's *Nick of the Woods* is the "granddaddy" of the dime novel is an important contribution in Thomas D. Clark, "Virgins, Villains & Varmints," *American Heritage,* III (Spring, 1952).

One popular dime novel writer, E. Z. C. Judson (Ned Buntline), received full biographical treatment in Jay Monaghan, *The Great Rascal* (Boston: Little, Brown and Company, 1951).

In the introduction to this volume the editor drew on two of his articles: "A General Classification of 1,531 Dime Novels," *The Huntington Library Quarterly,* XVII (May, 1954) and "Dime Novels: An American Heritage," *The Western Humanities Review,* IX (Winter, 1954-55).

The present text for *Seth Jones; or, The Captives of the Frontier* is from Beadle's Half-Dime Library, November 9, 1877; the text for *Deadwood Dick on Deck; or, Calamity Jane, the Heroine of Whoop-Up. A Story of Dakota* is from Beadle's Pocket Library, February 11, 1885.

SETH JONES.

BEADLE AND COMPANY.
NEW YORK: 118 WILLIAM ST. LONDON: 44 PATERNOSTER ROW.
L. Winch, Philadelphia

SETH JONES

or

The Captives of the Frontier

BY EDWARD S. ELLIS

Chapter 1

THE STRANGER

The clear ring of an ax was echoing through the arches of a forest, three-quarters of a century ago; and an athletic man was swinging the instrument, burying its glittering blade deep in the heart of the mighty kings of the wood.

Alfred Haverland was an American, who, a number of years before, had emigrated from the more settled provinces in the East, to this then remote spot in Western New York. Here, in the wilderness, he had reared a humble home, and, with his loving partner and a sister, laid the foundation for a settlement. True, this "settlement" was still small, consisting only of the persons mentioned, and a beautiful blue-eyed maiden, their daughter; but Haverland saw that the tide of emigration was rolling rapidly and surely to the west, and, ere many years, that villages and cities would take the place of the wild forest, while the Indians would be driven further on toward the setting sun.

The woodman was a splendid specimen of "nature's noblemen." His heavy coat lay upon a log a short distance away, and his swelling, ponderous chest was covered only by a close-fitting undergarment, showing the glowing neck and heaving breast. Substantial pants met the strong moccasins which incased his feet. A small raccoon-skin cap rested on the back of his head, exposing his forehead, while his black hair swept around his shoulders. His features were regular, and strongly marked. The brow was rather heavy, the nose of a Roman cast, and the eyes of a glittering blackness. So he stood with one foot thrust forward; his muscles, moving and ridging as they were called into play, betrayed their formidable strength.

Still the flashing ax sunk deeper and deeper into the oak's red heart, until it had gone clean through and met the breach upon the other side. Then the grand old forest-king began to totter. Haverland stepped back and ran his eyes to the top, as he noticed it yielding. Slowly it leaned, increasing each second, until it rushed seemingly forward, and came down to the earth with a thundering crash and rebound. He stood a moment, his hot breath issuing like steam from his chest, and then moved forward toward its branches. At that instant his trained ear detected a suspicious sound, and dropping his ax, he caught up his rifle and stood on the defensive.

3

"How de do? How de do? Ain't frightened, I hope; it's nobody but me, Seth Jones, from New Hampshire," said the new-comer in a peculiar accent. As the woodman looked up he saw a curious specimen of the *genus homo* before him. He is what is termed a *Yankee,* being from New Hampshire; but he was such a person as is rarely met with, and yet which is too often described nowadays. He possessed a long, thin Roman nose, a small, twinkling gray eye, with a lithe, muscular frame, and long, dangling limbs. His feet were incased in well-fitting shoes, while the rest of his dress was such as was in vogue on the frontiers at the time of which we write. His voice was in that peculiar, uncertain state, which is sometimes seen when it is said to be "changing." When excited, it made sounds singular and unimaginable.

The woodman, with characteristic penetration, read the man before him at a glance. Changing his rifle to his left hand, he extended the other.

"Certainly not, my friend; but then, you know, these are times in which it behooves us all to use caution and prudence; and where one is placed in such a remote section as this it would be criminal to be careless, when more than one life is dependent upon me for support and protection."

"Very true, very true; you're right there, Mr.—ah! I declare I don't know your name."

"Haverland."

"You're right, as I said, Mr. Have-your-land, or Haverland, as the case may be. I tell *you* these *are* dubious times—no disputin' that, and I was considerably s'prised when I heard the ring of an ax down in these parts."

"And I was equally surprised to meet your visage when I looked up. Jones, I believe you said was your name?"

"Exactly—Seth Jones, from New Hampshire. The Joneses are a numerous family up there—rather too many of them for comfort—so I migrated. Mought be acquainted, perhaps?"

"No, I have no acquaintance to my knowledge in that section."

"Haven't, eh? Thought that Joneses were pretty generally known through the country. Some remarkable geniuses have sprung from the family. But what under the sun keeps you out in this heathen country? What brought you here?"

"Enterprise, sir; I was tired of the civilized portion of our country, and when such glorious fields were offered to the emigrant as are here spread before him, I considered it a duty to avail myself of them, and I have done so. And now, sir, be equally frank with me, and let me know what induced you to visit this perilous region when you had no reason to suppose that a settlement had yet been commenced by the whites. You look to me as if you were an Indian-hunter or scout."

"Wal, perhaps I am. At any rate, I have been. I was a scout among the Green Mountain Boys, under Colonel Allen, and stayed with them till the Revolution was finished. After that I went to work on the farm and worked a while with the old man. Something occurred in our neighborhood that led me to think it was best for me to leave: I won't say what it was, but I will say it was no crime I committed. I stopped at the settlement down the river a few days, and then come to the conclusion to take a tramp in these parts."

"I am very glad you have come, for it isn't often we get sight of a white face. I hope you will take the welcome of a backwoodsman, and and make your home with us as long a time as you can—remembering that the longer you stay the more welcome you will be."

"I shall probably stay till you git tired of me, at any rate," laughed the eccentric Seth Jones.

"As you are from the East, probably you can give information of the state of feeling among the Indians between that section and us. From your remarks, I should infer, however, that nothing very serious threatens."

"Don't know 'bout that," replied Seth, shaking his head and looking to the ground.

"Why so, my friend?"

"I will tell you what, you, I heerd orful stories 'long the way. They say since this war, the darned red-coats have kept the Injins at work. Leastways, it's pretty sartin they are at work, anyhow."

"Are you sure?" asked the woodman, betraying an anxiety in his speech.

"Purty sure. There's a little settlement down here some miles (I have forgot the name,) sot on by the imps and burned all up."

"Is it possible? Reports have reached me during the past three or four months of the deadly hostility existing between the whites and reds, but I was glad to doubt it. Although I sometimes felt it was wrong."

" 'Twas so; and if you vally that ar' wife of your bussum, and your little cherubims, (as I allow you've got,) you'd better be makin' tracks for safer quarters. Why, how have you stood it so long?"

"My conduct toward the Indians has ever been characterized by honesty and good-will upon my part, and they have ever evinced a friendly feeling toward me and my helpless ones. I place great reliance upon this state of feeling—in fact my *only* reliance."

"Just so; but I tell you, it won't do to trust an Injin. They're obstropertous. Go to put your finger on them, and they ain't thar. Jest so, by gracious."

"I fear there is too much truth in your suspicions," replied Haverland, in a saddened tone.

"I'm glad I've tumbled onto you, coz I begin to git skeerish, and I like to do a feller a good turn, and I'll stick to you, bein' I've found you."

"Thank you, friend, and let us now proceed homeward. I intended to spend the day in work, but your words have taken away all desire."

"Sorry to do it; but it's best, ain't it?"

"Certainly; it would have been wrong had you not warned me of impending danger. Let us go home."

So saying, Alfred drew on his coat, slung his rifle and ax over his shoulder, struck into a path in the forest, which he himself had worn, and with a thoughtful tread, made his way homeward. Close behind him followed his new-made friend.

Chapter 2

THE DARK CLOUD

During the walk homeward, Haverland spoke but few words, although his loquacious friend kept up a continual unremitting stream of talk. The woodman's heart was too heavy to join him in his humorous, pointless words. Although dark and fearful suspicions had flitted before him, he had closed his eyes upon them until he could no longer shun them; they appeared at every turn, and now assumed a terrible certainty.

Although at the time to which we refer, the Revolutionary struggles of the colonies had closed, and their freedom was placed on a firm basis, yet universal peace by no means reigned. Dark, sanguinary and bloody tragedies were constantly enacted upon the frontiers for a generation afterward. The mother country failing in her work of subjugation, continued to incite the Indians to revolting barbarities upon the unoffending inhabitants. They found them too-willing instruments, and, instigated by them, a protracted war was long maintained; and, when the inciting cause was removed, the savages still continued the unequal conflict. As every one acquainted with our history must know, the war on the frontiers has been an almost interminable one. As the tide of emigration has rolled westward, it has ever met that fiery countersurge, and only overcome it by incessant battling and effort.

And even now, as the distant shores of the Pacific are well-nigh reached, that resisting wave still gives forth its lurid flashes of conflict.

In a pleasant valley stood the humble home of Alfred Haverland. His own vigorous arm had cleared off a space on all sides so that his residence stood at some distance from the forest, which rolled away for miles. In the clearing still remained the stumps of the fallen trees, and in some places the rich virgin soil had been broken, and was giving signs of the exhaustless wealth it retained in its bosom, waiting only for the hand of man to bring it forth.

The house itself was such as are generally found in new settlements. A number of heavy logs, placed compactly together, with an opening for a door, and one for a window, were all that could attract attention from the outside. Within, were two apartments, the lower and upper. The former was used for all purposes except that of sleeping, which, of course, was done in the upper. In building it, Haverland had made little preparation for defense, as he fondly hoped it would never be needed for such, and it seemed to him that the idea of danger would ever be before him, should he construct it thus. And, besides, should he use his utmost skill in the purpose mentioned, he knew it would avail him little. He had no means of withstanding a protracted siege, and a handful of assailants could bring him to any terms.

As he stepped forth into the clearing, Ina, his daughter, caught sight of him, and bounded out the cabin to meet him.

"Oh, father! I am glad you have come back so soon, but dinner isn't ready. Did you think it was? I was just telling mother—"

She paused suddenly, as she caught sight of a stranger, and with her hand on her mouth, stood, fearing to approach, and afraid to yield to the impulse of turning, and running into the house again.

"No, I didn't think dinner-time had come, but as I had a friend to visit me, I thought I could entertain him at home better than in the woods. But where is your kiss, dear?"

The father stooped, and touched his lips to the ruby ones of his blooming child, and taking her hand, moved forward toward the cabin.

"Whey! if that ain't a purty flower, then kick me!" exclaimed Seth Jones, in admiration. "Was she originated in these parts? Darter, I s'pose? Perhaps not, though?"

"Yes, she is my daughter, although she was not born in these parts."

"Dew tell. Darned if she ain't a beauty, and that makes what I said —"

The father motioned to him that the theme was forbidden, and they walked silently toward the house.

It was no wonder that Ina Haverland drew forth such encomiums from Seth Jones. She was, indeed, a beautiful creature. She had seen some fifteen or sixteen summers, several of which had been spent in the wilderness, which was now her home. She was rather small in stature, but graceful as a gazelle, free from the restraints which the conventionalities of life impose on those of her age. She had dark hair, gathered in a roll behind, fine expressive blue eyes, a perfect Grecian nose, thin lips, and a full chin, rendering the profile perfectly straight from the forehead downward. Her face was oval, and her complexion almost too light for a full enjoyment of health. Her dress was a semi-civilized one, consisting of a short skirt, with leggings beautifully wrought, and a loose sack, similar to the ones worn at the present day. Her small feet were incased in tiny moccasins, elaborately wrought with beads and Indian ornaments, and a string of wampum hung around the neck.

She led the way toward the house, and the three entered.

Haverland introduced his friend to his sister and wife, as a man who had chanced down in this direction, and who would probably tarry a few days. But the quick eye of his wife caught the thoughtful expression upon her husband's face, and she felt there was something yet unrevealed—something deeper and more important that was to be disclosed. She, however, forbore questioning or hinting, knowing that he would communicate what was necessary when he deemed the proper time had come.

A commonplace conversation was maintained until the meal was prepared by the busy housewife, when they all gathered around the board. An earnest blessing was invoked upon the humble food, and it was partaken of in silence.

"Wife," said Haverland, tenderly, "I will depart awhile with this friend here, and you and Mary may busy yourselves as you think best till I return. Probably I will not be back until toward night. Take no anxiety upon my account."

"I will endeavor not to; but, dear husband, go not far from home, for strange fears have come over me since morning."

Even the usually staid and calm face of Mary betrayed an unusual expression of anxiety.

"Fear not, wife, I will not go far."

Haverland now stepped outside, where he saw Seth, all agape, gazing at Ina, as she passed to and fro in the house.

"By gracious, you, I'm goin' to fall in love with that gal. No 'bjections, I hope?"

"No," answered Haverland, with a faint smile. "her heart is unfettered and I hope it will remain so for a long time."

"Oh! I don't mean to love her as you dew yer old woman—yer wife. I mean just as I would my darter, yer know. She's too small to think about lovers *yit*. Don't you let *sich* a thing git inter her head for five years or more."

"I'll try not to; but let us take a walk. I have something to say, which I would that they should not know for the present."

"All right—but jest hold on a minute."

At this juncture, Ina appeared with a small vessel, as if she intended bringing some water from some spring nigh at hand.

"Hold on a minute, gal, my beauty," said Seth, stepping forward, and reaching for the pail. "That's too big a load for you to carry."

"No, I have done it often, thank you, but it is no work for me."

"But jest let me fetch it *this* time, if only to show my good will, and my activity."

Ina laughingly yielded the vessel, and watched him as he took long, awkward strides toward the point where the path led into the forest.

"How far is it off?" he asked, turning round, as he reached the point mentioned.

"A short distance," answered Haverland; "the path leads to it."

Seth made some unintelligible answer, as he jerked his head back and disappeared.

This simple occurrence that we have just narrated, although trivial in itself, was one of the circumstances which often control important acts, and which seem to show that an all-wise Ruler orders them to suit his purposes, and to bring about good in the end. Seth Jones had no object other than a little amusement in his course, yet before he returned, he saw how fortunate it was.

He strode rapidly forward, and after passing a short distance, reached the spring. As he stooped, he was sure he heard a movement in the bushes beyond; and, as he was about to dip the vessel, he saw, in the smooth face of the water, a movement in the shrubbery. He had too much cunning and prudence to affect knowledge of it, and he filled the vessel without betraying any signs of suspicion. As he rose to the upright position, he gave an apparently careless sweep of his vision, and not twenty feet distant he saw the crouching forms of two Indians! As he turned his back, there was a peculiar, uncomfortable feeling, as he knew that it was the easiest matter in the world to receive one or two cold bullets. He, however, quickened his steps not in the least, and manifested no uneasiness, as he came to view in the clearing and laughingly handed the water to Ina.

"Come, let us go," said Haverland, moving toward the spring.

"Not that ar' way, by a long shot," said Seth, with a meaning shake of his head.

"Why not?"

"I'll tell you, purty soon."

"Let us to the river, then."

"That'll do, 'specially *as it ain't fur from your house!*"

Haverland looked searchingly at him, and saw there was a deep meaning behind those words, yet he said nothing, and led the way toward the river.

This stream was but a few hundred yards from the house, and flowed in a northerly and southerly direction. It was very smooth at this point, and not very wide, yet a mile or so further down it debouched into a large, broad, and deep river. The banks were lined, most of the distance, by close, impenetrable shrubbery, overarched by lofty trees, which were the edges of the almost interminable wilderness that then covered this part of the State, and of which great portions remain unto the present day.

Haverland moved to a spot where he had often stood and conversed with his wife, when they first entered the place. Resting his rifle upon the earth, and folding his arms over the muzzle, he turned around and looked Seth full in the face.

"What did you mean by telling me not to *go far from* the house?"

"Jest hol' on a bit," replied Seth, bending his ear as if to listen. Haverland watched him earnestly, and he also heard something unusual—as if some one were rowing a canoe in the water. His companion then stepped down to the water's edge, and signaled for him to approach. Haverland did so, and looked down the river. Some hundred yards off, he saw a canoe rapidly moving down-stream, impelled by the oars of three Indians.

"That is what I meant," said he, in a whisper, stepping back.

"Did you see them?" asked Haverland.

"I reckon I did. They were at the spring watching for your gal to come, so that they mought run off with her."

~~~~~~

Chapter 3

THE DARK CLOUD BURSTS

"Are you certain?" asked Haverland, with a painful eagerness.

"As sure as I live!"

"How? when? where did you see them? Pray, answer quick, for I feel that the lives of precious ones stand in peril."

"The facts are few—they are. When I went down to the spring, I see'd them pesky varmints thar, and I knowed they war waitin' for your little booty, 'cause if they wa'n't, they'd have walloped me, thunderin' soon. I see'd 'em sneakin' 'round, and purtended as though I didn't s'picion nothin'. They've found I's about, and have gone down for more help. They'll be back here to-night with a whole pack. Fact, by gracious!"

"You speak truly; and as matters stand thus, it is time for *action*."

"Exactly so; and what is it you propose to dew?"

"As you have offered me such signal aid thus far, I must again ask you for advice."

"Pshaw! don't you know what to dew, man?"

"I have a plan, but I would hear yours first."

"Wal, I can give it purty soon. You know well enough you're in tight quarters, and the best thing you can do is git away from here a leetle quicker nor no time. You know the settlements ain't more nor twenty miles off, and you'd better pack up and be off, and lose no time, neither."

"That was my plan, exactly. But hold! we must go by water, and will it not be best to wait and go by night, when we will have the darkness to protect us? We have just learned that the river contains enough enemies to frustrate our designs, should they be known. Yes, we must wait till night."

"You're right there; and, as there is no moon, we'll have a good chance, especially as we have to go down-stream instead of up. I tell *yeou*, the war *is* going on. When I left home, I had an idee things could be fixed so as to stop these infarnal red-skins from committin' on their depredations, although they looked mighty squally; but 'tain't no use, and it won't do to trust these critters."

Shortly after, Haverland turned and entered the house, followed by Seth. He called his wife and sister in, and explained, in a few words, the circumstances. It was but a realization of the fears entertained, and no time was lost in useless laments. Preparations were immediately made for the removal. The woodman owned a large boat, somewhat similar to the flatboats seen at this day upon the western waters. This was hauled in beneath the shrubbery which overhung the bank, and into this their things were placed. During the removal Seth remained along the riverbank, keeping watch of the stream, lest their enemies might return unawares.

The removal occupied most of the afternoon, and it was not until the shadows were lengthening across the river that the last article was placed on board. This completed, all seated themselves in the boat and waited for the rapidly-approaching darkness, to glide out into the stream.

"It is hard," said Haverland, somewhat moodily, "to leave one's home after all the difficulty in rearing it is finished."

"Fact, by gracious!" added Seth, whom Mary eyed very closely, as if not satisfied with the fellow's ways and looks.

"But it is best, dear husband. Let us hope, now, that the war is ended, and that, as we have passed through as great dangers as those that now threaten us, the time is not far distant when we may return to this spot with safety."

"We can die but once," said Mary, abstractedly, "and I am ready for any fate."

Seth studied her face with a quick keen glance, then smiled, and said: "Oh, you look a-here. I am captain here, by your leave, my dears, and I ain't goin' to allow any sick stomachs in this here crew." His sunny face seemed greatly to encourage the little band.

"I wouldn't fear to remain here now," said Ina, bravely; "I am *sure* we soon may return. I *feel* it."

Haverland kissed his child, but made no further reply, and all relapsed into stillness, and ceased further conversation. There was something in the gathering gloom around, something in the peculiar situation in which they were placed, that imparted a despondency to all. The boat was still fastened to the shore, and the time for loosening it was close at hand. Mrs. Haverland had passed within the rude cabin, the door of which remained open, while Seth and the husband remained in the stern. Ina sat near at hand, and had fallen into the same silence that rested upon the others.

"Doesn't it look dark and awful, back there?" she asked, in a whisper, of Seth, pointing toward the shore.

"It does, somewhat, I think."

"And yet I wouldn't be afraid to go back to the house."

"You'd better stay in the boat, young 'un."

"You think I am *afraid*, do you?" she said, bounding out of the boat to the shore.

"Ina! Ina! what do you mean?" asked the father, sternly.

"Oh, nothing; only I want to take a little run to ease my limbs."

"Come back here, instantly!"

"Yes—oh, father! quick! quick! come and take me!"

"Seize the oar and shove out!" commanded Seth, springing into the water, and shoving the boat off.

"But, for God's sake, my child!"

"You can't help her—the Injins have got her. I see 'em; drop quick, they're going to fire! look out!"

At that instant there was the sharp crack of several rifles from the shore, and several tongues of fire flamed from the darkness, and the wild yell of a number of Indians pealed out in horrid strength.

Had it not been for Seth all would have been lost. He comprehended everything in an instant, and saved the others.

"Oh, father! mother! The Indians have got me!" came in agonized accents from the shore.

"Merciful God! must I see my child perish without heeding her cry?" groaned Haverland, in spirit.

"No, they won't hurt her, and we must take care of ourselves while we can. Don't stand up, for they can see you."

"Father, will you leave me?" came again in heartrending tones.

"Don't be scart, young 'un," called out Seth; "keep up a good heart. I'll git you ag'in ef you behave yourself. I will, as sure as I am Seth Jones. Just keep up pluck, little one." The last words were shouted loudly, for the boat was fast gliding into the stream.

The mother had heard all, and said nothing. She comprehended it, and with a groan sunk back upon a seat. Mary's eyes flashed like a tigress at bay; and she did not cease to cast looks of indignation at Seth, for leaving the child to her horrid fate so coolly. But she said nothing—was as quiet and pale as a statue. Seth eyed her like a lynx; his eyeballs seemed like fire. But he was as cool as if at his ease perfectly; and he quickly made all feel that he was born for such appalling emergencies.

They were now in the center of the stream, and moving quite rapidly. The darkness was so great that the shores were now vailed from sight. And with hearts in as deep a gloom, the fugitives floated downward.

Chapter 4

THE LOST HOME AND A
FOUND FRIEND

It was on the morning of the day which we have just seen close. As will be remembered, the air is clear and the day one of the most beautiful and pleasant of the year. The air was perfectly still, and had that peculiar, bracing sharpness which is only felt when it is in a perfect state of rest. It was such a morning as would make every healthy person feel that to merely *live* was pleasure.

That part of the State of New York in which the first scenes of this life-drama are laid, was a country at this time cut up and diversified by numerous streams—the greater number of comparatively small size, but a few of considerable magnitude. Skirting and between these were thousands of acres of thick, luxuriant forest, while in some places were plains of great extent entirely devoid of timber.

It was about the middle of the day referred to, that a single horseman was slowly skirting one of these open patches of country, a few miles distant from Haverland's home. A mere glance would have shown that he had come a great distance, and both he and the animal he bestrode were jaded and well-nigh worn out. He was a young man, some twenty or twenty-five years of age, attired in the costume of a hunter; and, although fatigued with his long ride, the watchfulness of his motions would have shown any one that he was no stranger to frontier life. He was rather prepossessing in appearance—had fine dark eyes, curly hair and whiskers, and expressive Roman nose, and small and finely-formed mouth. In front, a long, polished rifle rested across the saddle, ready for use at a second's warning. His horse's sides were steaming and foamy, and the animal made his way along with painfully evident weariness.

As the day waned, the traveler looked about him with more interest and eagerness. He carefully examined the streams he crossed, and the pieces of wood, as though searching for some landmark or habitation. At length he manifested a pleasure in what he saw, as though the signs were as he wished, and hurried the lagging steps of his animal.

"Yes," said he to himself, "the woodman's house cannot be far from this. I remember this stream, and that wood yonder. I shall then be able to reach it by night. Come, my good horse, go ahead with better spirits, for you are near your journey's end."

A short time after, he crossed a small stream that dashed and foamed over its rocky bed, and entered the broad tract which led to the clearing in front of Haverland's door. But although he had a tolerably correct idea of his situation, he had sadly miscalculated the distance. It was already dusk when he struck the stream several miles above where we have seen the fugitives take it. This river, or creek, he knew led directly by the cabin he was seeking, and he determined to keep it until he had reached his destination. His progress was now quite tardy, from being often obliged to pass around the thick undergrowth which lined the river; and, when he reached a point that he knew was a mile distant from Haverland's cabin, it was far in the night.

"Come, my good horse, we have had a longer tramp than I expected, but we are now very near the termination of our journey. Heigh! what does that mean?"

This last exclamation, or question was caused by seeing directly ahead of him, a bright, lurid glare shoot high into the heavens.

"Can it be that the woodman's house is fired? Impossible! and yet, that is the precise spot. Heavens! something is wrong!"

Agitated by strong and painful emotions, Everard Graham (such was his name) now hurried his horse toward the spot from which the light emanated. In a short time he had proceeded as far as he dared with his horse, then dismounting, he tied him, and made his way cautiously forward on foot. The light was so strong that he found it necessary to pick his way with the greatest care.

A few moments sufficed to show him all.

He saw the house of Haverland, the one in which he expected to pass the night, but one mass of flame. And around it were a score of dark forms, leaping and dancing, and appearing, in the ghastly light, like fiends in a ghostly revel.

Graham stood a moment spell-bound with horror and amazement. He expected to see the reeking bodies of Haverland and his family, or hear their groans of agony; but, as he continued gazing, he became convinced that they were either slain or had escaped, as there were no signs of their presence. He could not think they had escaped, and was compelled to believe they had been tomahawked, and had perished in the flames.

It was a ghastly and almost unearthly sight—the small cabin, crackling and roaring in one mass of living flame, throwing strange shadows across the clearing, and lighting up the edges of the forest with a brightness almost as great as the sun at noonday—the score of dusky beings, leaping and shouting in wild exultation, and the vast wilderness, shutting down like an ocean of darkness around.

Gradually the flames lessened, and the woods seemed to retreat into the gloom; the shouts of the savages ceased, and they, too, disappeared; and the building, which hitherto was a mass of crackling fire, was now a heap of slumbering coals and embers, which glowed with a hot redness in the darkness.

An hour or two afterward, a shadowy form could have been seen gliding stealthily and silently around the glowing ruins. He appeared like a specter as seen by the reflected light of the slumbering coals, or might have been taken for the shadow of some ruin of the building. At intervals he paused and listened as though he half expected to hear the footfall of some one, and then again continued his ghostly march around the ruins. Several times he stopped and peered into the embers, as though he supposed the whitened bones of some human being would greet his vision, and then he recoiled and stood as if in deep and painful thought. It was Everard Graham, searching for the remains of Haverland and his family.

"I see nothing," he said musingly, "and it may be that they have escaped, or their bodies are now cooking in that heap of coals, and yet something tells me that they are not. And if it is not thus, what can have become of them? How could they have eluded the malignant vengeance of their savage foes? Who could have warned them? Ah, me! in spite of the unaccountable hope which I feel, my own sense tells me there are no grounds for it. Sad is the fate of the unprotected at this time."

"Fact, by gracious!"

Graham started as though he had been shot, and gazed around. A few yards off he could just discover the outlines of a man standing as if he were contemplating himself.

"And who are you?" he asked, "that appears upon this spot at such a time?"

"I am Seth Jones, from New Hampshire. Who mought be you that happens down in these parts at this pertickler time?"

"Who am I? I am Everard Graham, a friend of the man whose house is in ruins, and who, I fear, has been slaughtered with his family."

"Exactly so; but don't speak so loud. There mought be others about, you know. Jist let's step back here, where 'tain't likely we'll be obsarved."

The speaker retreated into the darkness, while Graham followed him. At first he had some slight misgivings, but the tones and voice of the stranger reassured him, and he followed him without distrust or hesitation.

"You say you're a friend of Haverland's, eh?" asked Seth, in a whisper.

"I am, sir; I was acquainted with him before he moved out in these parts. He was an intimate friend of my father's, and I promised to pay him a visit as soon as I could possibly do so, and I am here for that purpose."

"Jest so; but you took a rather ticklish time for it, I reckon."

"So it seems; but, if I wished to wait until it would be perfectly safe, I'm afraid my visit would never be made."

"Fact, by gracious!"

"But allow me to ask whether you know anything of the family?"

"I reckon that, perhaps, it mought be possible I do, seein' as how I've been around these times."

"Are they slain, or captives?"

"Neyther."

"Is it possible they have escaped?"

"Jest so. I helped 'em off myself."

"Thank Heaven! Where are they?"

"Down the river, at one of the settlements."

"How far distant is it?"

"A dozen miles, p'raps, though it mought be more, and then ag'in it mightn't."

"Well, let us then hasten to them, or, let me, at least, as I have nothing to detain me here."

"I'm willing," said Seth, moving forward, "but I forgot to tell you the darter's 'mong the Indians. I didn't think of that."

Graham started; for, perhaps, the shrewd reader has already suspected he had more than a passing interest in the fate of Ina. Visions of a fair, childish face *had* haunted him, and his perilous journey was owing much to their enchantment. He had played with her in childhood, and while they were yet children they had separated; but they had pledged their hearts to each other, and looked hopefully forward to a reunion in later years. Graham had dreamed of this meeting a long time; and, now that it was so cruelly thwarted, he felt agonized indeed. Years before, when still a boy, although quite a large one, he had visited this section, and the memory of that visit had ever been a bright dream in the past. He mastered his emotion in a moment, with a strong effort, and asked his companion, calmly:

"What tribe has captured Ina?"

"Them infarnal Mohawks, I believe."

"How long ago did it occur?"

"Only a few hours, as you can see by them coals there."

"Will you be kind enough to give me the particulars?"

"Sartinly."

And thereupon Seth proceeded to narrate the incidents given in the preceding chapter, adding, however, that the parents and sister were safe. He had accompanied them himself down to the settlement mentioned, where, leaving them, he had made all haste back again, and had arrived just in time to meet Graham. At first, he said, he mistook him for a savage, and as he was alone, he came very near shooting him; but, as he heard him communing with himself, he discovered at once that he was a white man.

"And what has brought you back here?" asked Graham, when he had finished.

"That's a pooty question to ax me, I swow! What has brought me back here? Why, the same thing, I cac'late as has brought you—to find out what is to be found out 'bout Ina, that purty darter."

"Ah—pardon me, friend, I am glad to hear it, and I am free to confess that that inducement has had more in bringing me here than anything else. From your starting alone to rescue her, I presume you entertained hopes of recovering her, and, as you, alone, entertained such hopes, I judge there is greater room for them, when another one joins you."

"Did I say, stranger, I 'spected to git that gal again?" asked Seth, in a low tone.

"You did not say so in words, it is true; but from *what* you said, I judged such was your intention. Was I mistaken?"

"No, sir; that's what I meant."

"I see no reason why we should not be friends, as we are both actuated by a desire to rescue an unfortunate one from the horrors of Indian captivity, and I trust, without that fact, we would find nothing distasteful in each other."

"Them's my sentiments, 'zactly. Give us your hand."

The two closed hands with a true friendly gripe, and could each have seen the other's face in the darkness, he would have beheld a radiant expression of friendship. They then retired further into the wood and continued the conversation.

We may mention in this place, that the Indians who had captured Ina were, as Seth had remarked, members of the Mohawk tribe. This tribe itself was a member of the "Five Nations," including with them the Seneca, the Cayuga, Onondaga, and Oneida tribes, which have become quite famous in history. They are known among the French as the *Iroquois*, and among the Dutch as *Maquas*, while at home they are called Mingoes, or *Agamuschim*, signifying the *United People*. The Mohawks, or *Wabingi*, first existed separately and alone. The Oneidas then joined them, and these, in turn, were followed by the Onondagas, Senecas, and Cayugas. In the beginning of the last century, the Tuscaroras of the South joined them, after which they took the name of the Six Nations. Of course, they were all united, and war made upon one tribe, was made upon all. They were truly a formidable confederation, and the Revolution testifies to what deeds they were sufficient when instigated by the British. During the predatory warfare which long existed upon the Old Frontier, the white settlers relied mainly upon stratagem to outwit their foes, and it was by this means alone that Seth Jones hoped to rescue Ina from their hands.

~~~~~~

Chapter 5

ON THE TRAIL, AND A SUDDEN
DEPARTURE FROM IT BY SETH

"The Mohawks, you say, have then captured her?" remarked Graham, after a moment's pause.

"Yes; I know it's them."

"Did you get a glimpse of them?"

"I came up as soon as possible, and they were leaving at that moment. I saw one or two of them, and know'd it was them, sure 'nough. Howsumever, that don't make no difference, whether it's the Mohawks, Oneidas, or any of them blasted Five Nation niggers. They are all a set of skunks, and one would just as lief run off with a man's gal as not. There ain't any difference atwixt 'em."

"I suppose not. The same difficulties would have to be surmounted in each case. The point is not whether one shall make an attempt at a rescue, but how it shall be done. I confess I am in a maze. The Mohawks are an exceedingly cunning people."

"That's a fact—that needn't be disputed."

"But then, you know, if we outwit them, we will not be the first whites who have done such a thing in their day!"

"That's a fact, too. Now, jest hold on a minute, while I think."

Graham ceased talking for a moment, while Seth remained as if in deep and anxious thought. Suddenly lifting up his head, he remarked:

"I have it."

"Have what? The plan which must be pursued by us?"

"I ca'c'late I have."

"Well, out with it."

"Why, it's this. *We've got to git that gal,* an' no mistake."

Despite the gloominess which had been upon Graham, he could not help laughing outright at the serious tone in which this was uttered.

"What are you laughing at?" indignantly demanded Seth.

"Why, I thought we had arrived at that conclusion long since."

"I didn't think of that; so we did. Howsumever, I've thort further—hey, what's that off yonder? Nother building burning?"

Graham gazed in the direction indicated, and saw that day was breaking. This he remarked to his companion.

"Yes, so 'tis; and I'm glad of it, for we want some light on this subject."

In a short time, the sun appeared above the forest, and poured a flood of golden light above the woods and streams. Birds were singing their morning songs in every part of the wood, and everything wore as gay a look as though no deed of blood had been committed during the night. As soon as it was sufficiently light, Seth and Graham made their way toward the stream.

"As we shall shortly start," remarked the latter, "I will attend to my horse, which I brought with me. He is but a short distance away, and I will be back in a moment."

So saying, he departed in the wood. He found his horse completely worn out, asleep on the ground. He unloosened his fastening, and as there was abundant provender around in the shape of young and tender twigs and luxuriant grass, he removed the saddle and bridle, and concluded to allow him free scope of the wood until his return, trusting to the rather doubtful chances of ever recovering him again. This done, he returned to his companion.

He found Seth leaning upon his rifle and gazing meditatively into the silent stream flowing before him. Graham looked curiously at him a moment and then said:

"I am ready, Seth, if you are."

The individual addressed turned without a word and strode toward the clearing. When the ruins of the house were reached they both halted, and in an undertone he said:

"Hunt up the trail."

Each bent his head toward the ground and moved in a circle around the clearing. Suddenly Graham paused and proceeded quickly several yards in the wood, halted and exclaimed:

"Here it is, Seth."

The latter hastened to his side, and stooping a moment, and running his eye along the ground, both forward and backward, replied:

"This is the trail! They ain't very keerful 'bout it now, but I reckon it'll make us open our peepers wider to see it, after we get into the wood."

"Well, as the starting-point is now reached, we must perfect our arrangements. You must take the lead in following this up."

"Can't you?" asked Seth, looking up in his eyes.

"Not as well as you. From what little I have seen of you, I am sure you excel me in the knowledge of the forest. I have had some experience in fighting, but very little in tracing a foe through such a wilderness as this."

"Don't say? That's just where you an' I disagree. I was always the one to track the tories or red-coats for old Colonel Allen, and I remember one time—but I guess I won't go to telling stories now, being as I haven't much time; but I can say, though p'raps I oughtn't to, that I can foller any red-skin as far as he can go, and I don't care how much pains he takes to cover up his tracks. You see, if I undertake to foller this, I've got to keep my nose down to the ground, and won't be likely to see any danger we're running into; that'll have to be your business. You just hang close to my heels, and keep your eyes traveling all over."

"I'll endeavor to do my part, although I shall expect some aid from you."

"I may give some, as I can tell purty near 'bout when the imps have gone over the tracks I'm looking at. And now we must start. I promised Haverland that I wouldn't show myself again until I could tell him something about his darter, and I swow, I won't. Come ahead."

With these words, Seth started ahead on a rapid walk. He was slightly inclined forward, and his keen gray eye was bent with a searching look upon the ground. Graham followed him a few feet distant, with the barrel of his rifle resting in the hollow of his left arm, while the stock was held in his right, so as to be ready at a moment's warning.

The signs that led Seth Jones forward were faint, and to an ordinary observer, invisible. The Indians, although they had little fears of pursuit, were yet too cunning and experienced to neglect any caution that would mislead what enemies might be disposed to follow them. They traveled in Indian file, each one stepping in the track of the one before him, so that, judging from the tracks made, it would appear that but a single savage had been journeying in these parts. Ina was compelled to walk in this manner, and more than once when she inadvertently made a misstep, a cruel blow warned her of her task.

Sometimes the leaves, as they lay, appeared perfectly devoid of the slightest depression or disturbance, yet, had one stooped and carefully scrutinized the ground, he would have seen the faint outlines of a moccasin defined upon it, or observed that a leaf had been displaced, or perhaps a slender twig had not yet recovered the position from which it had been forced by the passing of human feet. All these were trifling indications, it is true, yet they were unerring ones to the practiced eye of the hunter, and as plain as the footprints upon the dusty roads. Soon Seth paused, and raising his head, turned toward Graham.

"We are gaining on 'em."

"Ah—are we? Glad to hear it. When is it probable we shall overtake them!"

"Can't exactly say, but not for a considerable time yet. They are tramping at a purty good gait, and they only halted last night to rest Iny now and then. Darn 'em! she'll want rest, I ca'c'late, mor'n once afore she's done with 'em."

"Can't you conjecture their number?"

"There's somewhere in the neighborhood of twenty of the best warriors of the Mohawks. I can tell that by their tracks."

"How is that? They make but a single one, do they?"

"Of course not, but I rayther ca'c'late they make that a little different, fur all that, from what one would. Are you hungry?"

"Not at all; I can stand it till noon, without the least inconvenience."

"So can I; keep a good look-out, and now ahead again."

With these words, Seth again plunged into the woods, and the two prosecuted their journey much as before. The sun was now high in the heavens, and its warm rays pierced the arches of the forest at many points, and there were golden patches of light scattered over the travelers' path. Several times they crossed small, sparkling streams, where sometimes could be seen signs of the pursued having slaked their thirst, and more than once the frightened deer bounded ahead, and paused and gazed in wonder at them, then leaped away again. Graham could hardly resist the temptation of bringing one of them down, especially as he began to feel a desire to taste them; but he too well knew the danger of risking a shot, when it might bring down their most mortal enemies in a moment down upon them.

All at once Seth halted and raised his hand.

"What does this mean?" he asked, gazing off in a side direction from the trail.

"What is it!" queried Graham, approaching him.

"The trail divides here. They must have separated, though I can't see what has made them."

"Isn't it a strategem of theirs to mislead pursuers?"

"I believe it is! Here, you follow the main trail, while I take the side one, and we'll soon see."

Graham did as directed, although it cost him considerable trouble to perform his part. It proved as they expected. In a short time, the two trails united again.

"We must look out for such things," remarked Seth. "I've got to watch the ground closer, and you must look out that I don't pitch heels over head into a nest of hornets."

They now proceeded cautiously and rapidly forward. About the middle of the afternoon, they halted beside a stream of considerable size. Seth produced a quantity of dried venison, which he had brought with him from the settlement, and of this they made a hearty meal. This done, they arose and again proceeded on their journey.

"See there!" said Seth, pointing to the middle of the stream. "Do you see that stone there? Notice how it is marked, and observe that print of a moccasin beside it. One of their number has slipped off of it. Let us be keerful."

He stepped into the water, and made his way carefully across, followed by Graham. When they stepped upon dry land again, the shades of evening were gathering over the forest, and already the birds had ceased their songs. There was, however, a bright moon—in fact, so bright, that they determined to keep up their pursuit.

The progress was now necessarily tardy, as it required the utmost of Seth's vision to keep the trail, and had it not been for the friendly openings in the wood, where it was as plain as at mid-day, they would have been compelled to abandon it altogether until morning. Several times Graham was compelled to stand, while Seth, almost on his hands and knees, searched out the "signs." They came across no evidence of the Indians having encamped, and judged from this that they either intended reaching their tribe before doing so, or that they were somewhere in the vicinity. The latter was the most probable supposition, and prudence demanded them to be cautious and deliberate in their movements.

Suddenly Graham noticed the woods appeared to be growing thinner and lighter in front, as though an opening was at hand. He called the attention of Seth to this, who remarked that it was very probable. In a few moments they heard a noise as of flowing water, and immediately after stood upon the bank of a large creek, or more properly a river. The current was quite rapid, yet, without much hesitation, they plunged boldly in and swam across. The night being warm and moderate, they suffered little inconvenience from their wet and clinging clothes, as the exercise of walking kept them sufficiently warm.

As they ascended the bank, they stood upon a vast and treeless plain, over which the trail led.

"Must we cross this?" asked Graham.

"I don't see any other way. There ain't any chance to skirt it, 'cause it appears to run up and down about four thousand three hundred miles, while you can see the other side."

This was true—that is, the latter part of his assertion. The plain before them, from all appearances, was a prairie of great length, but comparatively narrow breadth. The dark line of the woods upon the opposite side could be plainly seen, and did not appear more than a good hour's walk away.

"I don't see any other way," repeated Seth, musingly, to himself. "It's got to be crossed, though it's a ticklish business, I swow!"

"Wouldn't it be better to wait until morning?" asked Graham.

"Why so?"

"We may walk into danger without seeing it, in the night."

"And how do you s'pose we're going to walk over here in daylight, without being targets for all the Injins that are a-mind to crack away at us?"

"Can we not pass around it?"

"Stars and garters! hain't I told you it reaches five thousand miles each way, and it would take us three years to get half-way round?"

"I was not aware that you had given me such interesting information, until just now; but, as such is the case, of course nothing is left for us but to move forward, without losing time talking."

"The trail goes purty straight," said Seth, turning and looking at the ground, "and I've no doubt it heads straight across to the other side. Hope so, 'cause it'll be convenient."

"You must help me keep watch," said Graham; "you will not need to watch the ground all the time, and you will need to keep a look-out elsewhere."

As might naturally be supposed, our two friends, although quite experienced backwoodsmen, had miscalculated the distance to the opposite side of the prairie. It was full midnight ere they reached its margin.

All was silent as death, as they cautiously and stealthily entered the wood again. Not a breath of wind stirred the boughs on the tree-tops, and the soft murmur of the river had long died away into silence. There were a few flying clouds that obscured the moon at intervals, and rendered its light uncertain and treacherous. Seth still pressed forward. They had gone a few hundred yards, when they heard voices! Cautiously and silently they picked their way, and soon saw the light of a fire reflected against the uppermost limbs of the trees. The fire itself was invisible, although it could not be far distant. Seth whispered for Graham to remain quiet, while he moved forward. He then stepped carefully ahead, and soon reached a massive embankment, up which on his hands and knees he crawled. He peered carefully over this, and saw, down in a sort of hollow, the whole Indian encampment! There were over twenty gathered around, most of whom were extended upon the ground asleep, while several sat listlessly smoking and gazing into the fire. Seth looked but a moment, as he knew there were watchful sentinels, and it was fortunate that he had not been discovered, as it was. Carefully retreating, he made his way down again to Graham.

"What's the news?" asked the latter.

" 'Sh! not so loud. They're all there."

"*She,* too?"

"I s'pose, though I didn't see her."

"What do you intend doing?"

"I don't know. We can't do nothin' to-night; it's too near morning. If we git her, we couldn't git a good 'nough start to give us a chance. We've got to wait till to-morrow night. There's a lot of 'em on the watch, too. We've got to lay low till daylight, and foller 'long behind 'em."

The two made their way off in a side direction, so as not to be likely to attract notice in the morning, should any of the savages take the back trail. Here they remained until daylight.

They heard the Indians, as soon as it was fully light, preparing their morning meal; and as they deemed they could see them without incurring great peril, they determined to obtain a glimpse of them, in order to assure themselves whether Ina was among them or not. Each had suspicion the company had separated, and that their trail had been overlooked in the darkness.

Accordingly, the two crept noiselessly to the top. There was a heavy, peculiar sort of brier growing on the summit of the embankment, which was fortunately so impenetrable as to effectually conceal their bodies. Seth pressed against this and peered over. His head just came above the undergrowth and he could plainly see all that was transpiring. Graham, with an unfortunate want of discretion, placed his arm on Seth's shoulder and *gazed over him!* Yet, singularly enough, neither was seen. Graham was just in the act of lowering his head, when the briers, which were so matted together as to hold the pressure against them like a woven band, gave way, and Seth rolled like a log down the embankment, directly among the savages!

Chapter 6

A RUN FOR LIFE

When the sad event just chronicled took place, and Seth made a rather unceremonious entrance into view of the savages, Graham felt that he too was in peril, and his life depended upon his own exertions. To have offered resistance would have been madness, as there were fully thirty Indians at hand. Flight was the only resource left, and without waiting to see the fate of Seth, our hero made a bound down the embankment, alighting at the bottom, and struck directly across the plain, toward the timber that lined the river. He had gained several hundred yards, when several prolonged yells told him that he was discovered, and was a flying fugitive. Casting his eye behind him, he saw five or six Indians already down the embankment and in full chase.

And now commenced a race for life and death. Graham was as fleet of foot as a deer, and as well trained and disciplined, but his pursuers numbered five of the swiftest runners of the Mohawk nation, and he feared he had at last found his match. Yet he was as skillful and cunning as he was sinewy and fleet of foot. The plain over which he was speeding was perfectly bare and naked for six or eight miles before him, while it stretched twice that distance on either hand before the slightest refuge was offered. Thus it will be seen that he took the only course which offered hope—a dead run for it, where the pursuers and pursued possessed equal advantages.

He was pretty certain that his pursuers possessed greater endurance than himself, and that in a long run he stood small chance of escape, while in a short race he believed he could distance any living Indian. So he determined to try the speed of his enemies.

As he heard their yells, he bounded forward almost at the top of his speed. The pursuers, however, maintained the same regular and rapid motion. Graham continued his exertions for about a half-mile, making such use of his arms and limbs as to give the impression that he was doing his utmost. Toward the latter part of the first mile, his speed began to slacken, and his dangling limbs and furtive glances behind him would have convinced any one that he was nigh exhausted.

But this was only a stratagem, and it succeeded as well as he could have wished. The Indians believed he had committed a common and fatal error—that of calling into play the uttermost strength and speed of which he was master at the outset, and that he was wearied out, while they themselves were just warming into the glow of the chase. Seeing this, they sent up a shout of exultation, and darted ahead at the top of their speed, each endeavoring to reach and tomahawk him before his companion.

But their surprise was unbounded when they saw the fugitive shoot ahead with the velocity of a race-horse, while his veins, too, were only filling with the hot blood of exertion. They saw this, and they saw, too, that should such speed continue long, he would be far beyond their reach, and all now ran as they never ran before.

We say Graham's stratagem succeeded. It did, and it gave him the knowledge he wished. It showed him that he had met his match! His pursuers, at least one or two of them, were nearly as fleet as was he; and, although he might distance them for a time, yet ere half the race was finished he would inevitably lose his vantage ground!

Could one have stood and gazed upon this race of life, he would have seen a thrilling scene. Far ahead, over a vast plain, a fugitive white man was flying, and his swift, steady gait showed that his limbs were well trained and were now put to their severest test. As his feet doubled with such quickness beneath him as to be almost invisible, the ground glided like a panorama from under them.

Behind were a half-dozen savages, their gleaming visages distorted with the passions of exultation, vengeance, and doubt, their garments flying in the wind, and their strength pressed to its utmost bounds. They were scattered at different distances from each other, and were spreading over the prairie, so as to cut off the fugitive's escape in every direction.

Two Indians maintained their places side by side, and it was evident that the pursuit would soon be left to them. The others were rapidly falling behind, and were already relaxing their exertions. Graham saw the state of things, and it thrilled him with hope. Could he not distance these also? Would they not leave him in such a case? And could he not escape ere he was compelled to give out from exhaustion?

"At any rate I will try, and God help me!" he uttered prayerfully, shooting ahead with almost superhuman velocity. He glanced back and saw his followers, and they seemed almost standing still, so rapidly did he leave them behind.

But as nature compelled him to again cease the terrific rate at which he was going, he saw his unwearied pursuers again recovering their lost ground. The parties now understood each other. The Indians saw his maneuvers, and avoided the trap, and kept on in the same unremitting, relentless speed, fully certain that this would sooner or later compel him to yield; while Graham knew that the only chance of prolonging the contest rested in his dropping into and continuing his ordinary speed.

They now sunk into the same steady and terribly monotonous run. Mile after mile flew beneath them, and still so exact and similar were their relative rates, that they were absolutely stationary with regard to each other! The two Indians now remained alone and they were untiring—they were determined to hold out to the end!

At last, Graham saw the friendly timber but a short distance from him. The trees seemed beckoning him to their friendly shelter, and, panting and gasping, he plunged in among them—plunged right ahead till he stood upon the bank of a large and rapidly-flowing stream.

When the Anglo-Saxon's body is pitted against that of the North American Indian, it sometimes yields; but when his mind takes the place of contestant, it *never* loses.

Graham gazed hurriedly around him, and in the space of a dozen seconds his faculties had wrought enough for a lifetime—wrought enough to save him.

Throwing his rifle aside, he waded carefully into the stream until he stood waist deep. Then sinking upon his face, he swam rapidly upward until he had gone a hundred yards. Here he struck out into the channel, swimming *up*-stream as well as *across* it, so as not to reach the bank at a lower point. The current was very swift, and required an exhausting outlay of his already fainting frame before he reached the opposite bank. Here he immediately sprung upon the shore, ran quickly a short distance down the stream, making his trail as plain as he could; and then springing into the water, swam rapidly upward, remaining as close to the shore as possible, so as to avoid the resisting current. The reason of these singular movements will soon be plain.

The shore was lined thickly by overhanging bushes, and after swimming until he supposed it time for his pursuers to come up, he glided beneath their friendly shelter, and awaited the further development of things. Almost immediately after, both appeared upon the opposite bank, but at a point considerably lower down. Without hesitation, they sprung into the stream and swam across. As they landed, they commenced a search, and a yell announced the discovery of the trail. Instantly after, another yell proclaimed their disappointment, as they lost it in the river.

The savages supposed that the fugitive had again taken to the water, and had either drowned or reached the other side. At any rate, they had lost what they considered a certain prey, and with feelings of baffled malignity they sullenly swam back again, searched the other side an hour or so, and then took their way back to their companions.

Chapter 7

THE EXPERIENCE OF SETH

"By gracious! stars and garters! &c.! &c.! This is a new way of introducing one's self!" exclaimed Seth, as he sprawled out among the savages around the council-fire.

The consternation of the Indians at this sudden apparition among them may well be imagined. The crackling of the undergrowth above had aroused them, yet the advent of Seth was so sudden and almost instantaneous that ere they could form a suspicion of the true nature of things, he was among them. Their habitual quickness of thought came to them at once. Graham was seen as he wheeled and fled, and as has been shown, a number sprung at once in pursuit, while a dozen leaped upon Seth, and as many tomahawks were raised.

"Now jest hold on," commanded Seth; "there ain't any need of being in a hurry. Plenty time to take my hair. Fact, by gracious."

His serio-comical manner arrested and amused his captors. They all paused and looked at him, as if expecting another outburst, while he contented himself with gazing at them with a look of scornful contempt. Seeing this, one sprung forward, and clenching his hair in a twist, hissed:

"Oh! cuss Yankee! we burn him!"

"If you know what's best, ole chap, you'll take yer paw off my head in a hurry. Ef you don't you mought find it rather convenient to."

The savage, as if to humor him, removed his hand and Seth's rifle, too. Seth gazed inquiringly at him a moment, and then, with an air of conscious superiority, said:

"I'll lend that to you awhile, provided you return it all right. Mind, you be keerful now, 'cause that ar' gun cost something down in New Hampshire."

From what has just been written, it will doubtless be suspected that Seth's conduct was a part which he was playing. When thrown into peril by the impatience of his companion, he saw at once that an attempt at flight was useless. Nothing was left but to submit to his misfortune with the best grace possible; and yet there was a way in which this submission could be effected which would result better for himself than otherwise. Had he offered resistance, or submitted despairingly, as many a man would have done, he would doubtless have been tomahawked instantly. So with a readiness of thought which was astonishing, he assumed an air of reckless bravado. This, as we have shown, had the desired result thus far. How it succeeded after, will be seen in the remaining portion of this history.

Seth Jones was a man whose character could not be read in an hour, or day. It required a long companionship with him to discover the nicely-shaded points, and the characteristics which seemed in many cases so opposite. United with a genial, sportive humor and apparent frankness, he was yet farseeing and cautious, and could read the motives of a man almost at a glance. With a countenance which seemed made expressly to vail his soul, his very looks were deceptive; and, when he chose to play a certain *role*, he could do it to perfection.

Had any one seen him when the conversation above recorded took place, he would have unhesitatingly set him down as a natural-born idiot.

"How you like to burn, eh, Yankee?" asked a savage, stooping and grinning horribly in his face.

"I don't know; I never tried it," replied Seth, with as much *nonchalance* as though it was a dinner to which he was referring.

"E-e-e-e! you will try it, Yankee."

"Don't know yet; there are various opinions about that, p'raps. When the thing is did I mought believe it."

"You *sizzle* nice—nice meat—good for burn!" added another savage, grasping and feeling his arm.

"Just please do not pinch, my friend."

The savage closed his fingers like iron rods and clenched the member till Seth thought it would be crushed. But, though the pain was excruciating, he manifested not the least feeling. The Indian tried again, and again, till he gave up and remarked, expressive of his admiration of the man's pluck:

"Good Yankee! stand pinch well."

"Oh! you wa'n't pinching me, was you? Sorry, I didn't know it. Try again, you mought p'raps do better."

The savage, however, retired, and another stepped forward and grasped the captive's hand.

"Soft, like squaw's hand—let me feel it," he remarked, shutting his own over it like a vise. Seth winced not in the least; but as the Indian in turn was about to relinquish his attempt at making sport for his comrades, Seth said:

"Your paws don't appear very horny," and closed over it with a terrific gripe. The savage stood like a martyr, till Seth felt the bones of his hand actually displacing, and yielding like an apple. He determined, as he had in reality suffered himself, to be revenged, and closed his fingers tighter and more rigid till the poor wretch sprung to his feet, and howled with pain!

"Oh! did I hurt you?" he asked, with apparent solicitude, as the savage's hand slid from his own with much the appearance of a wet glove. The discomfited Indian made no reply but retired amid the jeers of his comrades. Seth, without moving a muscle, seated himself deliberately upon the ground, and coolly asked a savage to lend him a pipe. It is known, that when an Indian sees such hardihood and power, as their captive had just evinced, he does not endeavor to conceal his admiration. Thus it was not strange that Seth's impudent request was complied with. One handed him a well-filled pipe, with a grin in which could be distinctly seen admiration, exultation, and anticipated revenge. From the looks of the others, it was plain they anticipated an immense deal of sport. Our present hero continued smoking, lazily watching the volumes of vapor, as they slowly rolled before and around him. His captors sat about him a moment, conversing in their own tongue (every word of which, we may remark, was perfectly understood by Seth), when one arose and stepped forward before him.

"White man strong; him pinch well, but me make him cry."

So saying he stooped, and removing the captive's cap, seized a long tuft of yellow hair which had its roots at the temple. A stab in the eye would not have caused an acuter twinge of pain; but, as he jerked it forth by the roots, Seth gave not the slightest indication save a stronger whiff at the pipe. The savages around did not suppress a murmur of admiration. Seeing no effect from this torture, the tormentor again stooped and caught another tuft that grew low upon the neck. Each single hair felt like the point of a needle thrust into the skin, and as it came forth, the Indians seated around noticed a livid paleness, like the track of a cloud, quickly flash over their captive's countenance. He looked up in his tormentor's eyes with an indescribable look. For a moment he fixed a gaze upon him, that, savage as he was, caused a strange shiver of dread to run through him.

To say that Seth cared nothing for these inflicted agonies would be absurd. Had the savage dreamed what a whirlwind of hate and revenge he had awakened by them he would not have attempted what he did. It was only by an almost unaccountable power that Seth controlled the horrible pains of both body and mind he suffered. He felt as though it was impossible to prevent himself from writhing on the ground in torment, and springing at his persecutor and tearing him limb from limb. But he had been schooled to Indian indignities, and bore them unflinchingly.

His temple had the appearance of white parchment, with innumerable bloody points in it, as the blood commenced oozing from the wound, and his neck seemed as though the skin had been scraped off! His momentary paleness had been caused by the sickening pain and the intensest passion. His look at the savage was *to remember him*. After the events which have just transpired they remained seated a moment in silence. At last one who appeared to be the leader, addressed, in an undertone, the Indian whom we have just seen retire from the post of tormentor. Seth, however, caught the words, and had he not, it is not probable he would have successfully undergone the last trying ordeal.

The same savage again stepped forward in the circle before the helpless captive, and removing the cap which had been replaced, clinched the long yellow locks in his left hand and threw the head backward. Then whipping out his scalping-knife, he flashed it a second in the air, and circled its cold edge around his head with the rapidity of lightning. The skin was not pierced, and it was only an artifice. Seth never took his eyes from the Indian during this awful minute.

The tormentor again retired. The savages were satisfied, but Seth was not. He handed his pipe back, replaced his cap, and rising to his feet, surveyed for a few seconds the group around. He then addressed the leader.

"Can the white man now try the redman's courage?"

The voice sounded like another person's. Yet the chief noticed it not, and nodded assent to the request, while the looks of the others showed the eagerness and interest they felt in these dreadful proceedings.

The savage who had inflicted all this agony seated himself directly beside the chief. Seth stepped to him, and grasping his arm pressed moderately. The Indian gave a scornful grunt. Seth then stooped and gently took the tomahawk from his belt. He raised it slowly on high, bent down till his form was like the crouching panther ready to spring. The glittering blade was seen to flash as it circled through the air, and the next instant it crashed clean through the head of the unsuspecting savage!

Chapter 8

AN UNEXPECTED MEETING

Wearied and exhausted, Graham crawled forth from the water, and lay down awhile to rest himself upon the soft, velvety carpet of grass. Here, overcome by the terrific strain which his system had undergone, he fell into a deep and lasting sleep. When he awoke, the day had far advanced, and the sun was already past the meridian. After fully awakening, and fervently thanking Heaven for his remarkable preservation and escape, he commenced debating with himself upon the best course for him to pursue. He was now alone in the great wilderness, and what step should he next take? Should he endeavor to hunt up his friend Haverland, or should he press on in the pursuit of the object which had led him thus far?

While these questions were yet unanswered, he mechanically cast his eye up the river, and started as he saw a small canoe coming around a bend quite a distance from him. He had just time to see that there were two beings in it, when prudence warned him to make himself invisible. He stepped behind the trunk of a massive king of the forest, and watched with eager interest the approach of the new-comers. The light canoe shot rapidly over the placid surface of the river, and in a few moments was abreast of him. He saw that the two occupants were white men, and he scanned their countenances with deep interest. The stronger of the two was seated in the center of the light vessel, and dipped the ashen blades deep into the water at every stroke. The other, seemingly an older man, was seated in the stern, and while he controlled the actions of the other, scanned either shore with the experienced eye of the frontiersman. Graham believed, though he knew he had been careful, that his presence was suspected, as the canoe, apparently without any intent of its occupants, sheered off toward the opposite shore. He remained concealed until it was directly abreast of him, when a sudden suspicion flashed over him that one of the men was Haverland, although it was so long since he had seen him that it was impossible to satisfy himself upon that point without a closer view. However, they were white men, and he determined to risk the probabilities of their being friends. In a subdued voice, without coming into view himself, he called to them. He knew he was heard, for the man at the oars halted a second, and glanced furtively toward the shore; but at a slight sign from the other he again bent to them, and they both continued, as though they suspected no danger.

"Hallo, my friends!" called he, in a louder tone, but still concealing himself. There was no notice, however, taken of him, save he fancied a quicker propulsion of the boat forward. He now stepped boldly forth and called:

"Do not be suspicious; I am a friend."

This brought them to a pause, while the one in the stern spoke:

"We are not satisfied of that: for what business have you here?"

"I might with equal justice put that question to you?"

"If you choose to give no answer, we can't wait to bandy words with you. Go ahead, Haverland."

"Hold! Is that Alfred Haverland with you?"

"Suppose it is? What is that to you?"

"He is the man whom, above all others, I wish to see. I am Everard Graham; and, perhaps he remembers the name." The woodman now turned toward the shore with a stare of wonder. A minute sufficed.

"It's he, Ned, sure enough."

With these words he turned the canoe toward shore. A few strokes sent it up against the bank, and he sprung out and grasped the hand of his young friend.

"Why, Graham, what in the name of the seven wonders has brought you here? I forgot—you *did* promise me a visit somewhere about this time, but so many other things have transpired as to make it slip my mind altogether. And I can assure you, I have had enough to break the heart of any ordinary mortal," he added, in a choking voice.

Explanations were then given; and the wonder, gratitude, and apprehension, that followed Graham's story, may be imagined. Before these were given, Haverland introduced his companion, Ned Haldidge.

"Seth promised to bring Ina back," said he, "but I could not bear to remain idle while he alone was searching for her. This good friend here, who has had much experience in border warfare, willingly joined me. I suppose you would like to see the mother; but if you did, you would see a well-nigh broken-hearted one, and I cannot bear to meet her until I have learned more of our darling daughter."

"And if them cowardly Mohawks don't rue the day they commenced their infernal work, then Ned Haldidge is mightily mistaken!" exclaimed that individual, warmly.

"I don't know," smiled Graham, "but that with our present number and present feelings, we might make an open attack upon them, especially as we have a friend in the camp."

"No, sir; that'll never do!" replied the hunter, with a shake of the head. "They can never be overcome in that way. We could have brought a dozen men with us who could have blown the cowards to atoms, but 'twouldn't do."

"You then rely wholly upon stratagem, eh?"

"Nothing else will do with *them* critters."

"And Heaven only knows whether that will," remarked Haverland, in a desponding tone.

"Ah! don't give way, Alf; wait till it's time."

"You must pardon my exhibition of weakness," said he, recovering himself. "Though I feel the strength of an army in these limbs of mine, yet I have the heart of a *father* in this bosom, and I can do any thing for the recovery of my darling daughter. Oh! I can hear her screams yet, as she was torn from us on that night."

Graham and Haldidge remained silent, respecting his deep and moving grief. Soon the father spoke again, and this time his voice and manner were changed.

"But why stand we here idle? Is there nothing for us to do? Are we to remain desponding, when a single effort may save her?"

"That's just what I've been thinking ever since we stopped here," replied Haldidge. "I don't see any use in waiting, especially when there *is* use in doing something."

"Let us depart, then. You will accompany us, of course, Graham?"

"Certainly; but I should like to inquire your intentions?" asked he, pausing on the bank a moment, as the others seated themselves.

"I should think you would remember we can have but *one* intention," answered Haverland, in a tone of slight rebuke.

"That is not exactly what I meant. Of course, I knew your ultimate intention, but I wished to inquire what course you intended to pursue."

"Oh, that's it" replied Haldidge. "I've been considerable among the red-skins of this region, and know that they can be sooner reached by going down the river some distance further—several miles below this bend—and taking the land."

"But my experience tells me you are mistaken this time. Ina's captors are now at no great distance, and the shortest course to them, you will find, is a direct line from here, across the open prairie, the other side of the river."

"At any rate, we will cross to the opposite bank; so step in."

"Wait a minute. What does that mean?"

As Graham spoke, he pointed quickly up the river. From the position of the two within the boat, they could discern nothing.

"Jump ashore, quick, and pull the boat out of sight. There's something afoot, and you mustn't be seen," exclaimed Graham, excitedly, in an undertone, as he stooped and grasped the prow of the canoe. The men sprung ashore, and in an instant the vessel was hauled up out of sight, while the three made themselves invisible, and from their hiding-places eagerly watched the river.

The object which had arrested the attention of Graham was a second canoe, which was just making its appearance round the bend above, which had first brought his friends to view. This latter one was of about the same size, and could be seen to hold either three or four persons. The dark-tufted heads of the occupants, rising like statues in the boat, showed unmistakably that they were Indians.

As it came nearer and nearer, Haldidge whispered there was a fourth person in the stern, *and she was a female*. Haverland and Graham breathed hard, for a wild hope filled the heart of each; but as the canoe came abreast of them, while they could plainly distinguish the features of the three savages, they could not gain a glimpse of the fourth person. She was covered by an Indian shawl, and her head was bowed low upon her bosom, as though in painful thought.

"Let us fire and send these three dogs to eternity," whispered Graham.

Haldidge raised his hand.

" 'Twon't do; there may be others about, and if that other one is Ina, it may only be the means of her destruction. Alf, do you think that is her?"

"I can't tell—yes, by Heaven, 'tis her! Look! she has moved her shawl. Let us rescue her at once!" exclaimed the father, rising, and about to start.

"Hold!" imperatively and half angrily commanded Haldidge, "you will spoil all by your rashness. Don't you see it is near night? They are now below us, and we cannot get them in such a range as to insure us each of them. Wait till it is darker, and we will pursue them. I have a plan which I think cannot fail. Just restrain yourself for a short time, and I will bring things about in a manner that will surprise them as much as it will you."

Haverland sunk down again beside the others. The night was now fast coming on, and in a few minutes the light birch canoe was shoved noiselessly into the water, and the three made ready for the race for life and death.

Chapter 9

THE CHASE

The night was even closer at hand than our friends suspected. In the forest, where the withdrawal of the sun was almost simultaneous with darkness, it came without much warning. The gloom was already settling over the water, and Haverland instantly shot the canoe from under the shrubbery out into the stream. There were rowlocks and oars for a second person, and Graham took up a couple of them and joined his labors with his friend, while Haldidge took the steering-oar. As they passed boldly into the channel, the canoe ahead was just disappearing around a bend below.

"Come, this won't do; we mustn't let them keep out of our sight," said Haverland, dipping his oars deep into the water.

A heavy darkness was fast settling over the river, and our friends noted another thing. A thick, peculiar fog, or mist, such as is often seen of summer nights, upon a sheet of water, was already beginning to envelope the bank and river. This, as will be evident, while it would allow the pursuers to approach the Indian canoe much closer than otherwise, still gave the latter a much greater chance of eluding them. Haldidge hardly knew whether to be pleased with this or not.

"It may help us in the beginning, boys, but we've got to hold on till it's fairly down on us. If the rascals catch a glimpse of us before, they'll give us the slip as sure as fate. Just lay on your oars a few minutes. We can float down with the current."

"I allow it's the best plan, although I am much in favor of dashing ahead, and ending the matter at once," remarked Graham, nervously handling his oars.

"And while I think of it," pursued Haldidge, "I don't see as it would do any hurt to muffle the oars."

Before starting they had abundantly provided themselves with means for this, and in a few moments a quantity of cloth was forced into the rowlocks, so as to be able to give full sweep to the oars without making enough noise to attract suspicion from the shore, unless an ear was listening more intently than usual.

By this time, too, the thick mist mentioned had enveloped the river in an impenetrable cloud, and they shot boldly into it. The light vessel flew as swiftly and noiselessly as a bird over the water. Haldidge understood every turn and eddy in the stream, and guided the canoe with unerring certainty around the sharp bends, and by the rocks whose black heads now and then shot backward within a few feet of their side.

In this way a mile was passed, when he raised his hand as a signal for them to cease efforts for a moment.

"Listen!" he uttered.

All did so, and faintly, yet distinctly and distantly, they heard the almost inaudible dip of oars, and the click of the rowlocks.

"Is that above or below?" asked Haverland, bending his head and intently listening.

"I think we have *passed* them, sure enough," replied Graham.

The sound certainly appeared to come from above them, and all were constrained to believe that, rowing as swiftly and powerfully as they did, they must have swept by them in the darkness without suspecting their proximity.

"Can it be possible?" questioned Haldidge, wonderingly and doubtingly.

But such was the character of the river-banks at this point, that all had been deceived in listening to the sounds, and the Indians were all the time leaving them far behind. It was not until they heard unmistakably the sounds receding in the distance that they became conscious of the true state of matters. At that moment, as they were dying out, they all heard them plainly enough far below.

"We might have known it," said Haldidge, in vexation. "You've got to lay to it, to catch them now."

"But is there not danger of running afoul of them?"

"Not if we are careful. I think they will run in to shore, soon, and if so, it will be the eastern bank. I will hug that closely, and keep my ears open.

The two now bent to their oars with redoubled powers. They dipped the ashen blades deeply and pulled until they bent dangerously, while the water parted in foam at the rushing prow, and spread away in a foamy pyramid behind.

The effect of this was soon apparent. The rattle of the oars ahead grew plainer and plainer at each stroke, and it was evident they were gaining finely. Haverland's arm was thrilled with tenfold power, as he felt that he was rushing to the rescue of his only darling child, and he only wished he might have the chance to spring upon her abductors and rend them limb from limb. Graham's heart beat faster as he reflected that, perhaps, in a few moments, he should be face to face with her who had hovered about his pillow, in visions, for many a night.

Haldidge sat perfectly cool and possessed. He had formed his plan and imparted it to the others; it was to pursue the canoe noiselessly until they were almost upon it, when the instant they were near enough to distinguish forms, they would fire upon the Indians, and dash ahead and rescue Ina at all hazards.

This Haldidge, who has been introduced to notice in this chapter, was a middle-aged man, who ten years before had emigrated from the settlements along the Hudson, with a company which had formed the settlement from which he started, and where we saw Haverland and his wife and sister safely domiciled. He was a married man, and his cabin happened to be on the outskirts of the village. He joined and led the whites in several forays against the savages, when the latter became too troublesome; and in this way became a prominent object for the Indians' hatred. His residence became known to them, and one dark, stormy night a half-dozen made a descent upon it. By the merest chance, Haldidge was in the village at that time, and thus escaped their malignant revenge. Being disappointed of their principal prey, they cowardly vented their hatred upon his defenseless wife and child.

When the father returned, he found them both tomahawked, side by side, and weltering in each other's blood. So silently had this onslaught been made, that not a neighbor suspected anything wrong, and were horror-struck to find that such deadly peril had been so near their own doors. Haldidge took a fearful vengeance upon the destroyers of his happiness. He succeeded, a couple of years afterward, in discovering them, and, before six months were over, shot them all. As may be supposed, his natural aversion to the race was intensified by this tragical occurrence, and had become so distinguished, that his name was a terror to the savages in that section. This will account for his readiness in accompanying Haverland upon his perilous expedition.

As was said, our friends were rapidly gaining upon the Indian canoe. At the rate at which they were going, they would be up to them in the course of half an hour. They were so close to the shore, as to see the dark line of the shrubbery along the bank, and several times an overhanging limb brushed over their heads. Suddenly Haldidge raised his hand again. All ceased rowing and listened. To their consternation not the slightest sound was heard. Graham leaned over, and placed his ear almost to the water, but detected nothing but the soft ripple of the stream against the roots and dipping branches along the shore.

"Can it be?" he asked, with a painful whisper, as he raised his head, "that we have been heard?"

"I do not think so," replied Haldidge, apparently in as much doubt as the rest.

"Then they have run in to shore, and departed."

"I fear that has been done."

"But we have kept so close to the shore, would we not have seen or heard the boat?"

"Provided they landed at once. They may have run in this very minute, and may not be more than a few yards off."

"If so, we must hear them yet, and it won't do to slide down upon them in the manner we are now going, or we shall find ourselves in the same fix we expected to get them in."

"Very true, and a good suggestion," remarked Haldidge, and as he did so, he reached up and caught an overhanging limb, and held the canoe still.

"Now, boys, if you've got ears—"

"Sh! Look there!" interrupted Haverland, in an excited whisper.

Each turned his head, and saw what appeared to be a common lighted candle floating upon the surface of the stream. It was a small point of light which at intervals glowed with a fuller redness, and which for a time completely confounded our friends. On it came as noiselessly as death, gliding forward with such a smooth, regular motion as to show that it was certainly borne by the current.

"What in the name of—"

"Stop!" cried Haldidge; "that's the canoe we're after! It's the light of one of their pipes we see. Are your guns ready?"

"Yes," replied the two, just loud enough for him to hear.

"Make right toward it, then, and fire the instant you see your mark. Now!"

At the same instant he released his hold upon the limb, and they threw all their force upon the oars. The canoe bounded like a ball directly ahead, and seemed about to cut the other in twain. A minute after, the shadowy outlines of three forms could be dimly seen, and the avenging rifles were already raised, when the beacon-light was suddenly extinguished and the Indian canoe vanished as if by magic.

"It's one of their tricks!" excitedly exclaimed Haldidge. "Dash ahead! Curse them; they can't be far off."

The two dropped their rifles, and again seized the oars, and Haldidge sheered it abruptly up-stream, for he fancied they had turned in that direction. He bent his head forward, expecting each moment to see the forms of their enemies loom up to view in the mist, but he was mistaken; no savages greeted his anxious vision. He guided his boat in every direction—across the stream, up and down—but all to no purpose. They had surely lost their prey this time. The Indians had undoubtedly heard the pursuers—had muffled their own oars, and so proceeded as silently as they.

"Hold a minute!" commanded Haldidge.

As they rested, they listened deeply and intently.

"Do you hear anything?" he asked, leaning breathlessly forward. "There! Listen again."

They could distinguish the ripple of water, growing fainter and fainter each minute.

"They are below us again, and now for a trial of speed."

The two needed no more incentives, and for a time the canoe skimmed over the water with astonishing speed. The moon was now up, and there were patches in the stream, where the wind had blown away the fog, and being exposed to the light, were as clear as midday. Now and then they crossed such spots, sometimes but a few feet wide, and at others several rods. At these times the shore on either side was perfectly outlined, and they glided over with a sort of instinctive terror, as they felt how easily an enemy might be concealed.

In crossing one of these, broader than usual, a glimpse of the Indian canoe showed itself, just disappearing upon the opposite side. They were not more than a hundred yards apart, and they bounded toward it with great rapidity. The patches of light became more frequent, and the fog was evidently disappearing. Quite a breeze had arisen, which was fast sweeping it away. Haldidge kept close in to the eastern shore, feeling sure that their enemies would land upon this side!

Suddenly the whole mist lifted from the surface of the water in a volume, and rolled off toward the woods. The bright moon was reflected a long distance, and the pursuers gazed searchingly about, fully expecting to see their enemies not a dozen rods away. But they were again doomed to disappointment. Not a ripple disturbed the waters, except their own canoe. The moon was directly overhead, so that there was not a shadow cast along the bank, sufficient to conceal the slightest object. The Indians had evidently landed, and were far distant in the forest.

"It's no use," remarked Haverland, gloomily, "they are gone, and we might as well be too."

"It is a sore disappointment," said Graham.

"And as much so to me as to either of you," said Haldidge. "I have an old score against the infernal wretches that will take many years to wipe out. I hoped to do something toward it tonight, but have been prevented. There is no use of hoping more at this time; they have eluded us, that is self-evident, and we must try some other means. No doubt you are wearied in body as well as in mind, and don't fancy particularly this remaining out in the river here, a shot for any one who might possess the will; so let us go into shore, have a rest, and talk over things."

Dispiritedly and gloomily the trio ran the canoe to the bank and landed.

Chapter 10

A COUPLE OF INDIAN CAPTIVES

So sudden, so unexpected, so astonishing was the crash of Seth's tomahawk through the head of the doomed savage, that, for a moment after, not an Indian moved or spoke. The head was nearly cleft in twain (for an arm fired by consuming passion had driven it), and the brains were spattered over a number of those seated around. Seth himself stood a second to satisfy himself the work was complete, when he turned, walked to his seat, sat down, coolly folded his arms and *commenced whistling.*

A second after, nearly every savage drew a deep breath, as if a load had been removed from his heart; then each looked at his neighbor, and in the scowling, ridged brows, the glittering eyes, the distorted visages, the strained breathing through the set teeth, could be read the fearful intention. Every face but that of the chieftain's was livid with fury. He alone sat perfectly unagitated. Three Indians arose, and, grasping their knives, stood before him waiting for the expected words.

"Touch him not," said he, with a shake of the head; "him no right here."

As the chief spoke, he tapped his forehead significantly with his finger, meaning that the prisoner was demented. The others believed the same, still it was hard to quell the pent-up fire which was scorching their breasts. But his word was law inviolate, and without a murmur, they seated themselves on the ground again.

Seth, although his eye appeared vacant and unmeaning, had noted all these movements with the keenness of the eagle. He knew that a word or sign from the chief would be sufficient to hack him to a thousand pieces. When he stood before his inhuman tormentor, with the keen tomahawk in his hand, the certainty of instant death or prolonged torture would not have prevented him taking the savage vengeance he did. Now that it was over, he was himself again. His natural feelings came back, and with it the natural desire for life. The words of the chief convinced him that he was regarded as either insane or idiotic, and consequently as not deserving death. Still, although saved for the present, he ever stood in imminent peril. The fallen savage had living friends, who would seize the first opportunity to avenge his death. At any rate, let matters stand as they might, Seth felt that he was in hot quarters, and the safest course was to get out of them as soon as possible.

It was perhaps ten minutes after the horrid deed, that the savages commenced bestirring themselves. Several arose and carried their comrade to one side, while the others commenced preparations for taking up the day's march. At this moment, the runners who had pursued Graham to the water's edge, returned, and the tragical occurrence was soon made known to them. A perfect battery of deadly, gleaming eyes were opened upon Seth, but he stood it unflinchingly. The Indians would have relished well the idea of venting their baffled vengeance upon the helpless captive in their hands; but the commanding presence of their chief restrained the slightest demonstration, and they contented themselves with meaning looks.

One thing did not escape Seth's notice from the first, and it was an occasion of wonder and speculation to him. Nothing could be seen of Ina. In fact, the appearance of things was such as to lead one to believe that the savages knew nothing of her. Could it be that he and Graham had been mistaken in the party? Could some other tribe have made off with her? Or, had they separated, and taken her in another direction? As he ruminated upon these questions, he became convinced that the last suggested the certain answer. They could not have mistaken the party, as they had never lost sight of the trail since taking it; and, moreover, he had noticed several slight occurrences, since his advent among them, that satisfied him, beyond a doubt, of the identify of the party with the one which had descended upon the home of the woodman. From the caution which the aggressors had evinced in their flight, together with the haste with which it had been conducted, it was plain they had some fears of pursuit; and to guard their treasure, a number had left them at a favorable point, intending to join the main body where pursuit was not to be expected, or where the pursuers had been sufficiently misled to warrant it. As he reflected, Seth was satisfied that this was the only and true explanation of her nonappearance.

The preparations were soon completed, and the Indians commenced moving forward. If Seth had entertained any doubts of their intention relating to him, they were soon dispelled by his experience. It was not at all likely that he would be reserved as a prisoner, unless they intended to put him to some use. Accordingly he found himself loaded down with an enormous burden, consisting mostly of food, in the shape of deer's meat, which the savages had brought with them. They buried their fallen comrade, without the ceremony and mourning which might be expected. The North American Indian rarely gives way to his emotions, except upon such occasions as the burial of one of their number, a "war-dance," or something similar, when the whole nest of devilish passions is allowed free vent. They indulged in no such ceremonies—if ceremonies they may be called—at this time. A comparatively shallow grave was dug, and into this the fallen one was placed in an upright position, his face turned toward the east. His rifle, knives, and all his clothing were buried with him.

The day was a suffocating one in August, and Seth's sufferings were truly great. He was naturally lithe, wiry, and capable of enduring prolonged exertion, but, unfortunately for him, the savages had become aware of this and loaded him accordingly. Most of the journey was through the forest, where the arching tree-tops shut out the withering rays of the sun. Had they encountered any such open plains as the one passed over near their encampment, Seth would have never lived through it. As it was, his load nearly made him insensible to pain. A consuming thirst was ever tormenting him, although he found abundant means to slake it in the numberless rills which gurgled through the wilderness.

"How Yankee like it?" grinned a savage by his side, stooping and peering fiendishly into his face.

"First rate; goes nice. Say, you, s'posen you try it?"

"Ugh! walk faster," and a whack accompanied the word.

"Now I calc'late, I'm going to walk just about as fast as I durned please, and if you ain't a mind to wait, you can heave ahead. Fact, by gracious."

And Seth did not hasten his steps in the least. Toward noon he found he should be obliged to have a short rest or give out entirely. He knew it would be useless to ask, and consequently he determined to take it without asking. So, unloosing the cords which bound the pack to his back, he let it fall to the ground, and, seating himself upon it, again went to whistling.

"Go faster, Yankee—you no keep up!" exclaimed one giving him a stunning blow.

"See here, you, p'raps you don't know who it mought be you insulted in that way. I'm Seth Jones, from New Hampshire, and consequently you'll be keerful of tetching me."

The savage addressed was upon the point of striking him insolently to the earth, when the chieftain interfered.

"No touch pale-face—him tired—rest a little."

Some unaccountable whim had possessed the savage, as this mercy was entirely unexpected by Seth, and he knew not how to account for it, unless it might be he was reserving him for some horrible torture.

The resting-spell was but a moment, however, and just as Seth had begun to really enjoy it, the chieftain gave orders for the replacement of the load. Seth felt disposed to tamper awhile, for the sake of prolonging his enjoyment, but, on second thought, concluded it the better plan not to cross the chief who had been so lenient to him thus far. So, with a considerable number of original remarks, and much disputation about the placing of the burden, he shouldered it at last and trudged forward.

Seth was right in his conjectures about Ina. Toward the latter part of the day, the three Indians, who had been pursued by our other friends, rejoined the main party, bearing her with them. She noticed her companion in captivity at once, but no communication passed between them. A look of melancholy relief escaped her as she became assured that her parents were still safe, and that only she and her new friend were left to the sufferings and horrors of captivity. But there was enough in that to damp even such a young and hopeful spirit as was hers. Not death alone, but a fate from the sensuous captors far worse than death itself, was to be apprehended. In the future, there was but one Hand that could sustain and safely deliver them, and to that One she looked for deliverance.

Chapter 11

STILL IN PURSUIT

"It seems the devil himself is helping them imps!" remarked Haldidge, as they landed.

"But I trust Heaven is aiding us," added Haverland.

"Heaven will, if we help ourselves, and now as I'm in this scrape, I'm bound to see the end. Look for trail."

"It's poor work I'm thinking we'll make, groping in this moonlight," said Graham.

"While there's life there's hope. Scatter 'long the bank, and search every foot of land. I'll run upstream a ways, as I've an idea they landed not fur off."

The hunter disappeared, with these words, and Graham and Haverland commenced their work in an opposite direction. The branches overhanging the water were carefully lifted up, and the muddy shore examined; the suspicious bending or parting of the undergrowth was followed by the minutest scrutiny, and although the heavy darkness was against them, yet it would have required a most guarded trail to have escaped their vision. But there efforts were useless; no trail was detected; and convinced that the savages must have landed upon the opposite side, they turned to retrace their steps. As they did so, a low whistle from the hunter reached their ears.

"What does that mean?" asked Graham.

"He has discovered something. Let us hasten."

"What is it, Haldidge?" asked Haverland, as they reached the hunter.

"Here's their tracks as sure as I'm a sinner, and it's my private opine they ain't fur off neither."

"Shall we wait till daylight before we undertake to follow it?"

"I am much afraid we shall have to, as there may be signs which we might miss in this darkness. Day can't be far off."

"Several hours yet."

"Well, we will make ourselves comfortable until then."

With these words the trio set themselves upon the earth, and kept up a low conversation until morning. As soon as the faint light appeared, they detected the Indian canoe a short distance up the bank, secreted beneath a heavy, overhanging mass of undergrowth. As it was during the summer season, their pursuit was continued at an early hour, so the savages could have had but a few hours' start at the most. With Ina they could not proceed very rapidly, and our friends were sanguine of overtaking them ere the day closed.

The only apprehension the pursuers felt, was that the three savages, fully conscious now that their enemies were upon the trail, might hasten to rejoin the main body, and thus cut off all hope. They could not be many miles apart, and must have made some preparation for this contingency.

The trail to the hunter's eye was distinct and easily followed. He took the lead, striding rapidly forward, while Haverland and Graham were continually on the look-out for danger. Haverland was somewhat fearful that the savages, finding they could not avoid being overtaken, would halt and form an ambush into which the hunter would blindly lead them. The latter, however, although he appeared culpably rash and heedless, understood Indian tactics better; he knew no halt would be made until the savages were compelled to do so.

"Ah!—see here!" exclaimed Haldidge, suddenly pausing.

"What's the trouble?" queried Graham, stepping hastily forward with Haverland.

"Their camping-ground; that is all."

Before them were more visible signs of the trail than they had yet witnessed. A heap of ashes was upon the ground; and as Haverland kicked them apart, he discovered the embers still red and glowing. Sticks were broken and scattered around, and all the varied evidences of an Indian camp were to be seen.

"How long ago was this place vacated?" asked Graham.

"Not three hours."

"We must be close upon them."

"Rather, yes."

"Let us hasten forward, then."

"You see by these coals that they didn't start until daylight, and as
that gal of yourn, Haverland, can't travel very fast, of course they've
had to take their time."

"Very true; although disappointment has attended us thus far, I
begin to feel a little of my natural hope return. I trust that this opportunity will not escape us."

"Ah! more signs yet," exclaimed Graham, who had been examining
the ground for several yards around.

"What now?"

"That's a piece of her dress, is it not?"

And he held up a small, fluttering rag in his hands. The father eagerly took it, and examined it.

"Yes; that is Ina's; I hope no violence has placed it in our hands,"
and several involuntary tears coursed down his cheeks at the illusion.

"I'm thinking she left it there on purpose to guide us," remarked
Graham.

"She must have seen us, of course, and has done all she could to
guide us."

"Very probable; but it strikes me rather forcibly that we are gaining
nothing in particular by remaining here. Remember, the savages are
going all the time."

Thus admonished, the three set rapidly forward again, the hunter
taking the lead as before. The pursuit was kept up without halting
until near noon. Conscious that they were rapidly gaining upon the
fugitives, it was necessary to proceed with the extremest caution. The
breaking of a twig, the falling of a leaf, startled and arrested their
steps, and not a word was exchanged except in the most careful whisper. Haldidge was some dozen yards in advance, and the eyes of his
companions were upon him, when they saw him suddenly pause and
raise his hand as a signal for them to halt. They did so, and stooping
downward, he commenced examining the leaves before him.

A moment sufficed. He turned and motioned his two companions
forward.

"Just as I feared," he moodily exclaimed, in a half whisper.

"What's the matter?" asked Haverland, anxiously.

"The two trails join here," he answered.

"Are you not mistaken?" asked Haverland, knowing that he was not,
and yet catching at the faintest hope held out to him.

"No, sir; there's no mistake. Instead of three Indians, we've got over
forty to follow up now."

"Shall we do it?"

"Shall we do it? Of course we shall; it's the only chance of ever getting a sight of Ina again."

"I know it, and yet the hope is so faint; they must know we are in pursuit, and what can we do against ten times our number?"

"No telling yet; come, strike ahead again."

With these words, the hunter turned and plunged deeper into the forest. Graham and Haverland silently followed, and in a few minutes the three were proceeding as carefully and silently as before through the dense wood.

As yet our friends had partaken of nothing, and began to experience the pangs of hunger; but, of course, in the present instance, these were disregarded. Somewhere near the middle of the afternoon, they came upon another spot where the savages had halted. Here, if Haverland and Graham had any lingering doubts of what the hunter had said, they were soon removed. It was plain that a large Indian party had halted upon this spot but a few hours before, and it was equally evident that they had taken no pains to conceal the traces they had made. If they had any suspicions of pursuit, they had no apprehensions of the consequences, as they were well aware of the disparity between the two forces, and scorned the whites.

This was gratifying on the other hand to the hunter. He knew well enough that as matters stood at present, he could hope for nothing except through his own cunning and stratagem; and, for this reason it was very probable that the Indians were satisfied no attempt would be made. They did not take into consideration that there was an enemy in their camp.

Considerable remains of the meal were discovered, and served to satisfy the wants of our friends for the present. The early time in the afternoon showed them that thus far they had gained quite rapidly upon the savages. It was the earnest wish of the three that they should come up to the Indian party by nightfall; but this expectation was doomed to a sudden disappointment; for in a few hours they reached a point where the trail *divided again.*

This was unaccountable even to the hunter, and for a few moments our friends stood perfectly nonplused. They had not looked for this, and knew not the slightest reason for it.

"This beats all creation!" remarked Haldidge, as he again examined the trail.

"Depend upon it, there is something meant in this," observed Haverland, with an air of deep concern.

"It is some stratagem of the imps which we must understand before going further."

"They must entertain different ideas of us from what we thought. You may safely believe that this is some plan to mislead us, and if there is ever a time when our wits shall be demanded it has now come."

During this fragmentary conversation, the hunter was minutely examining the trail. Graham and Haverland watched him a few seconds in silence, when the latter asked:

"Do you make anything of it?"

"Nothing more. The trail divides here; the main body proceeds onward in a direct line, while the minor trail leads off to the west. The division must have been very unequal, for as near as I can judge the smaller party does not number over three or four at the most. No efforts have been made to conceal their traces, and there is either a deep-laid scheme afloat, or they don't care a fig for us."

"Very probably both," remarked Graham. "They care enough for us to take good care to remain out of our reach, when they do not possess advantages over us, and have already shown their skill in not laying but in executing schemes."

"If we could only give that Seth Jones an inkling of our whereabouts and intentions, I should feel pretty sanguine again," said Haverland.

"Very likely if that Jones could give us an inkling of his whereabouts and experiences, you would lose a little of that expectation," rejoined the hunter, with a meaning emphasis.

"But this is a waste of time and words," said Graham; "let us lay our heads together and decide at once what is to be done. As for me, I'm in favor of following the smaller party."

"What give you that idea?" asked Haverland.

"I confess I cannot give much reason for the notion, but somehow or other it has struck me that Ina is with the smaller party."

"Hardly probable," returned Haverland.

"It don't seem so, I allow," remarked the hunter, "but queerly enough the same notion has got into my head."

"Of course you can then give some reason."

"I can give what appears to have a show of reason to me. I have been doing a big amount of thinking for the last few minutes, and have almost reached a conclusion. I believe that the gal is with the smaller party, and it is the wish of the savages that we shall follow the main body. We will thus be drawn into ambush, and all further trouble from us would be removed."

"It seems hardly probable that the savages would run such a risk of losing their captive when there is no occasion for it," remarked Haverland.

"It don't seem probable, but it ain't the first thing they've done (providing of course they've done it), that would make you open your eyes. I believe these Mohawks are certain we won't suspect they've let the gal go off with two or three of their number, when there were enough to watch her and keep her out of the hands of a dozen such as we are. Feeling certain of this, I say they have let her go; and being sure also that we'll tramp on after them, they have made arrangements some distance away from here to dispose of us."

"Sound reasoning, I admit, but here's something to offer on the other side," said Graham, producing another fluttering rag from a bush.

"How is that upon the other side of the question?" queried the hunter.

"If you will notice the bush from which I took this, you will see it is upon the trail of the larger party, and consequently Ina must have been with that party to have left it there."

"Just show me the exact twig from which you took it," quietly asked Haldidge. Graham led the way a few yards off and showed him the spot. The hunter stooped and carefully examined the bush.

"I'm not satisfied," said he, "that I was right. This rag was left there by a savage for the express purpose of misleading us. We must seek Ina in another direction."

"Haldidge," said Haverland, earnestly, "I place great reliance upon your skill and judgment, but it strikes me at this moment that you are acting capriciously against reason."

"There's but one way to decide it; will you agree to it?" asked the hunter, smiling. The other two expressed their willingness, and he produced his hunting-knife. For fear that some of our readers may be apprehensive of the use to which he intended putting it, we will describe his *modus operandi* at once. Stepping back a pace or two, the hunter took the point of his knife between his thumb and forefinger, and flung it over his head. As it fell to the earth again, the point was turned *directly toward the trail of the lesser party*.

"Just what I thought," remarked the hunter, with another quiet smile. The mooted question was now settled to the satisfaction of all, and our three friends turned unhesitatingly to the westward upon the trail of the smaller party.

How much sometimes hangs upon the slightest thread! How small is the point upon which great events often turn! The simple fact of the direction in which the blade of the hunting-knife remained when it fell, decided the fate of every character in this life-drama. Had it pointed to the northward, an hour later the three would have walked into an ambush intended for them, and everyone would have been massacred. The hunter was right. Ina Haverland had gone with the smaller party.

Chapter 12

PENCILINGS BY THE WAY

We have said the hunter was right. By the accidental turning of the hunting-knife, he had not only saved his life, but his efforts had been turned in the right direction.

It must be confessed that Haverland himself had some misgivings about the course which they were taking. He could not believe that the savages were short-sighted enough to place a captive, who was secure in their possession, into the hands of one or two of their number, when they were conscious they were pursued. But the decision of the hunting-knife could not be appealed from, and in a moody silence he followed in the footsteps of the hunter.

It was now getting far along in the afternoon, and the pursued savages could be at no great distance. Their trail was plain, as no efforts had been made to conceal it; but, although Haldidge strove his utmost to detect signs of Ina's delicate moccasin, he failed entirely, and was compelled, in spite of the assurance which he manifested at the start, to take some misgivings to himself.

The hunter, notwithstanding the consummate cunning and skill he had shown thus far in tracing up the savages, had made one sad mistake. He had been misled altogether in the number of the smaller party. Instead of three or four Indians, there were six: he began to think he had undertaken a more difficult matter than he anticipated. Still there was no time for halting or faltering, and he strode resolutely forward.

"Ah—some more signs," exclaimed he, stopping suddenly.

"What are they?" queried his companions, eagerly.

"Just notice this bush, if you please, and tell me what you make of it?"

The two friends did so, and saw that one of the branches of some sprouts of chestnut, growing round a stump, had been broken short off, and lay pointing toward the trail.

"I make it favorable. Ina has done this to guide us," said Haverland.

"My opinion exactly," added Graham.

"You are mistaken about one thing. *Ina did not do it.*"

"Did not do it?" exclaimed the others; "and who did then?"

"That's the question. I'm of the opinion that that white man you have told me about has done it."

"But it cannot be that he is with them too."

"Surely it is impossible that the Indians would allow *both* of their captives to be in charge of two or three of their number at the same time."

"As for two or three, there are six painted Mohawks ahead of us for that matter. I haven't detected the trail of the gal yet, but have discovered several times pretty convincing evidence that a white man is among them. If you will look at that stick again, you will see that it is not likely your gal broke it. In the first place I don't believe she is able; for notice how thick it is; and, if she could have done it, it would have taken so much time that she would have been prevented."

"Very probably Seth is among them, although it is singular, to say the least. Some unaccountable whim has taken possession of the Indians."

"But you say you discern nothing of Ina's trail?" asked Graham.

"Not as yet."

"Do you think she is among them?"

"I do."

"Where is her trail, then?"

"Somewhere on the ground, I suppose."

"Well, why have we not seen it, then?"

"I suppose, because it has escaped our eyes."

"A good explanation," smiled Graham; "but if we have failed altogether thus far to detect it, is it probable that she is among them?"

"I think so. You must remember that these half-dozen Mohawks are walking promiscuously and not in Ingin file, as is generally their custom. It is very probable that the gal is in front, and what tracks her little moccasin might make would be entirely covered up with the big feet of the Ingins."

"I hope you are not mistaken," returned Haverland, in such a tone as to show that he still had his lingering doubts.

"That matter cannot be decided until we get a peep at the dusky cowards, and the only course is for us to push ahead."

"It strikes me that they can be at no great distance, and if we are going to come upon their campfire to-night, we have got to do it pretty soon."

"Come on, then."

With this, the hunter again strode forward, but with more stealth and caution than before. He saw in the different signs around them unmistakable proof that the Indians were at no great distance.

Just as the sun was setting, the triumvirate reached a small stream which dashed and foamed directly across their trail. They halted a moment to slake their thirst, and the hunter arose and moved forward again. But Graham made it a point to search at every halting-place for guiding signs, and he called out to his companions to wait a moment.

"Time is too precious," replied he, "and you won't find anything here."

"Won't find anything here, eh? Just come and look at this."

The hunter stepped back over the stones in the brook, and with Haverland, approached Graham. The latter pointed to a broad, flat stone at his feet. Upon it was scratched, with some softer stone, the following words:

> Hurry forward. There are six Indians, and they have got Ina with them. They don't suspect you are following them, and are hurrying up for village. I think we will camp two or three miles from here. Make the noise of the whippowil when you want to do the business, and I will understand.
>
> Yours, respectfully.
>
> SETH JONES

"If I warn't afraid the imps would hear it, I would vote three cheers for that Jones," exclaimed Haldidge; "he's a trump, whoever he is."

"You may depend upon that," added Graham, "for what little I saw of him was sufficient to show me that."

"Let me see," repeated the hunter, again reading the writing upon the stone, "he says they will encamp two or three miles from here. The sun has now set, but we shall have light for over an hour yet, sufficient to guide us. It's best for us to be moving forward, as there is no time to spare."

"It beats my time how this Jones got into that crowd," said Graham, half to himself, as the three again moved forward.

"He's *there*, we know, and that is enough for the present; when we have the time to spare, we may speculate upon the matter. All ready?"

"Yes—but a moment. Haldidge, let us have some arrangement about the manner in which we are going to travel. Double caution is now necessary."

"I will keep my eyes upon the trail, as I have done all along, and see that we don't walk into a hornet's nest with our eyes shut. You can help keep a look-out, while you, Graham, who have been so lucky thus far in stumbling upon what neither of us saw, will watch for more signs. Just as like as not, that Jones has been clever enough to give us some more good directions."

Each understanding his duty, now prepared to fulfill it. The progress was necessarily slow, from the extreme caution exercised.

The hunter had proceeded but a short distance when he noticed his shadow was cast upon the ground; and, looking up, he saw, to his regret, that the full moon was in the heavens. This was unfortunate for them; for, although it discovered the trail with as much certainty as in the day, and thus assisted them in the pursuit, yet the chances of their approach being made known to the Indians was almost certain.

"Hist!" suddenly called Graham, in a whisper.

"What's up now?" asked the hunter, turning stealthily around.

"Some more writing from Seth."

Haverland and Haldidge approached. Graham was stooping beside a flat stone endeavoring to decipher some characters upon it. The light of the moon, although quite strong, was hardly sufficient. By dint of patience and perseverance they succeeded in reading the following:

> Be *very* careful. The imps begin to suspect; they have seen me making signs, and are suspicious. They keep a close watch on the gal. Remember the signal when you come up with us. Yours, in haste, but nevertheless with great respect,
>
> SETH JONES, ESQ.

It was now evident that they were in close proximity to the savages. After a moment's hurried debate, it was decided that Haldidge should walk at a greater distance ahead than heretofore, and communicate instantly with his companions upon discovering the camp.

Slowly, silently and cautiously the three moved forward. A half-hour later, Graham touched the shoulder of Haverland and pointed meaningly ahead. A red reflection was seen in the branches overhead; and as they stood in silence, the glimmer of a light was seen through the trees. The next instant the hunter stood beside them.

"We've come to them at last," he whispered; "see that your priming is all right, and make up your mind for hot work."

They had already done this, and were anxious for the contest to be decided. Their hearts beat high, as they realized how near the deadly conflict was, and even the hunter's breath was short and hurried. But there was no faltering or wavering, and they moved stealthily forward.

Chapter 13

SOME EXPLANATIONS

The village of the Mohawks was at a considerable distance from the spot where had once stood the home of the woodman, and incumbered as they were with plunder, their progress was necessarily slow; besides, knowing full well that pursuit would be useless upon the part of the whites, their was no occasion to hasten their steps. When, however, Seth Jones' unceremonious entrance among them, together with the escape of his new companion and the subsequent report of the smaller party with Ina, was made known, the old chief began to have some misgivings about his fancied security. It occurred to him that their might be a large party of whites on the trail, and in such case, his greatest skill was required to retain the captives. And here was the trouble. If he was pursued—and upon that point there could be no doubt—his progress must be hastened. His pursuers would follow with the swiftness of vengeance. With the plunder in their possession, the thing was impossible, and he saw, at length, that stratagem must be resorted to.

He selected six of his bravest and fleetest warriors—two of whom had been Graham's most troublesome enemies in his fearful chase—and placed Ina in their charge, with instructions to make all haste to the Indian village. Before starting, it occurred to him that the best plan would be to send the white man also with them. Were he to remain with the larger party, in case of attack, his presence, he had reason to fear, would be their own destruction, while six savages fully armed and ever vigilant, could surely guard an unarmed idiot and a woman.

The chief, as stated, was satisfied he was pursued. Hence, if he could throw his pursuers off the scent, their discomfiture would be certain. He believed this could be done. How well he succeeded, has already been shown. The six savages with their charge parted from the larger party, and struck off rapidly in a direction diverging to the north. Their trail was so concealed as to give the impression that there were but three, and this deception we have seen misled the hunter. A piece of Ina's dress was purposely lodged upon a bush, in the rear of the larger party: and promiscuously and hopefully, the chief leisurely continued his way with his dusky followers.

After the parties had parted company, the smaller one hastened rapidly forward. Ina, in charge of a stalwart, athletic Indian, was kept to the front, the more effectually to conceal her trail, while Seth kept his position near the center of the file. He was allowed the free use of his hands, though, as has been remarked, he was deprived of his weapons. As they journeyed hastily forward, he made it a point to enlighten them as much as possible by his conversation, and certain original remarks.

"If you have no objection, I wouldn't mind knowing your idea in thus leaving the other Injins, eh?" he remarked, quizzically, to the savage in front. No reply being given, he continued:

"I s'pose, you're thinking about that house you burnt down, and feeling bad—oh, you ain't, eh?" suddenly remarked Seth, as the Indian glared fiercely at him.

"It was a bad trick, I allow," he continued, "enough to make a fellur mad, I swow. That house, I shouldn't wonder now, took that Haverland a week to finish; 'twas an ugly piece of business—yes, sir."

At intervals the savages exchanged a word with each other, and once or twice one of them took the back trail, evidently to ascertain whether they had any pursuers. Finding they had not, they slackened their speed somewhat, as Ina had given signs of fatigue, and they believed there was really no occasion for hastening. But the weariness which the fair captive had endured, so increased, that long before the sun had reached its meridian, they halted for a half-hour's rest. This was at the crossing of a small, sparkling stream. As the sun was now quite hot, and the atmosphere thick and heavy, the rest in the cool shadows of the trees was doubly refreshing. Ina seated herself upon the cool moist earth, her captors preserving, singularly enough, a far more vigilant watch over her than over Seth Jones; but, for that matter, the latter was allowed no very special freedom. A couple of Indians again took the back trail, for prudent reasons, but met with nothing to excite their apprehensions.

In the meantime, Seth continued tumbling over the ground, occasionally giving vent to snatches of song, and now and then a sage remark. Without being noticed, he picked a small chalky pebble from the margin of the brook, and working his way to a large flat stone, executed, with many flourishes, the writing to which we referred in a preceding chapter. Although cleverly done, this latter act did not escape the eyes of the suspicious savages. One immediately arose, and walking to him, pointed down and gruffly asked:

"What that?"

"Read it fur yourself," replied Seth, innocently.

"What that?" repeated the savage, menacingly.

"A little flourishing I was executing, jist to pass away time."

"Ugh!" grunted the Indian, and, dipping his big foot in the brook, he irreverently swept it across the stone, completely wiping out Seth's beautiful chirography.

"Much obliged," said the latter; "saved me the trouble. I can write it on again when it gits dry."

But no opportunity was given, as a moment after the scouts returned, and the line of march was taken up. But Seth well knew he had accomplished all that could be desired. He had taken particular pains that the pebble should be flinty enough to scratch into the soft stone every word he wrote. Consequently the party had not been gone a half-hour when every letter came out as clear and distinct as before, despite the wet daub the indignant savage had given it.

Their progress for a time was quite rapid. Seth, somehow or other, was constantly pitching out of file, breaking down twigs along the way, stumbling against the stones which were not in the way, and, in spite of menaces and occasional blows of his captors, making the trail unnecessarily distinct and plain.

At noon another halt was made, and all partook of some food. Ina was sick at heart, and ate but a mouthful. An apprehension of her dreadful position came over her, and her soul reeled as she begin picturing what was yet to come. Seth quarreled with two of his captors, because, he affirmed, they took more than their share of the dinner; and, take it all in all, affairs were getting into as interesting a state as one could well conceive.

The meal finished, they again set forward. From the whispered consultation of the savages, as well as the words which reached Seth's ears, and their utter disregard of Ina's painful fatigue, he began to believe that the Indians suspected that their stratagem had not misled their pursuers, and were apprehensive of pursuit. Finally, Seth became satisfied that such was the case, and when they halted, toward the middle of the afternoon, he again gave vent to his thoughts upon a friendly stone which offered itself, and this, again, received a fierce wipe from the foot of the same savage, and the words again came out to view, and accomplished all that their ardent author could have desired.

These acts of Seth settled the suspicions of his captors into a certainty, and a closer surveillance was kept upon their refractory captive. No further opportunities were given him, and as he himself had expected this turn of matters, there was no need of it upon his part. Although he had but little reason to hope it, he did hope and believe that Haverland and Graham were upon the trail, and he felt that if the words intended for their eyes could only reach them, the fate of Ina and himself was determined.

The moon being at its full, and shining in unclouded splendor upon the forest, so lightened the way that the savages continued their flight —as it may now be called—for an hour or two in the evening. They would have probably gone further, had it not been painfully evident that Ina was ready to give out. The old chief had given them imperative commands not to hasten her too much, and to rest when they saw she needed it. Accordingly, though they were brutal enough to insult her with menaces, they were of no avail, and, finally they came to a reluctant halt for the night.

It will be necessary to understand the situation of these savages and their captives, in order to comprehend the events that followed.

A fire was started, and just within the circle of this, half reclining upon the ground, was Ina, with a heavy Indian shawl thrown around her. She had partaken of none of the food offered, and was already in a semi-unconscious state. On either side of her was seated a vigilant savage, well-armed and prepared for any emergency. Upon the opposite side was Seth, his feet firmly lashed together, while his hands were free. Two Indians were upon his right, and upon his left. The remaining one took his station about a hundred yards on the backtrail.

Here, lying flat on his face, he silently waited for the approach of the enemy.

Chapter 14

IN THE ENEMY'S CAMP

The savages, after starting the fire, allowed it to smolder and die out, for fear of guiding their enemies. Now this was the most fortunate thing that could have happened for their pursuers; for, in the first place, it burned long enough to give them a perfect knowledge of the position of Ina and Seth; and when its light could no longer be of any assistance, but would materially injure their hopes, the Indians were kind enough to let it fade entirely out.

Before giving the signal, the hunter deemed it best to ascertain the whereabouts of the savage missing at the camp-fire. Leaving his rifle in charge of Haverland, and cautioning them not to move, he crept stealthily forward. So silent and snakelike was his approach, that the savage lying directly in his path had not the slightest suspicion of his proximity. The first thing that attracted his attention was the *thought* that he heard a slight movement in front of him. Raising his head a few inches, he peered cautiously forward. Nothing meeting his keen vision he sunk back again.

The hunter and savage, both being on the ground, were in blank darkness, and although their forms, if standing on their feet, would have been plainly discernible, yet, under the thick shadows of the undergrowth, they might have touched each other without knowing it. The hunter, however, as he lay, caught the outlines of the savage's head against the fading light of the fire behind him, as he raised it. This gave him a knowledge of his position and determined his own mode of action.

Without the least noise, he slid slowly forward until he was so close that he could actually hear the Indian's breath. Then he purposely made a slight movement. The Indian raised his head, and was gradually coming to his feet, when the hunter bounded like a dark ball forward, clutched him by the throat, and bearing him like a giant to the earth, drove his hunting knife again and again to the hilt in his heart. It was a fearful act, yet there was no hesitation upon the hunter's part. He felt that it must be done.

He loosened his gripe upon his victim's throat, when there was not a spark of life left. Then casting his body to one side, he made his way back to his companions. Here, in a few words, he explained what had taken place. It was evident that the Indians were so cautious and alarmed, that the most consummate skill was required, to accomplish the work in hand.

Suddenly an ingenious plan occurred to Graham. It was to dress himself in the fallen Indian's dress, walk boldly into the camp and be guided by circumstances. After a moment's consultation, it was acquiesced in by all. Haldidge made his way to where the savage lay, and hastily stripping him, returned with his garments. These Graham donned in a few moments, and was ready. It was agreed that he should walk leisurely among them, while Haverland and Haldidge would follow him, and remain nigh enough to be ready at a moment's warning. If discovered, he was to seize Ina and make off in the woods, while his two friends would rush forward, free Seth, and make an onslaught upon the others.

The fire was now so low, that Graham had little fear of exposing himself, unless compelled to hold a conversation. The savages started as he came to view, but fortunately said nothing, as they supposed it to be their comrade. Graham walked leisurely to the almost dead fire, and seated himself by Seth. The savages continued placidly smoking their pipes.

"Ygh!" grunted Graham, peering into Seth's face. The latter started slightly, looked up, and understood all in a moment. Seth pointed to his feet; Graham nodded.

"Say, you, you was clever enough to tie up my feet, and now just have the kindness to move 'em a little nearer the fire. Come, do, and I'll remember you in my will."

Graham mumbled something, and, stooping forward, he moved the feet slightly, dexterously cutting the thong at the same moment.

"Much obliged," said Seth; "that'll dew; needn't take no further trouble, you old painted heathen."

Graham felt that if he could now put Ina upon her guard, all that would be necessary was—to act. But this was hardly possible. While ruminating upon the next step to be taken, an Indian addressed him in the Indian tongue. Here was a dilemma, and Graham was already mediating upon making the onslaught at once, when the ready wit of Seth came to his aid. Disguising most completely his voice, the eccentric fellow replied in the Indian tongue. This slight stratagem was executed so perfectly that not a savage entertained the slightest suspicion that another than their dead comrade had spoke to them. Another question was put, but before Seth could reply, there came a startling cry of the whippowil close at hand. All the savages sprung to their feet, and one held his tomahawk, ready to brain the captive Ina, in case they could not retain her. Another leaped toward Seth, but his surprise was great, when the man in turn sprung nimbly to his feet, and this surprise became unbounded, when, doubling himself like a ball, Seth struck him with tremendous force in the stomach, knocking him instantly senseless. Quick as thought, Graham felled the savage standing over Ina, and seizing her in his arms, plunged into the woods, setting up a loud shout at the same instant. The scene now became desperate. Haldidge and Haverland, fired almost to madness, rushed forward, and the former added his own yells to those of the savages. Ten minutes after, not an Indian was in sight. Finding it impossible to withstand this terrible onslaught, they fled precipitately, carrying with them several desperate wounds in body and feelings.

No lives were lost on either side, and not a wound worth mentioning was received by the assailants. The rout was complete.

But there was still danger, as the routed Indians could make all haste to the main body, and would in turn pursue the whites. This

Haldidge remarked, as he struck into the forest, and called upon the others not to lose sight of him. There was danger of this, indeed.

"By gracious! yew, Haverland, things begin to look up," exclaimed Seth.

"Thank God!" responded the father, with a trembling voice.

Ina, for a few moments after her recapture, was so bewildered as not to comprehend the true state of affairs. Finally, she realized that she was in the arms of friends.

"Am I safe? Where is father?" she asked.

"Here, my dearest child," answered the parent, pressing her to his heart.

"Is mother and aunty safe?"

"Yes, all—all safe, I trust, now."

"And who are these with you?"

"This is Haldidge, a dear friend of ours, to whom, under Heaven, your rescue is owing, and—"

"Just hold on, Alf, now, if you please; that's plenty," interrupted the hunter.

"Of course I did not mean to leave out Seth here, and—"

"No, by gracious, it wouldn't do, especially when you recollect how nice it was me and Graham gave 'em the slip."

"You and who?" eagerly asked Ina.

"Me and Mr. Graham—that fellow standing there—the one that has come out here to marry you. Haven't you heard of him?"

Ina stepped forward and scrutinized the face before her.

"Don't you remember me?" asked Graham, pleasantly.

"Oh, is it you? I am *so* glad you are here," she repeated, placing both her hands in his and looking up into his face.

"Now, just see here," said Seth, stepping earnestly forward, "I 'bject to this. 'Cos why, you haven't the time to go into the sparking business, and if you do, why, you'll be obsarved. I advise you to postpone it till you git home. What's the opinion of the audience?"

"Your suggestion is hardly necessary," laughed Graham. "The *business* you referred to shall most certainly be deferred until a more convenient season."

"It gives me great pleasure," remarked Haverland, "to witness this reunion of friends, and I thank God that my dear child, so nearly lost forever, has been restored to me; but there is another whose heart is nearly broken, who should not be kept waiting, and there is a long distance between us and perfect safety, which should be shortened as rapidly and quickly as possible."

"That's the idea," added Haldidge; "it won't do to consider yourself safe till you *are,* and that isn't yet."

"Just so exactly, and consequently all fall into line of march."

Our friends now set out on a rapid walk homeward. As has been remarked, there was yet a long distance to be passed, and even now, while surrounded by darkness, it was reckless to halt or lag upon the way. Haldidge, as well as Seth, resolved that they should not pause until it was evident that Ina needed rest. Both well knew that the Mohawks would not yield up their captives, as long as there was a chance to regain them.

Seth's only fear now was that they would be pursued and overtaken by some of the savages. That this apprehension was well-grounded, the events which we shall now record will plainly show.

Chapter 15

MANEUVERING AND SCHEMING

Through the entire night, with now and then an occasional halt of a few minutes each, the fugitives—for they may now be properly termed such—continued their journey. When day broke, they halted in a small valley through which a small, sparkling stream made its way. On either side, it was surrounded by dark, overhanging forest-trees, and heavier undergrowth, through which none but the eagle eye of the hunter or savage could discover their retreat.

Seth, when they first halted, made off in the woods, and in the course of a half-hour returned with a large fowl. The feathers were plucked from this, a fire kindled, and in a few moments it was cooked. It furnished all with a hearty, substantial and nourishing breakfast— what all needed. After this a short consultation was held, when it was determined that they should halt for an hour or two. Several blankets were spread upon the greensward, as a bed for Ina, and in ten minutes she was sound asleep.

Our friends had decided upon making their homeward journey upon foot for several reasons, any of which was sufficient to influence them. In the first place, their course would be much shorter and more direct, and was really attended with less danger; and even if they desired to take to the river there was no means to do it.

"By gracious!" remarked Seth, after a few minutes' deep thought, "I

feel, boys, as though we're to run into a scrape before we git home. I
tell *yeou* I do."

"And I do, too," added Haldidge. "I don't know why it is, and yet I
believe there is a reason for it. If there is any chance for them Mohawks to play a game of *tit for tat*, they'll do it; you can make up
your mind to that.

"Do you think the chance is given them?" queried Haverland.

"I am afraid we can't help it, any way we choose to fix it."

"What do you mean? What do you refer to!"

"You see, them Ingins can't help knowing the way we'll have to
take to reach home, and what is to hinder them from getting ahead of
us and giving us a little trouble?"

"Nothing at all, that's a fact. Our utmost vigilance will be required
at every step. Don't you think Seth, that one of us should act in the
capacity of scout?"

"I *know* it; not only one, but two. As soon as we start, I shall shoot
ahead and pilot you along, while one of you must flourish in the rear
to announce any new visitors. This is the only way we can ever expect
to move along with dignity."

"What course do you suppose the savages will take?" asked Graham.

"I guess they ain't in the neighborhood, though it's darned hard to
tell where they are. You can make up your mind that they'll show
themselves before we get any great distance ahead. They'll be dodging round in the woods till they find out where we are, and then
they'll use their wits to draw us into ambush, and I can tell *yeou*, too,
that 'cuter ones than we have walked right into the infarnal things."

An hour later, when preparations were making for resuming their
journey, Ina awoke. She was greatly refreshed by the sleep thus obtained, and the others felt cheered and hopeful at the prospect of a
rapid march for the day.

The burden and responsibility of this small band of adventurers naturally devolved upon Haldidge and Seth. Haverland, although a thorough hunter and woodsman, had but little or no experience in Indian
warfare, and accordingly showed himself to be devoid of that suspicious watchfulness which makes up the success of the frontier ranger.
As for Graham, he was suspicious enough, but he lacked also the great
teacher—experience. Seth and Haldidge thus thrown together, rapidly
consulted and determined in all cases the precautionary measures to
be adopted. In the present instant, it was decided that Haldidge
should linger some hundred yards in the rear, and use all the opportunities thus afforded of watching the actions or approach of their enemies. The same duty was imposed upon Seth at the front, with the

additional certainty upon his part, that the entire safety of the company rested with him.

Haverland and Graham generally walked side by side, with Ina between them, and as watchful as though they had none but themselves to depend upon. They seldom indulged in conversation, except now and then to exchange a few words or inquiries.

As Seth Jones was well satisfied in his own mind that the post of danger was held by him, we will follow his adventures. After emerging from the valley, in which the whites had encamped, their way for a considerable distance led them through the unbroken forest, without hill or vale, and pretty thickly crowded with bushy, yielding undergrowth. Had a person chanced to cross the path of Seth, the only evidence he would have had of the presence of a human being would have been the snapping of a twig now and then, or the flitting of his form like a shadow from tree to tree, and perhaps the shrill, bird-like whistle as he signaled to those in the rear.

Through the forenoon, nothing occurred to excite suspicion on his part, but at the period mentioned he arrived at a point where his alarm was excited at once. The place offered such advantages for an Indian ambush, that he gave the signal for those behind to halt, and determined to make a thorough reconnaissance of the whole locality before passing through it. The spot referred to, had the appearance of having formerly been the bed of some large-sized lake, the waters of which having dried up years before, left a rich, productive soil, which was now covered over with the rankest undergrowth and vegetation. Not a tree of any size appeared. The hollow, or valley, was so much depressed that from the stand-point of Seth, he obtained a perfect view of the whole portion. It was about a third of a mile in breadth, and perhaps a couple of miles in length.

Seth stood a long time, running his eye over it, scanning every spot where it seemed likely an enemy might lurk. Hardly a point escaped his keen vision.

It was while he stood thus, eagerly scanning the valley, that his looks were suddenly attracted toward a point near the center of the valley, from which a faint, bluish wreath of smoke was curling upward. This puzzled our friend greatly. He possessed the curious, investigating habits so generally ascribed to his race, and his curiosity was wonderfully excited by this occurrence. That there was some design in it, not understood yet, he was well satisfied, and he determined that, before allowing those behind him to venture into the valley, he would gain all the knowledge possible of it. His first step was to take his own trail backward until he reached Haverland and Graham, to whom he imparted his intention. This done, he set forward again.

Having arrived at the point where he first discovered this suspicious appearance, he paused again for further consideration. The smoke was still visible, rising very slowly in the clear air, and making so slight an appearance that even his experienced eye searched a long time for it. Seth watched for awhile, until he felt he could not understand the meaning of it without venturing into the valley. This conclusion arrived at, he hesitated no longer, but descended and entered at once the luxuriant growth.

When fairly within it, he make a *detour* to the right, so as to pass around the fire, and to avoid the path that one unsuspicious of danger would be apt to follow. As he made his way slowly and cautiously forward, he paused at intervals and listened intently. Sometimes he bent his ear to the ground and lay for minutes at a time. But as yet not the slightest sound had been heard. Finally he judged that he must be near the fire that had excited his apprehensions. The snapping of a burning ember guided him, and a few minutes later he stood within sight of it.

Here he met a sight that chilled him with horror!

Some wretched human being was bound to a tree and had been burned to death. He was painted black as death, his scalped head drooped forward, so that, from where Seth stood, it was impossible to distinguish his features; but he saw enough to make him shudder at the awful fate he had so narrowly escaped. Every vestige of the flesh was burned off to the knees, and the bones, white and glistening, dangled to the crisp and blackened members above! The hands, tied behind, had passed through the fire unscathed, but every other part of the body was literally roasted! The smoke in reality was the smoke from this human body, and the stench, which was now horrible, had been noticed by Seth long before he suspected the cause.

"Heavens and earth!" he muttered to himself, "this is the first time I ever saw a person burned at the stake, and I hope in God it will be the last time. Can it be a *white man?*"

After some cautious maneuvering, he gained a point from which he could obtain a veiw of the face, and he experienced considerable relief when he discovered that it was not a white man. He was probably some unfortunate Indian, belonging to a hostile tribe, who had been captured by his enemies, and upon whom they had thus wreaked their vengeance. Whether he was a Mohawk, or the member of another tribe, it was impossible for Seth, under the circumstances, to tell. But what was singular and unaccountable to Seth was, that there appeared to be no other savages in the vicinity. He knew it was not their custom to leave a prisoner thus, and the very fact of their being absent upon the present occasion made him doubly cautious and suspicious.

It was while he stood meditating upon the terrible scene before him, that he was startled by the report of Haldidge's rifle. He was satisfied that it was his as it was from that direction, and he could not be mistaken in its report. He had noticed it during the conflict the night before as having a peculiar sound, entirely different from either his own or the savages'. This was a new source of wonder and perplexity. He was completely puzzled by the extraordinary turn affairs were taking. Some unusual cause must have discharged Haldidge's rifle. What it was he could only conjecture.

Still doubting and cautious, he determined to reconnoiter his own position before returning. Stooping almost to the earth, he made his way stealthily around to the opposite side of the fire. Here he stretched out flat upon the earth, and bent his ear to the ground. A faint tremor was heard. He raised his head and heard the brushing of somebody through the wood. The next moment, five Mohawk warriors, in all the horrid panoply of warpaint, stepped into the open space in front of the Indian who had been burned at the stake.

The report of the rifle appeared to be the cause of the apprehension among them. They conversed earnestly, in a low tone at first, gesticulating violently, without noticing in the least the heart-sickening spectacle before them. Seth was satisfied that they had no suspicions of his own proximity, for they gradually spoke louder until he managed to hear the most of what they said. As he expected, it was the rifle report. They seemed to understand that it had not been discharged by one of their own number, and were afraid that their presence had been discovered. Seth learned further that there were at least a dozen Indians in the neighborhood, every one of whom was led thither by the one object.

Consequently he must have missed the others entirely in his movements, or else they were in the rear and had been discoverd by Haldidge. That the latter was the case seemed more than probable. A collision in all probability had occurred between them and the hunter, and Seth felt that his presence was needed. Accordingly he turned to retrace his steps.

His presence was indeed required, for danger, dark and threatening, surrounded the little band of whites.

Chapter 16

IN WHICH A HUNTER'S NERVES
ARE TESTED

In the morning when our friends started upon their day's march, Haldidge, as said, fell behind in order to guard against surprise from this direction. Although expecting as little as did Seth any demonstration from this quarter, still he was too much of a backwoodsman to allow himself to lose any of his usual suspicion and watchfulness. Sometimes he would take the back trail for a long distance, and then wander off to the right or left of it for perhaps a mile or more. By this means, he kept a continual watch, not only upon the trail itself, but upon the neighborhood for a long distance around it, and, in case of pursuit, made so many and conflicting tracks, that it could not but puzzle and delay their enemies.

Near noon, and at the very moment that Seth paused to take a survey of the suspicious valley-like depression, and when not more than a furlong in the rear, Haldidge caught sight of three Indians just ahead of him. They were sitting upon the ground, in perfect silence, and seemingly waiting for the approach of some one. The hunter found himself as much perplexed as was Seth to account for what he saw. Whether it was some stratagem to entrap himself or not he could not tell, but, before venturing further, he made up his mind to gain a further knowledge of their intentions.

Haldidge had one formidable difficulty to contend with: the wood at this particular spot was open, and almost devoid of the protecting undergrowth, so that it was about impossible to approach them closer without discovering himself to them. He noticed lying a short distance behind them a large, heavy log, apparently much decayed. In fact, this was so near them, that could he gain it, he could overhear everything said. He had a slight knowledge of the Mohawk tongue—not enough to converse in it—but still enough to understand the drift of a conversation. Accordingly he determined to reach the spot at all hazards.

Haldidge desired, if possible, to communicate with Haverland and warn him of the proximity of danger. To do this, it was necessary to make a long *detour*, and upon further consideration he decided not to attempt it. Lying flat upon his face, he worked himself toward the log mentioned, keeping it between himself and the Indians, and approaching it as silently and as steadily as a snake. So cautiously and carefully was it done, that it required at least twenty minutes to reach it, and all this time the Indians maintained the same unbroken silence. At length the concealment was reached, and the hunter noticed with pleasure that it was hollow. He lost no time in entering it, where, coiling himself up in as small a space as possible, he took himself to listening. As if to completely favor him, there was a small rent in the log, through which even the whispers of the savages could be heard, and which also admitted a thin ray of light.

Here Haldidge cramped himself up and listened intently. But not a word was exchanged between the Indians, who remained as motionless as statues. In the course of a few minutes he heard a footfall upon the leaves, and a second after several savages seated themselves upon the very log in which he had concealed himself! He judged that there were at least a half-dozen. Those whom he had first seen appeared to have risen, and, meeting the others, they had all seated themselves upon the log together.

They immediately commenced conversing in so low and gutteral tones, that their deep base voices communicated their tremor to the log. Haldidge started as he soon learned that they were conversing about himself and the three fugitives. Of Seth they seemed to have no knowledge. He discovered that they had lain in ambush a short distance ahead to entrap Haverland, Graham, and Ina, and they were debating how *he* should be disposed of. They knew that he was acting in the capacity of scout and sentinel, and were fearful that he might detect the ambush, or at least escape it himself.

At this point, one of the Indians, probably impelled by some whim, stooped and looked into the log. Haldidge knew, by the darkness thus occasioned, that one of them was peering in it, and he scarcely breathed for a few seconds. But the face was removed, and the hollow being dark within—the small rent being on the opposite side of the hunter—the savage felt reassured and resumed the conversation.

But Haldidge was doomed to have a trial of his nerves, of which he had little dreamed. When he entered the log, it was head foremost, so that his feet were toward the opening, and his face was in the dim light beyond. He judged the rotten cavity extended several feet further back; but, as there was no necessity for entering further, he did not attempt to explore it. It was while he lay thus, his whole soul bent to the one act of listening, that he was startled by the deadly warning of a rattlesnake. He comprehended the truth in an instant. *There was one of these reptiles in the log beyond him!*

It is difficult to imagine a more fearful situation than the hunter's at this moment. He was literally environed by death; for it was at his head, his feet, and above him, and there was no escape below. He had just learned that his death was one of the objects of the Indians, so that to back out into their clutches would be nothing less than committing suicide. To remain where he was would be to disregard the second and last warning of the coiled rattlesnake. What was to be done? Manifestly nothing but to die like a man. Haldidge decided to risk the bite of the rattlesnake.

Despite himself, the hunter felt that the reptile was exerting its horrible fascination over him. Its small eyes, gleaming like tiny yet fiery stars, seemed to emit a magnetic ray—thin, pointed, and palpable, that pierced right into his brain. There was a malignant subtlety—an irresistible magnetism. Now the small, glittering point of light seemed to recede, then to approach and expand, and then to wave and undulate all around him. Sometimes that bright, lightning-like ray would shiver and tremble, and then straighten out with metal-like rigidity, and insinuate itself into his very being, like the invisible point of a spear.

There was a desire on the part of Haldidge to shake off this influence, which wrapped him like a mantle. There was the desire, we say, and yet there was a languid listlessness—a repugnance to make the effort. The feeling was something similar to that produced by a powerful opiate, when we are first recovering from it. There was that dim consciousness—that indistinct knowledge of the outer world—that certainty that we can break the bond that holds us, by one vigorous effort, and yet the same sluggish indifference that prevents the attempt.

Haldidge drew his breath faintly and slowly, yielding more and more to that fatal, subtle influence. He knew he was charmed, and yet he couldn't help it. It was now impossible to shake off that weight which pressed him down like an incubus. That outer world—so to speak—had now receded, and he was in another, from which he could not return without help besides his own. He seemed to be moving, flitting, sinking, and rising, through the thin air, borne upward and downward, hither and thither, on a wing of fire. The spell was complete. That extraordinary power which instinct holds over reason—that wonderful superiority which a reptile sometimes shows he can exert over man, the snake now held over the hunter.

At this point, from some cause or other, one of the savages struck the log a violent blow with his hatchet. Haldidge heard it. He drew a long breath, closed his eyes, and when he reopened them, looked down at his hands upon which his chin had been resting.

The charm was broken! The hunter had shaken off the fatal spell!

Like the knocking at the gate in Macbeth; which dispels the dark, awful world of gloom in which murderers have been moving and living, and ushers in our own world, with all its hurrying tide of human life and passions; so this blow of the Indian's tomahawk broke the subtle, magnetic spell of the serpent, and lifted the heavy mantle-like influence which wrapped Haldidge in its folds.

He looked downward and determined not to raise his eyes again, for he knew the same power would again rise above him. The serpent, seemingly conscious of its loss of influence, rattled once more, and prepared to strike. Haldidge stirred not a muscle; in fact, he had scarcely moved since entering the log. But the snake did not strike. The continued death-like stillness of the hunter evidently seemed to the reptile to be death itself. He coiled and uncoiled himself several times, and then lifting his head, crawled directly over his neck and body, and passed out of the log! Here he was killed by the Indians.

Now that the hunter was himself again, he prepared for further action. The Indians had arisen from the log and were at some distance. He could hear the mumbling of their voices, but could not distinguish their words. After awhile these ceased, and he heard no more.

Haldidge was now filled with apprehension for the others. He had enough faith in the power and cunning of Seth to feel pretty confident that he would neither lead any one into ambush or fall into one himself, let it be prepared as skillfully as it might be; but then he could know nothing of the Indians in the rear, who might surprise Haverland and Graham at any moment.

The hunter at length grew so restless and uneasy that he emerged from his hiding-place as rapidly and silently as possible. He looked cautiously around, but no savage was in sight. Filled with the most painful apprehensions, he hastened through the wood, avoiding the trail of his friends, however, and finally came in sight of them. Before making himself known, he concluded to reconnoiter the place. While doing so, he saw the head of an Indian rise slowly above a bush, and peer over at the unconscious whites. Without losing a moment, he raised his rifle, took a quick but sure aim, and fired. Then calling out to Haverland and Graham, he sprung for an instant into view.

"Make for cover," he shouted; "the Indians are upon us."

In an instant every one of the whites was invisible.

‹‹

Chapter 17

ENCOMPASSED BY DANGER

At the first warning of Haldidge, Haverland comprehended the threatened danger in an instant. Catching Ina in his arms, he sprung into the wood, sheltering himself behind a tree so quickly that Ina, till that moment, did not comprehend the meaning of the startling movements around her.

"What is it, father?" she whispered.

"Keep quiet, daughter, and don't move."

She said no more, but shrunk beneath his sheltering form, believing that his strong arm was capable of protecting her against any foe, however formidable.

Graham, at the alarm, had leaped toward Haldidge, and the two sheltered themselves within a few feet of each other. The shot of the hunter had been fatal, for that yell which the North American Indian, like the animal, gives when he receives his death-wound, was heard, and the fall had also reached his ears.

Minute after minute passed away and nothing further was heard of the savages. This silence was as full of meaning, and as dangerous as any open demonstration upon the part of the Indians. What new plan they might be concocting was a mystery to all but themselves. At length Graham ventured to speak:

"What do you suppose they're up to, Haldidge?"

"Hatching some devilish plot, I expect."

"It seems it requires a good while to do it."

"Don't get impatient; they'll show themselves in time."

"Have you any idea of their number?"

"There was something like a half-dozen prowling around."

"There is one less now, at any rate."

"I suppose so; but there's enough left to occasion a little trouble at least. Where did Alf go with the gal?"

"Off yonder, a short distance. Hadn't we better get closer together?"

"No; I don't know as there is any necessity for it. We're as safe, drawn up in this style, as in any other I can imagine."

"I am afraid, Haldidge, they will make an attempt to surround us. In such a case, wouldn't Haverland be in great peril?"

"They can't get around him without running their heads in range with our rifles, and Alf is a man who'll be pretty sure to discover such a trick without any help."

"Where can Seth be?"

"Not very far off; that shot of mine will be pretty sure to bring him."

"Haldidge, how was it that you discovered these Mohawks? Did you know of their presence before you fired?"

"Yes, long before. I've an idea they've been tracking you for an hour or two."

"Why, then, was their attack deferred?"

"They have made no attack, remember. I don't believe they had any such intention. There is an ambush somewhere ahead that they have laid, and it was their idea to walk you into that."

"What was their notion in watching us so closely?"

"They were hunting for me, for I heard them say as much, and, I suppose, in case you didn't walk into their trap, why, they were going to make the attack."

"Can it be that Seth has fallen into the snare?" asked Graham in anxious tones.

"No, sir; such a thing can't be. He isn't such a fool as that amounts to. He is making himself generally useful; you can make up your mind to that. He's a smart chap, for all he is the most awkward, long-legged, gawky person I ever came across."

"I am puzzled to know who he is. It seems to me that he is only playing a part. Several times in conversing with him, he has used language such as none but a scholar and polished gentleman would use. At others and most of the time, he uses that ungainly mode of expression, which, in itself, is laughable. At any rate, whoever he may be, he is a friend, and the interest which he takes in the safety of Haverland and his family, is as efficient as it is singular."

"Maybe the interest is in Ina," said Haldidge, with a sly look.

"I understand you, but you are mistaken. He has assured me as much. No; there seems nothing of that feeling at all in him. He loves her as he would a child, but no more."

"How was it that he made that awkward tumble into the Indians' hands, when they gave you such a hard run for it?"

"That was all through my own blundering. He was cautious enough, but I became so impatient and careless that I precipitated him into the danger which would have been fatal to anyone else. It was no fault of his."

"I am glad to hear it, for it seemed odd to me."

This conversation which we have recorded, it must not be supposed, was carried on in an ordinary tone, and with that earnestness which would have lessened their habitual caution. It was in whispers, and hardly once during its progress did the two look at each other. Sometimes they would not speak for several minutes, and then exchange but a single question and answer.

It was now toward the middle of the afternoon, and it became pretty evident that night would have to be spent in this neighborhood.

"I do hope that Seth will make his appearance before dark," remarked Graham.

"Yes; I hope he will, for it will be dangerous when we can't see him."

"He must be aware of the threatened danger."

"Yes; I am pretty confident that he is not very distant."

"Hallo! what's that?" whispered Graham.

"Ah! keep quiet; there's something going on there."

A deathlike silence reigned for a few minutes; then a slight rustling was heard close by Haldidge, and as he turned his alarmed gaze toward it, the form of Seth Jones rose to his feet beside him.

"Where did you come from?" asked Graham, in astonishment.

"I have been watching you. In a little trouble, eh?"

"We've found out we've got neighbors."

"They're not very nigh neighbors, leastways."

"What do you mean?"

"There isn't one in a quarter of a mile."

Haldidge and Graham looked at the speaker in astonishment.

"I tell *you*, it's so, Hallo, Haverland!" he called out, stepping out from his concealment. "Come out here; there is nothing to be afraid of."

The manner of the speaker was singular, but the others well knew that he was not one to expose himself or others to danger, and accordingly all gathered around him.

"Are you not running great risk?" asked Haverland, still experiencing some slight misgivings at stepping upon a spot which he well knew was so dangerous a short time before.

"No, sir; I reckon you needn't be at all skeerish, for if there was any danger of them Mohawks, I wouldn't be standing here."

"It's getting toward night, Seth, and we should make up our minds at once as to what we are going to do or how we are going to spend it.

"Can you shoot a gun?" asked Seth, suddenly, of Ina.

"I don't believe you can beat me," she answered, lightly.

"That is good."

So saying, he stepped into the bushes, where the dead body of the

Indian was lying. Stooping over him, he removed the rifle from his
rigid grasp, took his bullet-pouch and powder-horn and handed them
to Ina.

"Now, there are five of us, all well armed," said he, "and if any of
them infarnal Mohawks gets ahead of us, we all desarve red night-
caps for it."

"How are we to prevent it, when there seems to be ten times our
number following us?" asked Haverland.

"The way on it is this 'ere; there is about a dozen trying to carcum-
vent us. They're now ahead of us, and have laid an ambush for us. If
we can pass that ambush we're safe as if we was home fair and sure.
And there must be no *if* about it, for that ambush must be passed to-
night."

Chapter 18

GETTING OUT OF THE WILDERNESS

Night, dark and gloomy, slowly settled over the forest. Nothing was
heard save the dull soughing of the wind through the tree-tops, or the
occasional howl of the wolf in the distance, or perhaps the near
scream of the panther. Heavy, tumultuous clouds were wheeling
through the sky, rendering the inky darkness doubly intense, and
shrouding even the clearings in impenetrable gloom.

By and by, the distant rumbling of thunder came faintly through
the air, and then a quivering fork of fire, like a stream of blood, trembling upon the edge of the dark storm-cloud for an instant. The heavy
clouds, growing darker and more awful, poured forward until they
seemed to concentrate in the western sky, where they towered aloft
like some old embattled castle. The thunder grew heavier, until it
sounded like the rolling of chariot-wheels over the courts of heaven,
and the red streams of liquid fire streamed down the dark walls of the
Storm Castle. Now and then the subtle element flamed out into a daz-
zling, instantaneous flash, and the bolt burst overhead.

"Keep close to me, and step light, for I tell *you* there's enough
lightning."

Seth had thoroughly reconnoitered the valley to which we have referred, and had found, as he had expected, that there was an ambush laid for them. There was a sort of footpath, apparently worn by the passing of wild animals, which nearly crossed the valley. It was here that the Indians supposed the fugitives would be entrapped, until the death of a too daring member of their party led them to suspect that their intentions were discovered.

The little band was hours in crossing this valley. Seth, with an almost inaudible "'sh!" would often pause, and they would stand for many anxious minutes listening intently for the dreaded danger. They would resume their march, stepping with painful slowness.

It was at least three hours after the fugitives commenced this journey, and when Seth judged that he must be nearly through it, that he suddenly discovered he was walking in the very path he had striven so carefully to avoid. He was considerably startled at this and left at once.

"'Sh! down!" he whispered, turning his face behind him.

They were not ten feet from the path, when they all sunk quietly to the earth. Footsteps were now audible to all. The darkness was too profound to discern anything, but all heard their enemies almost near enough to touch them with the outstretched hand.

The situation of our friends was immediately perilous. The Mohawks were not passing along the path as at first supposed, but evidently searching it! Haldidge and Seth felt that they could not be aware of their proximity, and yet they knew a discovery was unavoidable.

Seth Jones rose to his feet so silently that even Haldidge, who was within a foot of him, did not hear a rustle. He then touched Haverland's ear with his mouth, and whispered:

"Scatter with the gal as quick as lightning, for they must find us out in a minute."

Haverland lifted Ina in his strong arm—she needed no caution—and stepped forward. It was impossible not to make some noise, when the wet bushes brushed against them. The savages heard it and started cautiously forward. They evidently suspected it was the fugitives, and had no suspicion that any one was lingering in the rear. The first warning Seth had was of a savage running plump against him.

"Beg your pardon, I didn't see you," exclaimed Seth, as each bounded backward. "Curse you," he muttered, "I only wish I could sight you for a minute."

Seth, Haldidge and Graham were now maneuvering against some five or six Indians. Had a bright flash of lightning illuminated the scene, just at this time, it is probable that all would have laughed outright at each other's attitudes and movements. The Indians, upon finding how near they were to their deadliest enemies, immediately bounded backward several yards, in order to avoid a too sudden collision with them. The three whites did precisely the same thing, each in his own characteristic way. Seth leaped to one side, crouched down in his usual panther-like manner, with his rifle in his left hand and his knife in his right, waiting until he could settle in his mind the precise spot upon which one of the savages was standing before making a lunge at him.

It would be tedious to narrate the artifices and stratagem resorted to by these two opposing forces. Simon Kenton and Daniel Boone once reached the opposite sides of the Ohio river at the same moment, and at the same time each became aware of the presence of another person upon the opposite side. These two old hunters and acquaintances reconnoitered for over *twenty-four hours,* before they discovered that they were friends. For nearly two hours, the Mohawks and the whites maneuvered with the most consummate skill against each other; now retreating and leading, dodging and eluding, each striving to lead the other into some trap that was as skillfully avoided, until, judging that Haverland was safe, Seth concluded to retreat himself. Accordingly, he cautiously withdrew, and ten minutes later found himself upon the outermost edge of the valley.

Ten minutes after Seth departed, Haldidge moved off, of course unknown to himself, in precisely the same direction. Graham soon adopted the same course. They all came out of the dangerous valley within twenty feet of each other. It took them some time before they came together; but, as each suspected the identity of the other, this did not require as long as it otherwise would.

"Now, boys," whispered Seth, "I cac'late we're out of the Valley of Death. Best give it a wide berth, is the private opinion of Seth Jones."

"But how about Haverland?" Graham asked.

"I think they must have come out near that point," replied the other.

"Let us move round then, and we've got to be spry, for daylight can't be far off, and I'm thinking as how them Ingins will find out that we've absconded; and, my gracious! won't they feel cheap?"

Just as the light of morning appeared in the east, they came upon Haverland, and resumed their journey. No halt was made for breakfast, for they were all too anxious to get forward on their way. In the course of an hour or so, they struck a sort of path, made by the passage of wild animals, which, besides being so hardened as to conceal their trail, was easily traveled.

Seth and Haldidge were too experienced woodsmen to relax their vigilance. They maintained the same duty as before, the former taking it upon himself to lead the way through the wilderness, and the latter to guard against danger from behind. The settlement toward which they were so anxiously hastening, was still several days distant, and to reach it, it was necessary to cross a river of considerable breadth. This river was reached by Seth at noon.

"By gracious! I forgot about this!" he exclaimed to himself. "Wonder if the gal can swim? If she can't, how are we going to get her over? Put her on a chip, I s'pose, and let the breeze blow her across; the rest of us can swim, in course."

A few minutes later, our friends stood consulting upon the banks of the stream.

This consultation ended in active preparations for crossing on a raft. Hunting up material for constructing a raft now was the order of the hour. This was a work of extreme difficulty. They had no instruments except their hunting-knives, and these were little better than nothing. Large rotten limbs were broken from the trees, and placed together by Haverland, who took upon himself the task of lashing them with withes, while the others collected wood.

Haldidge went up the river, and Seth and Graham went down. Graham soon noticed a large, half-decayed log, partly lying in the water. "Just the thing, exactly! Why, it's a raft itself. This will save further trouble. Let us launch it at once, and float it up to the spot," he exclaimed delightedly.

The two approached it, stooped, and were in the very act of lifting it into the water, when Seth suddenly removed his shoulder, and arose to the upright position.

"Come, give us a lift," said Graham.

"Graham, I guess I wouldn't take the log, I don't think it will answer."

"Won't answer!" Why not? In the name of common sense, give some reason."

"Let that log alone! Do you understand?"

Graham looked up, and started at the appearance of Seth. His eyes fairly scintillated, and he seemed ready to spring upon him, for daring to utter a word of dispute.

"Come along with me!" commanded Seth, in a voice hoarse with passion.

It wouldn't do to disregard that command; and, taking up his rifle, Graham lost no time in obeying it. But he wondered greatly whether Seth was suddenly become crazy or foolish. He followed him a short distance, and then hastened up beside him. Seeing that his face had recovered its usual expression, he gained courage and asked what he meant by such commands.

"Didn't you take notice that that log was holler?"

"I believe it was, although I did not examine it closely."

"Wal, if you *had* examined it closely, or even loosely, so that you took a peep into the log, you'd have seen a big Mohawk curled up there snug and nice!"

"Is it possible? How came you to see him?"

"The minute I see'd the log was holler, I had my s'picions that there might be something or other in it, and I made up my mind that we shouldn't try to lift it till I knowed how it was. When I come to look closer, I knowed thar was something sure enough, for the way the bark was scratched at the mouth showed that plain enough. It wouldn't do, you see, to stoop down and peep in, for like as not the redskin would blaze away smack into my face. So I jest dropped my cap, and, as I stooped down to pick it up, I kind of slewed one eye 'round over my shoulder, and, as sure as blazes, I seen a big moccasin! I did, by gracious. I then proceeded to argufy the question; and, after considerable discussion, both in the affirmative and negative, I came unanimously to the conclusion that as I'd seen an Ingin's foot, if I'd foller it up, I'd be pretty sure to find the Ingin himself, and, moreover, also, if there was *one* Ingin about, you could make up your mind that there are plenty more not far off. By gracious! if I hadn't looked a little ramparageous, you wouldn't have let go that log so very quick, eh?"

"No; you alarmed me considerably. But what is to be done?"

"The cowards are poking around the woods, fixing out some plan to ambush us again. They've no idea we've smelt that rat that's brewing in the bud, and they're too cowardly to show their faces until they find they've got to, or let us slip."

"Shall we tell Haverland?"

"No; I will let Haldidge know of it, if he hasn't found it out already. The raft has got to be made, and we must keep on at it till it's finished, as though we knowed everything was right. Keep still, now, or Alf will notice our talking."

They were so close to the woodman that they changed their conversation.

"No material?" asked Haverland, looking up.

"It's rather scarce down where we've been," replied Graham.

"Sha'n't I help you?" asked Ina, looking up archly.

"I guess we won't need your help, as Haldidge seems to have enough already."

The hunter at this moment approached, bending under the weight of two heavy limbs. They were instantly lashed together, but it was found that the raft was much too weak and light, and more stuff was necessary before it would even float Ina. Accordingly, Haldidge plunged into the wood again. Seth walked beside him until they were a few yards away, when he asked:

"Do you understand?"

"What?" asked the hunter, in astonishment.

"Over there," answered Seth, jerking his thumb over his shoulder, toward the log mentioned.

"Red-skins?"

"I rather guess so."

"I smelt them a while ago. You'd better go back and watch Alf. I'll get enough wood. Danger?"

"No; they'll try some game; look out for yourself."

With this Seth turned on his heel, and rejoined Haverland. Graham was a short distance away cutting withes, which the woodman was as busily using. As Seth came up he noticed Ina. She was sitting upon the ground a few feet from her father, and her attention seemed wholly absorbed with something down the stream. Seth watched her closely.

"Isn't that a log yonder?" she asked.

Seth looked in the direction indicated. With no small degree of astonishment, he saw the identical tree which he and Graham disputed over, afloat in the river. This awoke his apprehensions, and he signaled at once for Haldidge.

"What's the row?" asked the hunter, as he came up.

Seth gave his head a toss down-stream, by way of reply, and added:

"Don't let 'em see you're watching it, for it might scare 'em."

Nevertheless Haldidge turned square around and took a long, searching look at the suspicious object.

"What do you make of it?"

"Them Mohawks are the biggest fools I ever heard of, to think such an old trick as *that* can amount to anything."

"What trick do you mean?" asked Haverland.

"Why, you see that log yonder, half-sunk in the water, that we are all looking at? Well, there are four or five Mohawks behind that, waiting for us to launch our raft."

"Maybe it's nothing more than a floating tree or log," said the woodman.

"Y-e-s," drawled the hunter, sarcastically, "*maybe* so; I s'pose a log would be very apt to float *up*-stream, wouldn't it?"

"Why is it approaching?" asked Graham.

"Not *very* fast," answered Seth, "for I guess it's hard work for them fellers to swim up-stream. Ah, by gracious! I understand the game. Look; don't you see it's further out than it was? They're going to get as near the middle as they can, and so close to us that when we undertake to cross, the current will carry us right down plump against 'em, when they'll rise up in their wrath and devour us. Fact, sure as you live!"

"We might as well understand matters at once," added Haldidge. "The plan of the Indians is undoubtedly the same as Seth suggests. In crossing, we cannot help drifting downward, and they are trying to locate themselves so as to make a collision between us. But they will make no attack until we are in the water. So you may keep at work upon the raft, Alf, without any fear, while Seth and I reconnoiter. Come, Graham, you may as well go along with us. Let us enter the wood separately at first, and we'll come together as soon as we can get out of sight. Act as though we didn't suspicion anything, and I'll wager my rifle here against your hat that we'll outwit the cowards after all."

The three entered the wood as proposed. After going a few yards they came together again.

"Now," whispered Seth, "by gracious, you will see fun. Follow close, boys, and keep shady."

Being now fairly within the wood, they proceeded in a direction parallel with the course of the river, using extreme caution, for it was more than probable that some of the Indian scouts were secreted in the wood. Keeping entirely away from the river until Seth judged they were below the suspicious log, they approached it. A reckless move, at this point, would have been fatal. Fortunately, there was a species of grass growing from the wood out to a considerable distance in the water. Through this they made their way much after the fashion of snakes. Seth, as usual, was in the front, and it struck Graham that he absolutely slid over the ground without any exertion on his part.

In a moment they were down to the river's brink. They now slowly raised their heads and peered over and through the grass out into the river. The log was a short distance above, and they had a perfect view of the side which was opposite to Haverland. Not a sign of an Indian was visible. The tree seemed anchored in the middle of the stream.

"There is something there," whispered Graham.

"'Sh! keep quiet and watch, and you'll see!" admonished Seth.

A moment more and the log, apparently without any human agency, slightly changed its position. As it did so, Graham saw something glisten on the top of it. He was at a loss to understand what it meant, and turned inquiringly toward Haldidge. The latter had his keen eyes fixed upon it, and there was a grim, exulting smile upon his face. He motioned for Graham to preserve silence.

As our hero turned his gaze once more toward the river, he saw that the log was still further into the stream. Something like polished metal was seen glistening even brighter than before. He looked carefully, and in a moment he saw that there were several rifles resting upon the surface of it.

While gazing and wondering where the owners of these weapons could conceal themselves, the water suddenly seemed to part on the side of the log toward them, and the bronzed face of an Indian rose to view. Up, up it went, until the shoulders were out of the water, when he remained stationary a moment, and peered over the log at Haverland. Seemingly satisfied, he quietly sunk down into the water again; but Graham noticed that he did not disappear beneath the surface, where he had hitherto kept himself, nestled in so close to the log that almost any one would have supposed that he was a part of it. His head resembled exactly a large black knot in the wood. Graham now noticed also that there were two other protuberances, precisely like the first. The conclusion was certain. There were three fully-armed Mohawks concealed behind the log, who were doing their utmost to steal upon the fugitives.

"Just exactly one apiece, as sure as you live," exclaimed Seth, exultingly. "Get ready, each of you, for your man. Graham, take the one nearest this way; you the next one, Haldidge, and I'll pick off the last one in the genuine style. Get ready, quick, for I've got to hurrah over the way things is coming round."

The three pointed their deadly instruments toward the unsuspicious savages. Each took a long, deliberate and certain aim.

"Now, then, together—*fire!*"

Simultaneously the three rifles flashed, but that of Seth missed fire. The others sped true to their aim. Two yells of deathly agony broke upon the air, and one of the savages sprung his entire length out of the water, and then sunk like lead to the bottom. The other clung quivering to the log for a moment, and then loosening his hold, disappeared beneath the water.

"Thunder and blazes!" exclaimed Seth, springing to his feet, "hand me your rifle, Graham. Something is the matter with mine, and that other imp will get away. Quick! hand it here!"

He took the rifle and commenced loading it as rapidly as possible, keeping his eye upon the Indian, who was now swimming desperately for the other bank.

"Is yer iron loaded, Haldidge?" he asked.

"No; I've been watching you and that chap's doubling, to see who'll get the best, so long, that I didn't think of it."

"Load again, for s'posen this gun should miss fire, too, he'd get off then, sure. Wal, my stars! if he isn't come out now!"

The Indian, as if scorning the danger, rose slowly from the water, and walked leisurely toward the shelter of the wood.

"Now, my fine feller, see if you can dodge this?"

Seth once more aimed at the retreating Indian, and this time pulled the trigger; but, to his unutterable chagrin, the rifle flashed in the pan! Before Haldidge could finish loading his gun, and before Seth could even reprime his, the Indian had disappeared in the wood.

"By the hokey-pokey! what's got into the guns?" exclaimed Seth, in a perfect fury. "That's *twice* I've been fooled. Worse'n two slaps in the face by a purty woman, I'll swow. Hallo! what's that?"

The discharge of a rifle across the river had sent the bullet so close to him as to whisk off a tuft of his long, sandy hair.

"By gracious; that was pretty well done," he exclaimed, scratching his head as though he was slightly wounded.

"Look out, for heaven's sake! Get down!" called Graham, seizing him by the skirt of his hunting-dress, and jerking him downward.

"Don't know but what it *is* the best plan." replied the imperturbable Seth, going down on his knees in time to avoid another foul shot. "There are plenty of the imps about, ain't there?"

The firing so alarmed Haverland that he desisted from his work, and sought the shelter of the wood. By this time, too, the afternoon was so far advanced that darkness had already commenced settling over the stream and woods. Crossing on the raft was now out of the question, for it would have been nothing less than suicide to have attempted it, when their enemies had given them such convincing evidence of their skill in the use of the rifle, even at a greater distance than to the middle of the stream. But the river had to be crossed for all that, and the only course left was to shift their position to some other place, build a new raft, and make another attempt.

There was no excuse for further delay, and the party immediately set forward. The sky again gave signs of a storm. Several rumbles of thunder were heard, but the lightning was so distant as to be of neither benefit or use to them. The sky was filled with heavy tumultuous clouds, which rendered the darkness perfectly intense and impenetrable; and, as none of them understood a foot of the ground over which they were traveling, it may well be supposed that their progress was neither rapid nor particularly pleasant. The booming of the thunder continued, and shortly the rain commenced falling. The drops were of that big kind which are often formed in summer, and which rattle through the leaves like a shower of bullets.

"Can you look ahead, Seth?" asked Graham.

"In course I can. The darkness don't make no difference not at all to me. I can see just as well on a dark night as I can in daylight, and, what is more, I *do*. I should like to see me make a misstep or stumble —."

Further utterance was checked by the speaker pitching, with a loud splash, head-foremost over and into something.

"*You* hurt, Seth?" asked Graham, in alarm, yet half tempted to give way to the mirth that was convulsing those behind him.

"Hurt!" exclaimed the unfortunate one, scrambling to his feet; "I believe every bone in my body is broken in two; and by gracious! my head is cracked, and both legs put out of joint, the left arm broke above the elbow, and the right one severed completely!"

Notwithstanding these frightful injuries, the speaker was moving about with wonderful dexterity.

"My gracious!" what do you suppose I've tumbled into?" he suddenly asked.

"Into a pitfall or a hole in the ground," replied Graham. "It's my opinion, too, that it will be very easy, with this noise we are making, to stumble into the Mohawks' hands."

"I should think you ought to know that I *didn't* fall," retorted Seth, angrily. "I happened to see sumthin', and I stepped forward to see if it would hold my weight. What are you laughing at, I should like to know?"

"What is it that you have stepped into?" asked Haverland.

"Why, it's nothing less than a *boat*, dragged up here by the varmints, I s'pose."

Such, indeed, was the case. There was a very large-sized canoe directly before them, and not a sign of the presence of others besides themselves. Not a more fortunate thing could have happened. Upon examination, the boat was found to be of unusual length and breadth, and amply sufficient to carry twenty men. It was quickly pushed back into the stream.

"Come, tumble in, and we'll set sail," said Seth.

The fugitives, without any hesitation, entered the boat, and Seth and Haldidge, lending their shoulders to it, shoved it into the river, and sprung in as it floated away.

Chapter 19

DENOUEMENT

The whites found in a moment that they had committed a great mistake in launching as they did. In the first place, there was not an oar in the boat, and, thus, not being able to "paddle their own canoe," they were also deprived of their ability to paddle one belonging to some one else. Besides this, the river was as dark as Styx, and the whole sky and air were of the same inky blackness, and not one in the boat had the remotest idea of where they were going, whether it was to pitch over some falls, down some rapids, or into the bank.

"I'm going to set down and consider which is the biggest fool, Haldidge, you or me, in starting out in this canoe which we *borrowed* for a short time."

So saying, Seth made his way to the stern of the canoe, where he rested himself—not upon the bottom of it, as he expected, but upon something soft, which emitted a grunt audible to all, as he did so.

"My gracious! what's under me?" he exclaimed, reaching his hand down and feeling around in the dark. "A live Ingin, as sure as my name is Seth Jones. Ah, you copper-headed monkey!"

It was as he said. An Indian had stretched out on his back, with his feet dangling over the edge of the canoe, and Seth, without the faintest suspicion of his presence, had seated himself square upon his breast. As may be supposed, this was not relished at all by the startled savage, and he made several strenuous efforts to roll him off.

"Now, just lay still," commanded Seth, "for I've an idea that I can't find a more comfortable seat."

The savage was evidently so thoroughly frightened that he ceased his efforts and lay perfectly quiet and motionless.

"Have you got a real Indian here?" asked Haldidge, as he came up to Seth.

"To be sure I have; just feel under me, and see if I hain't."

"What are you going to do with him?"

"Nothing."

"Are you going to let him off? Let's pitch him overboard."

"No you won't, Haldidge. I've two or three good reasons for not doing such a thing. In the first place, there ain't no need of it, the poor imp hasn't hurt us; and, for all I detest his whole cowardly race, I don't believe in killing them, except when they've done you some injury or are trying to. The most important reason, however, is that I don't want my seat disturbed."

"He is a cussed fool to let you sit on him that way. I'd give you a toss if I was in his place, that would send you overboard."

"Not if you knew what was best for you. Thunder!"

Perhaps the Indian understood the words of the hunter. At any rate, he made an attempt to carry out his suggestion, and well-nigh did it, too. Just as Seth gave vent to the exclamation recorded, he pitched headlong against Haverland, knocking him over upon his back, and falling upon him. At the same instant the savage sprung overboard, and swam rapidly away in the darkness.

"That's a mean trick," said Seth, as he recovered his sitting position. "I was jest setting on him to keep the rain off. Jest like the ungrateful dog!"

The attention of all was now directed to the progress of the canoe. Drifting slowly onward through the darkness, no one knowing whither, their situation began to assume a terrible form. There was no power in their hands to guide it, and should they run into any of the trees which had caught in the bottom, or upon a rock, they would be instantly swamped. But there was no help for it, and each one seated and braced himself for the shock which might come at any instant.

It was while they were proceeding in this manner, that they all heard the bottom of the canoe grate over something, then tremble for a moment, and suddenly come to a stand-still. The stern swung rapidly round and commenced filling.

"Overboard, men, all of you! We're sinking!"

Each sprung into the water, which was not more than two feet deep, and the canoe, thus lightened of its load, instantly freed itself, and floated off in the darkness.

"Don't move, till I take a few soundings," said Seth.

He naturally supposed that to reach the shore, he must take a direction at right-angles with the current. A few steps showed him that he was not in the river itself, but was walking in that portion which had overflowed its banks.

"Follow on, boys; we're right!" he called out.

Bushes and grass entangled their feet, and the branches overhead brushed their faces, as they toiled out of the water. A few moments and they were upon solid land again. The canoe had carried them safely across the river, so that this troublesome task was finished.

"Now, if we only had a fire," said Haverland.

"Yes; for Ina must be suffering."

"Oh! don't think of me!" replied the brave little girl, cheerfully.

Seth discovered with his customary shrewdness that the storm had been very slight in this section, and the wood was comparatively dry. By removing the leaves upon the surface of the ground, there were others beneath which were perfectly free from dampness. A quantity of these were thrown in a heap, a number of twigs found among them placed upon the top, and some larger branches placed upon these in turn. After great difficulty, Seth managed to catch a spark from his steel and tinder, and in a few moments they had a rousing, roaring, genial fire.

"That's fine," said Graham. "But won't it be dangerous, Seth?"

"Let it be, then; I'm bound to dry my skin tonight, if there's any vartue in fire."

But the Indians didn't choose to disturb them, although it was rather a reckless proceeding upon their part. It was more than probable, as Seth Jones remarked, that their pursuers had lost their trail, and would experience some difficulty in regaining and following it.

Morning at last broke upon the hungry, miserable, hopeful fugitives. As the light increased they looked about them and discovered that they had camped at the base of a large, heavily-wooded hill. It was also noticed that Haldidge, the hunter, was absent. While wondering at this, the report of his rifle was heard, and in a few moments he was seen descending the hill, bending under the weight of a half-grown deer. This was hastily dressed, several good sized pieces skewered and cooked in the flame, and our friends made as hearty and substantial a meal as was ever made in this world.

"Before starting upon our journey again," said Haldidge, "I want you all to go to the top of the hill, here, with me, and see what a fine view we shall have."   ,

"Oh! we've no time for views," replied Seth.

"I am afraid there is little spare time," added the woodman.

"But this is particularly fine, and I think you will be well pleased with it."

The hunter was so urgent that the others were finally obliged to consent. Accordingly they commenced the ascent, Haldidge leading them, and all anxiety, smiles and expectation.

"See how you like that view!" said he, pointing off to the west.

The fugitives gazed in the direction indicated. The prospect was indeed one which at that time pleased them more than could have any other in the universe; for below them, about half a mile distant, was the very village toward which they had been so long making their way. It looked unusually beautiful that morning in the clear sunshine. A score of cabins nestled closely together, and the heavy smoke was lazily ascending from several chimneys, while here and there a settler could be seen moving about. At one corner of the village stood the block-house, and the gaping mouth of its swivel shone in the morning sun like burnished silver. One or two small boats were visible in the water, their ashen paddles flashing brightly as they were dipped by strong and active hands. The river, down which the woodman and his wife and sister had escaped, flowed at the foot of the village, and its windings could be traced by the eye for miles. Here and there, scattered over the country, could be seen an enterprising settler's cabin, resembling in the distance a tiny beehive.

"You haven't told me how you are pleased with the landscape," said the hunter.

"Ah, Haldidge, you know better than to ask that question," replied Haverland, in a shaking voice. "Thank God that He has been so merciful to us!"

They now commenced descending the hill. Not a word was exchanged between them, for their hearts were too full for utterance. A strange spell seemed to have come over Seth Jones. At sight of the village, he had suddenly become thoughtful and silent, refusing even to answer a question. His head was bent down. Evidently his mind was engrossed upon some all-absorbing subject. Several times he sighed deeply, and pressed his hand to his heart, as though the tumultuous throbbing there pained him. The expression of his face was wonderfully changed. That quizzing, comical look was entirely gone, while wrinkles at the eyebrows and base of the nose could be seen no more. His face appeared to be positively handsome. It was a wonderful metamorphosis, and the question passed around unexpressed: "Is that Seth Jones?"

All at once, he seemed to become sensible that the eyes of others were upon him, and that he had forgotten himself. That old, peculiar expression came back to his face, and a few steps of the old straddling gait were taken, and Seth Jones was himself again!

The sentinels in the block-house had discovered and recognized the fugitives, and when they arrived at the palisade which surrounded the village, there were numbers waiting to receive them.

"I will see you all again!" said Haldidge, separating from the others and passing toward the upper end of the settlement.

After pausing a few moments to answer the inquiries of their friends, Haverland led the way toward the cabin where he had left his wife and sister. Here he found the good settlers had erected and presented him with a house. As he stepped softly to the door, intending to give his wife a playful surprise, she met him. With a low cry of joy, she sprung forward and was held in his arms, and the next instant she and Ina were clasped together and weeping.

"Thank Heaven! thank Heaven! Oh, my dear, dear child, I thought you lost forever."

Graham and Seth stood respectfully to one side for a few moments. The latter cleared his throat several times and brushed his arm across his forehead in a suspicious manner. As the mother regained herself, she turned and recognized Graham, and greeted him warmly.

"And you, too," she said, taking Seth's hand, and looking up into his face, "have been more than a friend to me. May Heaven reward you, for *we* never can."

"There! by gracious! don't say no more! boohoo! ahem! I believe I've caught a cold, being so exposed to the night air!"

But it was of no use; the tears *would* come; and Seth, for a few seconds, wept like a baby, yet smiled even through his tears. They all entered the house.

"Our first duty is to thank God for his mercy. Let us all do it," said the woman.

All sunk devoutly upon their knees, joining in fervent thanksgiving to the great Being who had shown his goodness to them in such a marvelous manner.

The settlers, with true politeness of heart, forbore to intrude until they judged the family were desirous of seeing them. After they had arisen from their knees, Mary, the sister of Haverland, entered. Graham chanced to glance at Seth, that moment, and was startled at the emotion he exhibited. He flushed scarlet, and trembled painfully, but, by a strong effort, recovered himself in time to greet her. She thanked him again, and began conversing, when she saw that he was embarrassed and ill at ease. A flash of suspicion crossed her fine, calm face, and it became pale and flushed by turns. What a riot of emotion was making in her heart only she herself knew; her face soon became passive and pensive; and a pathos gleamed from her sad eyes which sent Seth quickly out of doors to commune with the mysteries of his own thoughts.

The cabin was crowded until near midnight with congratulating friends. Prominent among these, was the man who officiated in the capacity of minister for the settlement. He was a portly, genial, good-natured man, of the Methodist persuasion, and a preacher for the times— one who could plow, reap, chop wood, and lead the settlers against their foes, when he deemed it necessary, or preach and practice the gospel before them.

It was a glad—a happy reunion—a night that was long remembered.

———

Just one week after the reunion the little party was seated in Haverland's home, composed of Ina, Seth Jones, the woodman, Mrs. Haverland and Mary. Seth sat in one corner, conversing with Ina, while the other three were also together. There was a happy look upon each face. Even the sweet, melancholy beauty of Mary was lighted up by a smile. She was beautiful—queenly so. Her hair, black as night, was gathered behind, as if to restrain its tendency to curl; but, in spite of this, a refractory one was constantly intruding itself. A faint color was visible in her cheeks, and her blue eye had in it something of a gleam of the common joy and peace.

Seth had remained most of the time with the woodman. Several times he had asked Mary Haverland to walk with him, and yet upon each occasion, when about to start, he became painfully nervous, and begged to be excused. And then his language was so different at times. Often he would converse with words so polished and well-chosen, as to show unmistakably that he was a scholar. Perhaps the reader has noticed this discrepancy in his conversation. It attracted attention, and strengthened many in their belief that for some unknown reason he was playing a part.

At the present time there was a nervousness in his manner; and, although he was holding a playful conversation with Ina, his eyes were constantly wandering to the face of Mary Haverland.

"And so you and Graham are going to be married to-morrow night?" he asked.

"You know, Seth, that we are. How many times are you going to ask me?"

"Do you love him?" he asked, looking her steadily in the face.

"What a question! I have *always* loved him, and *always* will."

"That's right; then marry him, for if man ever loved woman, he loves you. And, Alf, while I think of it," he spoke in a louder tone, "what has that big, red-haired fellow been hanging around here so much for the last day or two?"

"You will have to ask Mary," laughed the woodman.

"Oh, I understand, there'll be two weddings to-morrow night, eh? That's so, Mary?"

"Not that I know of; I have no expectation of becoming a wife for any one."

"Hain't eh? Why the man seems to love you. Why don't you marry him?"

"I am afraid Mary will never marry," said Haverland. "She has rejected all offers, though many were from very desirable men."

"Queer! I never heard of such a case."

"Her love was buried long ago," replied Haverland, in a lower tone, to Seth.

After a moment's silence, Seth arose, took his chair, and seated himself beside her. She did not look at him, nor did any one else. He sat a moment; then whispered:

"Mary?"

She started. Her eyes flashed like meteors in his face a moment; then she turned as pale as death, and would have fallen from her chair, had not Seth caught her in his arms. Haverland looked up in amazement; the whole family were riveted in wonder. Seth looked up from the face of the fainting woman, and smiled as he said:

"She is mine forever!"

"Merciful Heaven! Eugene Morton!" exclaimed Haverland, starting to his feet.

"It is so!" said the one addressed.

"Have you risen from the dead?"

"I have risen to life, Alf, but have never been with the dead."

Instead of the weak, squeaking tone which had heretofore characterized his speech, was now a rich, mellow base, whose tones startled Mary into life again. She raised her head, but he who held her would not permit her to rise. He pressed her fervently to his bosom. The ecstasy of that moment, only the angels in Heaven could fathom.

Haldidge and Graham entered, and the man in his true character, arose to his feet—a tall, dignified, graceful, imposing person.

"Where is Seth?" asked Graham, not noticing the apparent stranger.

"Here is what you have heretofore supposed to be that individual," laughed the person before him, enjoying greatly their astonishment.

"Seth, truly, but not Seth, either," exclaimed they both, with astonishment written on their faces.

"With a few words," he commenced, "all will be plain to you. I need not tell you, dear friends, that my character, since my advent among you, has been an assumed one. Seth Jones is a myth, and to *my* knowledge, no such person ever existed. My real name is Eugene Morton. Ten years ago, Mary Haverland and I pledged our love to each other. We were to be married in one year; but, when a few months of that time had elapsed, the Revolutionary War broke out, and a call was made upon our little village, in New Hampshire, for volunteers. I had no desire nor right to refuse. Our little company proceeded to Massachusetts, where the war was then raging. In a skirmish, a few days after the battle of Bunker Hill, I was dangerously wounded, and left with a farmer by the wayside. I sent word by one of my comrades to Mary, that I was disabled, but hoped to see her in a short time. The bearer of that message was probably killed, for it is certain my words never reached her, though a very different report did. We had a man in our company who was a lover of Mary's. Know-

ing of my misfortune, he sent her word that I was killed. When I rejoined my company, a few months after, I learned that this man had
deserted. A suspicion that he had returned home impelled me to obtain leave of absence to visit my native place. I there learned that
Haverland, with his wife and sister, had left the village for the West.
One of my friends informed me that this deserter had gone with them,
and, it was understood, would marry Mary. I could not doubt the
truth of this report, and, for a time, I feared I should commit suicide.
To soften this great sorrow, I returned at once, joined our company,
and plunged into every battle that I possibly could. I often purposely
exposed myself to danger, soliciting death rather than life. In the winter of 1776 I found myself under General Washington, at Trenton; I
had crossed the Delaware with him, and, by the time it was fairly
light, we were engaged in a desperate fight with the Hessians. In the
very heat of the battle, the thought suddenly came to me that the
story of Mary's marriage was untrue. Similarly enough, when the battle was over, I did not think any more of it. But in the midst of the
following engagement, at Princeton, the same thought came to me
again, and haunted me from that time until the close of the war. I determined to seek out Mary. All that I could learn was that Haverland
had emigrated 'out this way.' If she *had* married the deserter, I knew
it was under a firm belief that I was dead. Consequently, I had no
right to pain her by my presence. For this reason, I assumed a disguise. I discolored my now long-untamed hair. It so changed my
whole appearance that I hardly knew myself. War had changed my
youthful color into bronze, and sorrow had wrought its changes. It
was not strange, then, that any old friend should not know me, particularly when I could so successfully personate the 'Green Mountain
Boy,' in voice and manner. My identity was perfectly secure, I knew,
from detection. I came to this section, and, after a long and perse-
vering hunt, one day I found Haverland cutting in the wood. I introduced myself to him as Seth Jones. I found Mary. The report which
had reached me of her marriage was false; she was still true to her
first love. I should have made myself known then, had not the danger
which threatened Haverland come upon him almost immediately. As
his family were then tormented by the fate of Ina, I thought my recognition would only serve to embarrass and distract their actions. Besides, I felt some amusement in the part I was playing, and often en-
joyed the speculation I created by giving you, as it were, a glimpse
now and then into my real nature. I varied my actions and language
on purpose to increase your wonder." He here paused and smiled, as
if at the recollection of his numerous ludicrous escapades. He continued: "I have little more to add. I congratulate you, Graham, on the

prize you have won. You are to be married to-morrow night. Mary, will you not marry me at the same time?"

"Yes," replied the radiant woman, placing her hands in his. "You have my hand now, as you've had my heart through all these long, sorrowing years."

Morton kissed her forehead tenderly.

"Now congratulate *me*," said he, with a beaming face.

And they gathered around him, and such shaking of hands, and such greetings, we venture to say, were never seen before. Our friends experienced some difficulty at first in believing that Seth Jones was gone forever. They even felt some regrets that his pleasing, eccentric face had passed away; but they had gained in his place a handsome, noble-hearted man, of whom they were all proud.

The next day was spent in preparations for the great double wedding that was to take place that evening. Messengers were sent up and down the river, and back into the woods; there was not a settler within twenty miles who had not been invited. At nightfall, the company began to collect. Some came in boats, some on horseback, and others on foot. A double wedding rarely took place in the backwoods, and this occasion was too full of romance to be slighted by any, old or young.

When the lights were produced in the woodman's house there was a motley assemblage without and within. You could have heard old and middle-aged men talking about the prospect of the crops, and looking up to the sky and wisely predicting the probabilities of a change in the weather, or discussing, in anxious tones, the state of feeling among the Indians along the frontier; you could have heard— as they would be termed nowadays—"gawky" young men as sagely discoursing upon the same subjects, venturing a playful thrust, now and then, at one of their number about some "Alminy," or "Sera, pheemy," sweetheart.

The woodman's house had been much enlarged for the occasion. A long shed, amply sufficient to contain all the guests, was built along-side and connecting with it. After participating in a bountiful meal in this, the tables were removed, and preparation made for the marriage.

A sudden hush fell upon the assemblage. All eyes turned toward the door, through which Eugene Morton and Edward Graham, each with his affianced leaning upon his arm, entered.

"Ain't they purty?"

"Don't they look bootiful?"

"Golly! if they ain't *some*, then there's no use in talking."

Such and similar were the whispered remarks of admiration at the couple. Mary Haverland was dressed in a plain, light-colored dress without any ornament, except a single white rose in her hair, which now fell in dark masses over her shoulders. Her beauty was of the true regal type. She was very happy, yet seemed as if in a world of her own.

Morton was clad in gray homespun, which well became his graceful form. His whole appearance was that of the *gentleman* which he was—a brave soldier, a true-hearted man.

Ina, the sweet young heroine, was fascinating. Her dress was of the purest white. Her curls clustered around her shoulders, and were confined at the temples by a simple wreath of blue violets. There was a contrast between Ina and Mary, and yet it would have been a difficult task to have judged which was the most beautiful—the pure, queenly, trusting woman, or the purity and innocence of the young maiden. Graham was a worthy participant in the drama and pleased all by his goodness and intelligence.

In a few moments, a portly gentleman, with a white neckcloth, and all aglow with smiles, entered the room. Morton and Mary arose and stood before him, and amid the most perfect silence the ceremony commenced. The questions were put and answered in a firm voice, audible to every one in the room.

"What God hath joined together let not man put asunder."

And every voice said "Amen!" as they reseated themselves.

Haldidge, who had stood as groomsman to Morton, now signalled with a quiet smile, for Graham to take his position. The young hero did, and Ina, blushing deeply, and leaning on the arm of her bridesmaid, followed, and the ceremony commenced.

While this was proceeding, an interesting affair was occuring at the opposite end of the room. A large, bony, red-faced young man sat holding and squeezing the hand of a bouncing, buxom girl, and indulging in several expressive remarks.

"I swow, if they don't look purty. Wonder how the gal feels?"

"Why, happy, of course," replied his companion.

"By jingo, I bet *he* does; I know *I* would."

"Would what?"

"Feel glorious if I was in *his* place."

"What! marrying Ina Haverland?"

"No—I mean—ahem!—why, somebody else—that is—yes, *somebody* else."

"Who else do you mean?" asked the girl, looking him steadily in the face.

"Whey—ahem!—why, *you!* Darn it, now you know, don't you?"

" 'Sh! Don't talk so loud, Josiah, or they'll hear you."

"S'posen you was in her place, Sal, how would you feel?"

"Ain't you ashamed of yourself?" she asked reprovingly.

"No, darnation, I don't care. Say, Sal, how *would* you feel?"

"Do you mean if I was standing out there with you, and the minister talking to us?"

"Yes—yes; why don't you tell me?"

"You know well enough, Josiah, without asking me no such question."

Josiah commenced meditating. Some desperate scheme was evidently troubling him, for he scratched his head, and then his knees, and then laughed, and exclaimed to himself: "I'll do it, by George!" Then turning toward the girl, he said:

"Sal, let's you and I get married, won't you?"

"Why, Josiah!" and she hung her head and blushed, charmingly.

"Come, Sal, the old folks won't care. Let's do it, won't you?"

"Oh, Josiah!" she continued, growing nervous and fidgety.

"Come, say quick, for the dominie is near done, and he'll go home. Say *yes*, Sal, do."

"Oh, dear! oh, my stars!—YES!"

"Good, by jingo!" Hurry up there, Mr. Preacher."

At this point the good minister ceased his benediction upon the couples, and their friends commenced crowding around them. The minister started, not to go home, but to leave the room for a moment, when Josiah noticed it, and fearing that he was going, called out:

"Say, squire—you, dominie, I mean—just wait, won't you? Here's another job for you."

"Ah, I am glad to hear it," laughed the minister, turning round. "Are you the happy man?"

"Wal, I reckon so, and I calc'late as how Sal Clayton there is the happy gal."

All eyes were turned toward the speaker, and he stood their smiles unflinchingly. His face was of a fiery red, and a large flowing necktie hung disregarded over his breast.

"Go on, Josiah—that's you!" exclaimed several, patting him on the shoulder.

"Get out, all of you, till I'm through. Come up here, Sal; no use scroochin' now."

The females bore the blushing one forward, until she was near enough to Josiah to get hold of her hand.

"Now, go ahead, squire—you—minister, I mean, and don't be too thundering long about it, for I want to get married most terribly."

The company gave way, and the two stepped forward, and in a few moments were pronounced man and wife. When Josiah saluted his bride the smack was a telling one, and the congratulations of Morton and Graham were nothing to those which were showered upon the happy man.

Now the sport commenced. An old ranger suddenly made his ap-

pearance, bearing a violin under his arm—"a reg'lar old Cremony," as
he termed it. The word was given to "make ready for the dance." The
old folks disappeared and entered the house, where, with the minister,
they indulged in conversation, story-telling, nuts, apples and cider.

The fiddler coiled himself up on the top of a box, and commenced
twisting the screws of his instrument, and thumping the strings. The
operation of "tuning" was evidently a painful one, for it was noticed
that at each turn of the screw he shut one eye and twisted his mouth.

The violin was at length tuned, the bow was given two or three
sweeps across a lump of resin, and then drawn across the strings, as if
it said "attention!" As the couples were forming, the violinist slid partly down off the box, so that one foot could beat upon the sanded floor,
and then, giving his head a jerk backward, struck up a reel that fairly
set every heart dancing. The floor was immediately filled with the
young folks. Tall, strapping fellows plunged around the room, like
skeletons of India rubber, their legs bowed out, and sometimes trip-
ping over each other. Rousing, solid girls bounded round, up and
down, like pots of jelly, and "all went merry as a marriage-bell."

By and by the old folks made their appearance, "just to see the
boys and girls enjoy themselves." The fiddler at this moment shot off
on the "Devil's Dream." A timid elderly lady stepped up to him, and,
touching him softly on the shoulder asked:

"Is that a *profane* tune?"

"No, it's Old Hundred, with variations. Don't bother me," replied
the performer, relieving his mouth of a quantity of tobacco-juice at
the same time.

"Suppose we try it for a moment, aunt Hannah," said the minister
with a sly look.

The two stepped out upon the floor, the fiddler commenced another
tune, and they disappeared in the whirling mass. In a few moments
nearly all of the old folks, who had come just to "see them a minute,"
followed, and the way in which several elderly gentlemen and ladies
executed some of the reels of a half-century's memory, was a lesson to
the younger folks.

The company kept up their revelry until far beyond midnight. But
by and by they commenced withdrawing. It was proposed by several
to visit the different bridegrooms in bed, but, fortunately, the good
taste of the others prevailed, and they departed quietly homeward.

Slumber, with the exception of the sentinels at the block-house, fell
upon the village. Perhaps the Indians had no wish to break in upon
such a happy settlement, for they made no demonstration through the
night. Sweetly and beautifully they all slept; sweetly and peacefully
they entered upon life's duties on the morrow; and sweetly and peacefully these happy settlers ascended and went down the hillside of life.

SECOND EDITION.

Copyrighted, 1885, by BEADLE AND ADAMS. Entered at the Post Office at New York, N. Y., as Second Class Mail Matter. Feb. 11, 1885.

Vol. V. $2.50 a Year. Published Weekly by Beadle and Adams, No. 98 WILLIAM ST., NEW YORK. Price, Five Cents. No. 57.

DEADWOOD DICK ON DECK;

Or, CALAMITY JANE, The Heroine of Whoop-Up.

By E. L. Wheeler.

CALAMITY JANE.

DEADWOOD DICK ON DECK

or

Calamity Jane,
The Heroine of Whoop-Up

BY EDW. L. WHEELER

Author of "Deadwood Dick"
novels, etc., etc.

Chapter 1

BARKIN' UP THE WRONG TREE

Dashing along thro' the valley and vale,
From early morn till the day grows pale;
Into the 'pockets' framed in flowers—
Into the woodland's shady bowers;
Stopping anon by babbling streams,
Then darting on into rocky seams;
Free as the eagle in its flight,
Fearless in daylight, happy at night;
Ever unfettered to roam about—
Such is the life of the glorious scout.

Searching for gold in the waters clear,
Running a race with the mountain deer;
Profiting well by the miner's abuse,
Taming with spur the buckin' cayuse;
Paying one's way, taking no 'slack,'
Biting cold lead, and sending it back;
Friendly to friends, but deadly to foes,
Gay as a robin, hoarding no woes;
Such is the life of the scout, gay and free,
Such is the life that is suiting to me.

On the clear air of an August night these words were distinctly
wafted in melodious song—a wild, rollicking harmony of weird music,
such as none but a cultivated voice could produce. Mountains have
their peculiar facility of carrying and retaining sound, and it was long
ere the last quivering notes of the midsummer night's song had died
out. The tone of the singer had been one of those pure, intoxicating
rivals of the flute; clear and strong, with power of sustenation, and capable of instant modulation to the softest, sweetest degree.

Even after the singer had ceased in the song of the gay mountaineer, it seemed as if the long gulches and gloomy mountain defiles
had become enthused with the glorious melody, and the spectral pines
sighed a weird peculiar sound as if in a diapason accompaniment.

The screams of the night birds had been hushed; the noisy streams
and leaping cascades were seemingly less boisterous; two men sitting
down in the bottom of a narrow winding canyon or gulch, had ceased
smoking, to listen to the song of the unknown nightingale.

A little fire was burning in close proximity to a sharp bend in the course of the canyon, and near by was a single marquee of canvas, and a couple of superannuated-looking mules stretched out on the grass. A few yards to the left, as you looked up toward the bend in the canyon, rolled a wide, shallow stream of water, confined in its course by nearly perpendicular walls of rock, that towered aloft in rugged piles, until in natural grandeur they terminated in misty mountain peaks. The two men alluded to were sitting upon the bank of the stream, and they did not move until the songstress had ceased her melody; then they looked up and exchanged glances.

"Beautiful, wasn't it, Sandy?"

"Yes," replied the younger of the twain, as he resumed his pipe, his eyes roving out over the noisy river, dreamily. "I was not aware you had such musical stars out here in your mining districts. A woman, wa'n't it?"

"Yas, a woman," replied Colonel Joe Tubbs, knocking the ashes out of his pipe, and refilling it with chipped plug. "At least they say she's o' the feminine sex, fer w'ich I can't sw'ar, purtic'lar. An' ef she's a weemon, thar ain't many better lukers 'twixt hayr, Deadwood, an' ther risin' sun."

"What reason have you to doubt that she is not a woman, colonel?"

"Wal, Sandy, I ken't say as I really doubt et, fer I s'pect et's a solid fac' that she ar' one o'ther lineal descendents of thet leetle fruitful scrape in a certain garden, yeers ago, afore ther Antediluve. But ye see how it is: in the gelorious State o' Ohio, from which I war imported ter this side o' ther hemisphere, ther female sex ginnerally war begarbed in petticoats, an' left ther male representatives to wear ther breeches!"

"Humph!" and a little smile came to Sandy's lips, "then this nightingale who has just favored us, wears the breeches herself, does she?"

"You pile up yer chips an' bet thet she do, Sandy, and ef you warn't an Eastern chap, an' but leetle used ter sech weemon as we hev in this delectable Black Hills kentry, I'd say, 'Sandy, galoot, pile yer frunt foot for'a'd, and go in for Janie.'"

"Janie—that is her name, eh?"

"Wal, I reckon—Calamity Jane for short. I don't allow thar's many who do know who she is, aside from her title, Sandy, tho' she don't cum no furder off than up in Nevada. She's a brick, Sandy, and jest let et pop right inter yer noddle right hayr, that she ain't no fool ef she do wear breeches. An' ef ye ever have occasion ter meet ther gal, Sandy, jest remember ther words uv Colorado Joe Tubbs on thes 'ere eventful night—'Ther gal ain't no fool ef she do wear breeches.'"

"I will, pardner. I don't suppose because a woman wears male attire that she is necessarily a fool; though why a female must lower her sex by appearing in man's garb, I see not. She must be an eccentric creature—rather a hard case, is she not?" with a little curl of the lip.

"'Hard case,' Sandy?" and here the veteran paused to close one eye, and blow out a cloud of fragrant smoke; "wal, no, when ye ask my jedgment in ther matter. She's a woman, Sandy, an' tho' thar's many who lay claim ter that name who ar' below par, I don't reckon Janie ar' quite that fur gone. She's a dare-devil, Sandy, an' no mistake. She ar' the most reckless buchario in ther Hills, kin drink whisky, shute, play keerds, or sw'ar, ef et comes ter et; but, 'twixt you and me, I reckon ther gal's got honor left wi' her grit, out o' ther wreck o' a young life. Oncet an' awhile thar is a story whispered about that she war deserted up at Virginny City, an' tuk ter thes rovin' life ter hunt down her false lover; another thet she hed bin married ter a Nevada brute, an' kim over inter these deestrict ter escape him; then thar's bin sum hard stories o' her up at Deadwood an' Hayward, but I never b'lieved 'em 'case they were ginneraly invented by a gang o' toughs who hed a grudge ag'in' her. I never b'lieved 'em, Sandy, because she war a woman; an' once I hed a wife an' little golden-haired daughter— she luked like you, Sandy—an' I know'd 'em ter be good; thet's why I nevyr kim ter believe all about Calamity Jane!" and the old man bowed his head on his arm, at some sad recollection.

"No! no!" he went on, after a few moments of silence. "Janie's not as bad as ther world would have her; because she's got grit an' ain't afeared to shute ther galoot as crosses her, people condemn her. I reckon ye kno' how et is, out hayr in ther Hills, Sandy—ef a female ken't stand up and fight fer her rights, et's durned little aid she'll git."

"So I should conclude from what observations I have been able to make, since I came West," was the reply of the young miner. "Is this Calamity Jane pretty, colonel?"

"Wal, some might say so, Sandy; I am not partial ter givin' opinions o' ther external merits of ther female line, o' late years. Hed sum experience in thet line a couple o' years ago, afore I left Angelina, my second, ter come out hayr—war just tellin' her how purty a certain widder war, when—well, I never quite knew what struck me, but I finally waked up ter find myself carved up inter steaks an' ther ha'r on top o' my head gone. Likewise, my Angelina. She had eloped wi' another galoot. Since then I allus withhold my opinion on ther beauty or humblyness o' ther oppsite sex."

"Well, I suppose you wa'n't sorry, eh?" observed Sandy, as he arose, with a yawn, and picked up his handsome Sharpe's rifle.

"Wal, no; I ken't say's I am, sence et turns out thet ther Black Hills affords me more comfort an' enjoyment than hum uster wi' Angelina everlastingly browsin' me down wi' a mop-stick. Whar ye goin', Sandy, boy?"

"Just up to the bend and back, colonel, to see that all is right, before turning in for the night," was the reply, as the stalwart miner strode off, whistling softly some tune which was dear to the home in the East, which he had left to seek gold in the Black Hills country. After he had gone out of view in the darkness of the warm semi-tropical night, laden as it was with a strangely intoxicating perfume of many mountain flowers—for the Black Hills are truly the flower land of America—Colonel Joe Tubbs resumed his pipe, while he gazed thoughtfully out over the noisy, shallow waters of Canyon Creek. "A mighty good feller ar' thet Sandy, an' no mistake, but a queer stick, wi' all. Now, we've bin consolidated fer a couple o' months as pards, in a s'arch fer ther p'izen they call gold, an' I don't kno' nothin' about ther chap, 'cept thet he claims ter hev cum frum New York, an' ar' one o' the squarest galoots I ever fell in wi'. Quiet an' unobtrusive as a crippled cat—hain't much ov a talker neither; but them's often ther kind as hes got a sleepin' tiger in 'em."

Colonel Joe Tubbs had well described the young miner, Sandy, when he had said he was quiet and unobtrusive. He *was* quiet and unobtrusive—was deep and thoughtful—very seldom in a jolly spirit, though at all times pleasant and agreeable. Twenty-four or five years of life which had passed over his head had left a man in every sense of the word—a man in physical and mental development—a man in will and great force of character—a man so quiet and retired as to seem almost a recluse; yet, when gazing scrutinizingly at him, you could but be impressed with the peculiar force of the expression—"still waters run deep."

His form was stalwart and iron-cast, with strength delineated to the critical eye in every curve and muscle. His face was plain, yet rather attractive, with its firm mouth shaded by a heavy yellow mustache, eyes of a dusky brown, and hair light and worn long down over the shoulders. A face it was which a lady might admire, and a gentleman envy, even though Sandy would not have passed criticism as being handsome. His attire was plain, consisting of a buckskin suit, knee boots, and a slouch gray felt hat. He wore no belt; no other weapons than his rifle were visible about his person.

Tubbs was a short, stubby man, with a genial face, reddened somewhat by long exposure to the sun, and more so, perhaps, by a love for the miner's favorite, "tarant'ler juice," especially his nose. He was an eccentric, big-hearted fellow, past the middle age of man's wordly existence, who had had much experience in the Black Hills, and never laid by a cent.

This fact seemed to strike him very forcibly now, as he sat waiting for Sandy's return. Sandy was the name the colonel had given the young miner, when they had first met in Cheyenne, in lieu of another which the so-called Sandy had said was not for public ears—nor private, either.

"No, not a durned sum total o' one red hev ye laid by, Joe Tubbs, out o' all ther dust ye've handled. An' supposin' Angelina shed come back on ye fer support in yer old age? Lordy! whar'd ther ha'r be *then?*"

"Then, here's Sandy, too—squarest galoot in ther hills, an' I'll be on't—thar's Sandy; I orter leave him a leetle mite when I shuffle off, fer I got a peep at ther poor cuss's pocket-book, t'other day, an' 'twar flatter'n a flapjack. No use o' talkin'; responsibilities ar' rollin' on ye, Colonel Joe Tubbs, an' ye've got to clap yer hoof down an' bid farewell ter tarant'ler forever. Hello, Sandy, ar' that ye back a'ready?"

"Yes, colonel. Didn't know but I might see the nightingale, but was disappointed," was the reply, as the young miner sat down upon a camp-stool in the firelight. "Guess she did not know of our camp here."

"Don't you fool yourself, Sandy; thet gal knows every krook an' hoel in ther hull Black Hills proper, an' can lay her finger on any chap hayr ye kin name, wi'out any trouble. Hello! w'at hev ye got thar, pard?"—alluding to a small object that Sandy was turning over in his hands and inspecting admiringly.

"A piece o' rock that got dislodged somehow, up there around the bend, and rolled down in my path. Out of curiosity I fetched it in. What do you think of it colonel?" and with a peculiar smile, the young miner tossed the rock over to Tubbs.

"What! thunderation, Sandy, *it's gold! it's gold!*" and the colonel sprung hastily to the fire to examine the prize. "Yes, by thunder! et's gold, Sandy, an' as big as my fist; durn my ducats ef et ain't. Whar'd ye git et, boyee?—for Heaven's sake tell me whar? Why don't ye git exicited, Sandy, you galoot? It's gold! it's gold! Wurth a couple or three thousan' at least calcylation, I s'war!"

"No use of getting excited, is there, colonel?" and the miner stretched out with a yawn. "If it's gold, I don't suppose it will hurt anybody, and if there's gold in the mountain-side around the bend, it will not run away in affright."

"Sandy, ye're a cool 'un, an' no mistake. Ye'd freeze ice in fly-time, I do believe, ef ye were not in a kentry thet is next door neighbor ter purgatory etself. Thunderation, boyee, ef I only had a pint uv stiff old tarant'ler hyar, I'd celerbrate over yer discovery uv a rich 'find.' What shall we name et, Sandy?—ther place must have a name right in its infancy, just like leetle infant babbys hev."

"All right, colonel. Call it Satan's Bend. Sometime we may find a better name."

"Agreed. Satan's Bend et is, Sandy, an' but fer the want o' a pint o' good stiff tarant'ler, we'd hev a gelorious celebration."

After the conclusion of the beautiful yet weird mountaineer's song, which Joe Tubbs had declared came from the lips of Calamity Jane, a person on horseback descended a dizzy zig-zag path that led from one of the mountain peaks, into a narrow dark defile, but the matter of a mile or so above Canyon Gulch, and the infant city of Satan's Bend.

"Whoa! Steady, Trick—none o' yer funny business, now. Don't ye perceive thet ef yer were to tumble down this declivity with me, there'd be no guardian angel in the Black Hills?" and here a merry peal of laughter escaped the red lips of the speaker.

"Steady—a little further—there! Good for you, old fellow! We're on safe footing, at last. I wonder if any one's around in these parts?" and the dark eyes peered sharply into every shadow in her immediate vicinity. "No; I reckon the coast is all clear, and we must get a-going for Deadwood, Trick, for there is no telling how soon that delightful population may need us to quell some row or do a suffering pilgrim good."

We have described the eccentric dare-devil of the Black Hills in other works of this series, but as some may not have read them, it will require but little time to describe her again.

A female of no given age, although she might have ranged safely anywhere between seventeen and twenty-three, she was the possessor of a form both graceful and womanly, and a face that was peculiarly handsome and attractive, though upon it were lines drawn by the unmistakable hand of dissipation and hard usage, lines never to be erased from a face that in innocent childhood had been a pretty one. The lips and eyes still retained in themselves their girlish beauty; the lips their full, rosy plumpness, and the eyes their dark, magnetic sparkle, and the face proper had the power to become stern, grave or jolly in expression, wreathed partially as it was in a semi-framework of long, raven hair that reached below a faultless waist.

Her dress was buckskin trowsers, met at the knee by fancifully beaded leggings, with slippers of dainty pattern upon the feet; a velvet vest, and one of those luxuries of the mines, a boiled shirt, open at the throat, partially revealing a breast of alabaster purity; a short, velvet jacket, and Spanish broad-brimmed hat, slouched upon one side of a regally beautiful head. There were diamond rings upon her hands, a diamond pin in her shirt-bosom, a massive gold chain strung across her vest front.

For she had riches, this girl, and none knew better than she how to find them in the auriferous earth or at the gaming-table of Deadwood, the third Baden Baden of two continents.

A belt around her waist contained a solitary revolver of large caliber; and this, along with a rifle strapped to her back, comprised her outfit, except we mention the fiery little Mexican black she rode, and the accompanying trappings, which were richly decorated and bespangled, after lavish Mexican taste.

"I guess the coast is clear, Trick; so go ahead," and a jerk at the cruel Spanish bit and an application of spurs sent the spiteful cayuse clattering wildly down the canyon, while Calamity Jane rocked not ungracefully from side to side with the reckless freedom peculiar to the California buchario. Indeed, I think that any person who has witnessed the dare-devil riding of this eccentric girl, in her mad career through the Black Hills country, will agree with me that she has of her sex no peer in the saddle or on horseback.

The first time it was ever my fortune to see her, was when Deadwood was but an infant city of a few shanties, but many tents.

She dashed madly down through the gulch one day, standing erect upon the back of her unsaddled cayuse, and the animal running at the top of its speed, leaping sluices and other obstructions—still the dare-devil retained her position as if glued to the animal's back, her hair flowing wildly back from beneath her slouch hat, her eyes dancing occasionally with excitement, as she recognized some wondering pilgrim, every now and then her lips giving vent to a ringing whoop, which was creditable in imitation if not in volume and force to that of a full-blown Comanche warrior.

Now, she dashed away through the narrow gulch, catching with delight long breaths of the perfume of flowers which met her nostrils at every onward leap of her horse, piercing the gloom of the night with her dark lovely eyes, searchingly, lest she should be surprised; lighting a cigar at full motion—dashing on, on, this strange girl of the Hills went, on her flying steed.

The glowing end of her cigar attracted the notice of four men who were crouching in the dense shadows, further down the gulch, even as the hoofstrokes broke upon their hearing.

"That's her!" growled one, knocking the ashes out of his pipe, with an oath. "Reckoned she wouldn't be all night, ef we only hed patience. Grab yer weepons, an' git ready, boys. She mustn't escape us this time."

Calamity Jane came on; she was not aware of her danger, until she saw four dark shadows cross her path, and her cayuse reared upon its haunches.

"Whoa! Trick; don't git skeered; hold up, you devils. I reckon you're barkin' up ther wrong tree!" she cried.

Then there were three flashes of light in the darkness followed by as many pistol-shots—howls of pain and rage, and curses too vile to repeat here—a yell, wild and clear, a snort from the horse—then the dare-devil rode down the man at the bits, and dashed away down the canyon, with a yell of laughter that echoed and re-echoed up and down the canyon walls.

"I wonder who composed thet worthy quartette?" Calamity mused, as she gazed back over her shoulder. "Reckon at least a couple of 'em bit ther dust, ef not more. Could it have been—but no! I do not believe so. Deadwood Dick's men ain't on the rampage any more, and it couldn't hev been them. Whoever it was wanted my life, that's plain, and I shall have to look out fer breakers ahead, or next time I shall not get off with a simple scratch."

Chapter 2

HON. CECIL GROSVENOR— ALF. KENNEDY, DANITE

Ther world war made in six days,
'Took ther seventh fer Kaiser's pup.
We named this town in one day,
Ther next, we Whooped Her Up.

"Thet's a fact, stranger; me an' my man, Sandy, war ther originators o' this geelorious town o' Whoop-Up. We war ther fu'st mortals who evyer diskivered a'riferous in thes deestrict, an' we staked our claim, an' made our pile, you bet!"

The speaker, Colonel Joe Tubbs, stood in the doorway of one of two or three-score of large frame shanties that were strewn along through Canyon Gulch, in the immediate vicinity of what once—only a month before—had been called Satan's Bend. The gulch was now a successful mining strike, and boasted of the name of Whoop-Up.

Everything usually found in mining strikes could you find in Whoop-Up. It lacked none of the essential points requisite to make it a fast mining-town of the Black Hills. Saloons, groceries, dance-houses, gaming-dens, and other attractions, had sprung up along the bank of Canyon Creek, in anticipation of a rush of miners and adventurers into the new "locate;" the influx had come, and consequently the place was a city.

The population was heterogeneous, men and women of all nations, nearly, and all professions were here in Whoop-Up, to ply their vocations.

A Vigilance Committee had been one of the first organizations to spring up, and with Colonel Joe Tubbs as chief, there was a prospect of better order than in some of the towns of the Hills.

For a mile and a half along the only accessible shore of Canyon Creek, were strewn frame shanties and canvas tents almost without number, and the one street of the town was always full to overflowing with excited humanity. The monotonous grinding and crushing of ore-breakers, the ring of picks and hammers, the reports of heavy blasts in the rugged mountain-side, the shouts of rival stage-drivers, the sounds of music, and tipsy revelry from dance-houses and saloons; the boisterous shouts of the out-door Cheap John, dealer in "b'iled shirts" and miners' furnishing goods, the occasional reports of revolver-shots, may be heard in the streets of Whoop-Up, no matter, dear reader, if it be during the day or during the night, when you pay your visit.

For in this latest mining success of the country of gold, there is no suspension of bustle or business on account of night; in walking through the town you might wonder if these people never slept, because the long, thronged street is even livelier at any hour of the night than when the sun trails a pathway of light along the bottom of Canyon Gulch.

These plain board shanties you see are not dwellings, but devoted to "business" even though the business in many cases may be illegitimate.

It is in the white tents or skin-lodges that the miner stays, when at "home."

Poor homes, in many cases, but the best that could be afforded at present, for time meant money to these citizens and workingmen of Whoop-Up, and money was what they were after—gold! gold in its shining nuggets, in veins of quartz, or in glittering dust. Gold which men even risk death to obtain—which means murder on the soul of many a man, and dishonor and ruin to many a woman.

All these changes we have noted have occurred from the time of Sandy's first discovery of gold in the canyon, up to the time Colonel Joe stands in his saloon doorway, in company with a stranger, and looks up and down the busy, bustling main street.

Yes, and more!—for the mountain-side is covered with busy prospectors; here shafts penetrate into its bowels—there, 'way up a hundred feet above the town, a gang are working night and day, blasting out rich quartz rock, which another gang transports down an inclined plane, by car-loads, to the mighty quartz crushers in the bottom of the gulch. Everywhere the eye meets a scene of bustling activity and energetic labor on the part of those men who toil for gold.

Colonel Joe Tubbs no longer classes himself with the mining element, for as the single pard of Sandy, he is the richest man in the town, of course excepting Sandy. Upon discovering that they had chanced upon one of the richest quartz territories in the Hills, the two men had at once gone to work and staked off their claim, including in it over two miles of the canyon bottom, and a great share of the mountain-side; then when the rush came in a great voluminous tidal wave, they leased off a larger portion of their claim for high figures, reserving such portions for themselves as could be easiest worked and would be most profitable in yield.

Sandy's good fortune did not apparently affect him in the least.

He worked ten hours out of twenty-four, and was as quiet and un-demonstrative as when Tubbs had first met him.

He neither drank, caroused, nor gambled; minded his own business, and somehow contrived always to induce others to mind theirs.

He had money—over a half a million of it—but no one, not even old Joe Tubbs, knew where he kept it. The gang of miners who worked in his mine under him, were general favorites with him, and he with them.

Tubbs, in the sudden flush of his prosperity had abandoned the pick and cradle and started a "howtel," which, with one or two excep-tions, was the largest to be found in the magic city of Whoop-Up, and was liberally patronized, for a post-office on one end of the bar daily and nightly drew a crowd, and the lucky miner who got a letter from absent ones in the "States," was naturally expected to set up the ta-rant'ler liberal.

And in that city of Whoop-Up there were no less than half a dozen different post-offices, every mail-carrying stage line having a different depot for starting and arriving, which generally was at some saloon or grocery store. Consequently each stage line had its post-office.

This was the case in Deadwood, until Uncle Sam put in his say, and now there are but two post-offices there.

The stranger, who in company with Colonel Tubbs of the Mastodon Hotel, was surveying the scene upon the long street of the town, had registered himself as Honorable Cecil Grosvenor, of Washington—"a sort o' senator, ye see," Joe accepted, silently. He was a short, stout individual, with a well-fattened physique, a trimmed, iron-gray mus-tache, and hair to match; eyes of a steely, glittering gray, so cold and peculiar in their expression as to almost make one nervous; a general air of superiority over the average, being prevalent in the man's exteri-or. These were a few noticeable points, aside from the gentleman's elegant suit of broadcloth, silk hat, patent-leather boots, gloved hands, and gold-headed cane, along with a cluster diamond pin on his immac-ulate shirt front.

While the two men were standing and conversing, a rough-looking fellow came along and passed into the hotel, casting an inquiring glance at the Honorable Cecil, as he did so, and giving Tubbs a nudge.

"Tarant, Joe?"

"Go 'long in," was the gruff response; "thar's a bar inside, wi' a keeper."

And the miner passed in, with a strange glitter in his eyes.

"Thet old covey must be the pilgrim I want!" he muttered, "and if so, he looks in life like a purty fat lay-out, on w'ich ter make a spec'. Guess I'll lay low, an' watch fer him, an' see ef he knows who Arkansaw Alf is."

Outside, Honorable Cecil Grosvenor was speaking.

"Yes, it has the appearance of being a very lively strike!" he observed, setting his gold-rimmed glasses upon his nose, and gazing up the dizzy mountainside, where, hundreds of feet above, miners were toiling faithfully day and night.

"I suppose the place is controlled by corporations and companies, is it not? and there is plenty of land for cash?"

"Plenty o' land, yes, sir; but ther fac' is, et ain't sech as raised the a'riferous. Ner ther lodes ain't mostly controlled by corporations, nuther. When all these Hills war leased off, sar, me an' my pard, Sandy, we jest about hed ther old cat by ther tail, an' we give the poor man a show fer his money. Ef he didn't hev much, we couldn't give him much uv a stake, but give him as much as we ked. An' so we pieced et up, w'out lettin' one capitalist hev a smell. Thet's how me an' my man Sandy did it up brown, Sandy bein' a fine calkylater, stranger."

"You did wrong," Mr. Grosvenor said, with a shrug of his broad shoulders—"very wrong. One first-class corporation would have paid you more for your entire claim, by three-fold, than you received from the poor cusses you leased it to."

"Mebbe yer purty nigh right, stranger; but we pilgrims ain't ginerally hogs, an' we divide up ekal wi' ther boys. D'ye remember et, sir, I'd ruther 'a' not got a cent out o' ther hull business, than to have sold et ter men who'd hev hed et all under three or four piratical pairs o' fists, an' w'ile hoarding up their pile, ground ther workin' men down ter Chinamen's wages—'washee shirtee for fivee cents!' Mebbe ye cum frum out in Pennsylvania, whar they do thet kind o' playin', stranger, but et's most orful sure thet ye ken't play sech a trick out hyar among ther horny-fisted galoots o' this delectable Black Hills kentry—no sir-e-e-el!"

"Ha! ha! you are quite a working-man's enthusiast, I see, Colonel Tubbs," the Washingtonian said, with a hearty laugh; "but that is because you are unsophisticated yet. This man Sandy, of whom you speak, I dare say is of the same mind, eh?"

"Wah, I reckon he ain't far from et; an' as fer bein' unsophisticated, I reckon thar's them, an' not fur away, neither, who's probably got as many rocks ter ther square inch as all yer high-blooded Eastern corporative galoots."

"Oh, yes; no doubt!" Cecil Grosvenor replied, with a slight cough. "I am going down around the bend yonder, to take a look at the town. If any one should call and inquire for me, tell them I will soon return. Good-day, sir."

"Good-day ter ye," Colonel Joe replied, ingulfing a huge quid, and retiring into the bar-room of his famous "Mastodon." "Et kinder strikes me thet thet chap ain't ther pure quill, 'twixt me an' ther bar an' ther bedpost, an' I'd like my man Sandy ter see him, an' pass his jedgment. He hes got a sharp eye, hes thet Sandy, ef he is quiet, an' hayr's what don't believe ye ken fool him much. Charity Jim, ye posey, just hand me the brandy, an' charge et ter Colonel Joe Tubbs, fer et's a scandalous fac' thet I heven't hed more'n half a dozen decent swings this hull blessed forenoon."

James McGee, alias Charity Jim, obeyed with alacrity, for he knew that he had in all Whoop-Up no stronger or more liberal friend than the genial, cherry-nosed Tubbs.

"See hayr, pard, et's your treat, ain't it, seein' 's this ar' ther furst time we've met?" and the miner who had glanced so closely at the Honorable Cecil Grosvenor, stepped up to the bar, just as Colonel Joe was about dispatching a "quotation" from the bottle.

"You!" Joe said, lowering the bottle and staring at the individual in a mixture of amazement and commiseration. "You? Wal, now, ef thet ain't ther concentrated essence o' cheek, may I be etarnally banished from my blessed trant'ler! Who are you, pilgrim?"

"Wal, sir, old hoss, I reckon ef ye war ter arrange sev'ral letters together out o' ther classic shades o' a spellin'-book, an' pin 'em ter ther wall wi' lead punctuation p'ints, ye'd hev ther cognomenical discovery o' A'gustus Van Horn."

"Eh? Van Horn! Van Horn? I don't think I know ye, pilgrim, and I allus make it a p'int never ter swaller tanglefoot wi' a galoot as I don't know!"

After taking a slight nip at the bottle, the proprietor of the Mastodon returned it to Charity Jim.

The man who had thus styled himself Augustus Van Horn was dressed as a miner, and wore a small arsenal of weapons belted about his waist.

He was evidently about thirty years of age, with a brawny, iron-like form, the limbs especially being large and muscular, and a face that had a villainous and disagreeable expression, so red it was either from sun exposure or the effects of strong drink. His sensual mouth was shaded by a straggling, grindy mustache, his eyes were fierce and bloodshot and tigerish in their gleams. His hair was more the color of the inner side of hemlock bark than anything conceivable, and a deep, livid scar ran from his right cheek bone, near the eye, down across to the corner of his mouth—a scar so hideous in its aspect as to never be forgotten when once seen.

This much of his exterior Colonel Joe took in at a cursory glance, then walked away toward the door, in evident disdain. But the other was not to be bluffed so easily, for he stepped quickly in pursuit, and slapped one brawny hand down on the colonel's shoulder with force. And almost before he knew it Joseph Tubbs found himself ranged alongside the bar again, and confronted by his villainous-looking visitor.

"Now, jest yeou see hayr, old hoss!" the individual said, "get me a drink o' tarant'ler, an' don't be so danged imperdent, or ye might wake up wi' a hoel in yer constitutional system. Ye see, I war foolin' ye about my cognomistic appelation, fer ther name I give ye ar' foreign ter my ownership. By the way, did ye ever heer uv a shap who hes gained himself world-wide notoriety in ther Black Hills kentry o' gold, by ther name o' Arkansaw Alf Kennedy, the Ghoul—the leader of ther Dakota Danites?"

"Eh? what?—*you* that man?" Colonel Joe demanded, a strange terror seizing him, for he had heard of Arkansaw Alf, who, with his band of Danites, had hunted more than one victim to the death. Few, indeed, were there in all the Black Hills who had not heard of the Danite devil and his deadly backers.

"Yes, I'm Arkansaw Alf, old man, but mind, ef ye vally yer personal safety, mum's the word 'twixt you and me. Ef ye *dare* to betray me to the Vigilantes, of which you are a member, your doom is sealed. And you know a Danite-doomed galoot ain't noted fer a ripe old age after our deadly eyes are set upon him.

"Ef ye'll elongate yer ears toward my speaking trumpet, I'll orate a leetle fer yer personal eddification. D'ye kno' w'at a Ghoul is? Wal, ef ye don't, Webster defines et as an animal that feeds on flesh—a demon that feeds on ther dead. We're Ghouls an' Danites. Ghouls for the reason that we possess many demonistic gifts, an' ef et cums ter a famine in grub, I opine we would not be dissatisfied ef we had ter chaw away on a leetle human flesh. Danites ar' we, because as such we were reared from early childhood, under Brigham's watchful eye, until, at a still tender age, thar war sum thirty healthy females wanted

ter hitch 'emselves up in harness wi' us, an' we warn't agreeable, so
we sloped, an' sot up in business fer ourselves. Now, I reckon, ye hev
more enlightenment on ther subject than any other man in ther Hills,
outside o' the gang, an' ef ye don't play snide, your carcass is saved.
Keep yer whisky, old man—all I want is freedom in thes yere ranch,
an' silence on yer part. I'm playin' a leetle game, an' ef ye git obtru-
sive, most likely a Deadwood undertaker will have occasion to visit
Whoop-Up on a short notice. Good-day ter ye," and in the next moment the Ghoul had departed.

Chapter 3

A WAIF THAT SANDY FOUND

Whistling a merry tune, a man was descending the mountain on the
other side of Whoop-Up. He carried a Henry rifle in his hand, or
maybe now and then steadied himself with it to prevent plunging
down the dizzy decline, while at his feet trotted a large Newfoundland dog, nearly as large as a full-grown grizzly, but by no means as
clumsy.

The man was Sandy!

Looking fresh and healthy after a month in the bracing mountain
air, and not uncomely in his picturesque miner's suit; and then fortune's smile upon him had partly banished his old habitual soberness,
and made him a frank and pleasant companion, even though he generally bore that quite unobtrusive disposition toward all.

Few men in all Whoop-Up's mile and a half of single street could
say that they had ever chatted with or pried into any of Sandy's se-
crets—if, indeed, he had any, which was extremely doubtful, as he
never appeared to be troubled with a guilty conscience. He seemed to
avoid any unnecessary familiarity, unless he chanced upon some one
he particularly fancied. None of the women, of whom Whoop-Up had
an early and steady influx, ever attracted a second glance from Sandy
—with one exception. There were perhaps two out of a dozen who
were honest at heart, and had been drawn there with the golden delu-
sion of making money; the remaining ten out of a dozen were generally composed of that class found in every mining-city or settlement,
and classed as "doubtful."

We alluded to an exception, and she was a blonde proprietress of a gambling-den and dance-house combined—Madame Minnie Majilton, by name. She might have been classed among the doubtful by some; few knew anything about her more than that she ran the ranch known as the Castle Garden, and wore diamonds and silks. To be sure, the dance-house was of ill-repute, simply because the dancers were not over-bashful; but, said some, this did not necessarily make the madame bad.

She was a magnificent-looking woman, between twenty and thirty years of age—lovely both in face and form—a blonde beauty, such as was not to be found in all the city of Whoop-Up.

Sandy had met her once, on being advised to go to the Castle Garden to exchange the value of some gold for greenbacks, Madame Minnie ever having a plenty of the latter which she was willing to part with, dollar for dollar's weight.

And if Sandy's pulses had quickened at sight of the beautiful blonde, he was no more than a man—for all men in Whoop-Up worshiped at Madame Minnie's shrine, and siren that she was she had not the inclination, if the will, to repulse them for their volunteered admiration. So that it had come, that in passing the Castle Garden on his way to work, Sandy had grown accustomed to nod to the beautiful proprietress, who generally stood in the doorway about the time he passed, and on one or two occasions he had even astonished the town, by stopping to converse a moment.

If people nodded their heads and looked wise, Sandy made no point of it, but went on minding his own affairs after his old fashion.

And remarkable as it might seem, that individual had yet to come who had made it his business to cross the young miner or force him into a quarrel.

The bullying toughs who had any superfluous spite to vent upon their fellow-mortals, generally looked in an opposite direction from Sandy, seeming to avoid him as an unhealthy subject to tackle.

To-day he had been on an early-morning hunt, for squirrels, up among the beeches and redwoods which grew high up on the very dome of the mountain, and having bagged a full hand of game, was descending the declivitous siding opposite the Canyon Gulch wherein lay Whoop-Up, in the warm September sunshine.

Many times he would have lost his footing but for his gun, and at last, wearied by the exhaustion of his tiresome tramp, he sat down upon a beetling ledge of rock, allowing his feet to dangle over the precipice.

His faithful brute companion crouched silently by his side, and for many moments the two gazed off upon the grandeur of the wild scene, in which from deep dark defiles great mountains rolled and piled up in massive sublimity to such a height that their peaks were swathed in a flimsy mist as in cloudland. Great mountains of rugged rock, spotted here and there with chaparral and furze bushes, or peaked with grim, spectral pines.

"Nowhere does Nature so forcibly illustrate the power of the Divine Creator as in the mountainous regions," Sandy muttered, as he gazed dreamily off through an opening between the mountain peaks. "I sometimes wonder how it is that people do not more devoutly worship God in His works. Eh? Buffalo,"—with an approving glance at the great canine, who lay with his nose between his paws, his eyes shining, and great bushy tail wagging to and fro—"do you appreciate the magnificence of our surroundings? No! I hardly think you are educated up to that yet. But something is the matter, and it's below us, too, for I can see you squinting your eye down-hill. What is it, you rascal?"

A brighter expression came upon the countenance of the dog, and he opened and shut his mouth with a gape and a renewed wagging of his tail, while with one ear cocked forward and one eye half closed, he looked over the ledge into the gulch some fifty feet below.

In this direction Sandy gazed, going over every inch of the ground without discovering anything of particular moment. Then he went over it again, and made a discovery which elicited a startled exclamation from him. What he saw was the arm of some person protruding from a clump of furze bushes!

A person passing through the defile might have passed it time and time again without making the discovery which Buffalo's sharp eyes had made.

"It's a human arm, Buff!" Sandy said, "but we don't know whether it's a dead person or a living one. Come! let's go down but be careful to make no noise. It may be some one asleep!"

Silently the miner and his dog descend into the gulch, and creep stealthily toward the spot where the arm and hand protruded from the bushes. And the nearer they approached the greater was Sandy's assurance that the owner of the hand and arm was either asleep, or in the eternal sleep that knows no wakening.

It proved to be the former, when Sandy carefully parted the bushes, and gazed into the sheltered little nook, where a plump, graceful form was lying—that of a boy of eighteen, with a pretty, beardless face, which was so composed and at rest, in slumber, and curling chestnut hair which reached down upon the finely-shaped shoulders. A boy; *was* it a boy?

The form was clad in male habiliments, and there was a boyish look to the finely-chiseled features, which defied the suspicion of femininity in the sleeper.

A plain frontier costume of some coarse cloth, neatly fitting the graceful form of only medium height; the feet incased in knee-boots of a fine leather, and a Spanish wide-rim felt hat lying upon the grass, were items of the beautiful sleeper's outfit.

Weapons he carried none, outwardly exhibited—yet, here in the depths of the mountain, lying in sweet repose, was the youthful waif— who was it?

Sandy asked himself this question silently, over and over again, and Buffalo winked and blinked his eyes and shook himself, as if he were overjoyed at the result of his discovery.

Then, when Sandy's glance was most admiring, the heavy eyelashes seemed to unclose with a start; the eyes of deepest, intense hazel were revealed: there was a little gasp, and the form straightened into a sitting position. Terror and consternation were blended in the fair face, and the youth was tembling visibly.

"Don't be frightened, miss," Sandy said, respectfully, raising his sombrero and addressing her in a kindly tone. "I would not have intruded, only my dog discovered your presence here, and curiosity prompted me to come."

"You call me miss; please don't—anything but that," was the reply, in a pained, half-regretful tone. "How came you to know?" and with an effort the waif gained a standing position, and thereby the full beauty of the sylph-like form became apparent.

"I only surmised, because you did not correspond with your make-up—that is, you see, ma'am, you look too much like a girl to be a boy."

"And yet, I had the vain hope that I could pass myself off without being discovered. Oh! it's a bitter disappointment!" and the eyes filled with tears.

Sandy gazed at the ground, hardly knowing what to say or do. Here he was, in the presence of a beautiful young woman whom he had discovered in her masquerade—a dilemma such as he would never have imagined likely to occur.

"You are evidently a stranger in these parts, ma'am, are you not?"

"Oh! yes, sir. All this country is very wild and strange to me, and its people are even stranger. You must excuse me, sir, for not telling you of myself—it could not interest you, and I should be breaking a secret by telling. If—if I only could dare to hope that you would keep my secret, I would go on, and maybe I should not be so unlucky in the future."

"You need have no fear that I will betray you, ma'am," Sandy answered, so much compassion in his tone that it surprised even him, who was proof against emotion or excitement.

"It would be more to my notion to befriend you. You see, ma'am, that in these rough mining districts, a man's either got to have high honor, or none at all. There's no half-way business; you must be a man or a brute. I may say that I am looked upon as something above the average, though I don't say it in vanity. Now, though there is a little danger in it, I'll tell you what I'll do, and you can accept or refuse at your own option.

"I've got a little shanty down around the bend in Canyon Gulch, where I live—the only board dwelling, by the way, in the mines. Now, you are not fit to knock about here and there. If some one were to discover you, as I have done, it might go worse with you; and if you haven't any objections in particular, I'll take you in as a pard. I reckon a false mustache would make more of a man of you, and you would then pass muster. You can turn a hand at cooking, and occasionally, avoid suspicion, can peck away in the mines. As I always stick by a pard, ma'am, if you go in with me, you can depend upon it, you'll be sure of at least one friend!"

"Oh! thank God, sir; and I thank you, for your words are grateful to my hearing. A friend is something I have not had for many a long day, and I should be more than selfish if I did not accept and appreciate your kind offer. But, sir, there is danger that my identity might be discovered, and then your honor would be compromised."

"Forget that you are a woman, and all will go well."

"I will, sir, and may God bless you, for befriending one of whom you know absolutely nothing. May your hopes in me be fully realized."

"As I trust they shall. Now, as to the future; have you enemies likely to disturb you?"

"One only, sir, but he is powerful. Don't ask me to name him—I dare not; but I will watch for him, and steel myself. Oh! I have hopes that he will never dream of seeking me here, in this far-away mining country."

"Let us both hope so," Sandy responded, earnestly; "and, now, for a name. I will not ask you yours—perhaps you would not care to give it. As to me, you can call me Sandy; that is what they all call me. You—let me see;" and the miner reflected a moment; "we will call you Dusty Dick—'Dusty,' because of a little dust upon your garments or face, which can easily be arranged. Remember that hereafter we are pards, and only Dick and Sandy to each other, leaving off 'sirs,' 'ma'ams,' and other formalities which might arouse suspicion. Now, having arranged this, you may remain here in your retreat, while I go to Whoop-Up. As soon as possible I will return and bring with me such preparations as will effectually disguise you. Will you be afraid to stay alone over night, should I fail to get back to you?"

"I—I don't know; it would be very lonesome."

"Well, then, I'll leave Buffalo here for company and protection," Sandy replied, and bidding the huge dog remain behind, and shaking hands with his new pard, the miner shouldered his rifle and trudged off around the base of the mountain toward Whoop-Up.

Chapter 4

SANDY'S PARD—IN A TIGHT PLACE

And it came to pass that these people of Whoop-Up did not hear of Sandy's new pard for several days, after he had been installed in the miner's new home, and then they only gave the youth but a glance, for he was but ordinary-looking in his suit of miner's habiliments; and the little mustache which Sandy had dexterously fixed to his upper lip gave him a much more boyish look.

Very few comments were openly passed on Dick, who somehow always managed to work an extraordinary quantity of dust onto his hat, face and clothing, and he made bold to go about through the town and was unmolested.

He superintended the culinary department of Sandy's cabin, and at odd times, when he had nothing to do, would go into the mountain tunnel where Sandy and his men were blasting for gold, and look on, or maybe lend a helping hand, always waiting to accompany Sandy home at supper-time; for Sandy was the only mine-owner in Whoop-Up who did not work his mine night and day. He was content with the golden yield from seven to six—ten hours.

And well might he be, for his was the richest claim that had yet been opened, with a vein of the valuable ore that was seemingly inexhaustible.

Only one person questioned the young miner concerning his new pard, and that was the beautiful blonde proprietress of the Castle Garden, Madame Minnie Majilton. Sandy stepped into her establishment to get a cigar, one evening, on returning from the mine, and found the pretty proprietress behind the counter in person.

"Who is that you have waiting for you outside, Sandy—the one they

call your pard?" was the question put, as Madame Minnie handed out
a box of some choice *Reinas,* which she knew were the miner's favorites. "Rather a young tenderfoot to be buffeting about in this rough
country, not?"

"Well, yes," Sandy replied, lighting one of the weeds. "That's Dusty
Dick, my cook and pard—imported from the East, somewhere, I don't
know just where. Run across him by accident, you see; took a notion to
him and domesticated him."

"Ah! yes," Madame Minnie said, elevating her brows archly—"a
very fine person, no doubt; but do you know what I think, Sandy?"

"Well, no, can't say as I do—what?"

"Well, you see, between you and me—and I will assume that we are
good friends—I don't believe you are giving us people of Whoop-Up a
square deal, for a man calculated to be as honest and honorable as
you—though, of course, I wouldn't breathe such a word outside, for
the world."

"Eh?" the miner said, gazing at her in well-assumed amazement—
"what is this? Not giving you a square deal? What do you mean?"

"This, Sandy. I reckon Dusty Dick is no more of a man than I am."

"Dusty Dick a woman?" ejaculated the miner; then he went off into
a fit of laughter which seemed to convulse his whole frame—such
laughter as he had never before emitted since his residence among the
Whoop-Upians. "Why, you astonish me. Wait—Dick, come here. Con-
found it! where has the boy gone? Hold a bit, madame, and I'll bring
the boy and prove to you that your suspicions are unfounded," and
Sandy made a move as if to hasten out of doors in search of Dusty
Dick.

"No! no!" Madame Minnie made haste to interpose, almost scream-
ing, "don't don't, for the world. Just think how ashamed I should be! I
accept your word—indeed I do—only please do not call in the young
gentleman."

Sandy turned back with a smile, and leaned against the counter.

"By the way, ma'am, it just occurs to me that it would not be more
than fair, to ask if *you* are giving us a square deal, by keeping this
rather dizzy and doubtful establishment?"

"Why—why certainly: but really, you'll have to excuse me a moment, Sandy, as I see I am wanted in the ball-room. Come in some
other time, and I'll vindicate *my*self—come, and bring in your pard to
the ball," and then, with a gracious smile and bow, the charming proprietress fluttered lightly away into the adjoining apartment.

And she muttered to herself:

"Ah, yes, Sandy, you are as sharp as a needle, and a clever actor,
too, for such a quiet fellow, but you didn't deceive me concerning Mr.

Dusty Dick—oh, no; but I won't give you away—of course not, when you are the only man in the town worth two rows of pins, and the one I mean to extract a matrimonial offer from inside of a month. And will I be fool enough to refuse you? Humph! we shall see."

Meanwhile Sandy trudged homeward along the busy street, smoking his cigar meditatively.

"That woman is, in the vernacular of the mines, a 'brick!'" he muttered, "and likewise as handsome as an houri, though I am inclined to the opinion that houris are generally brunettes instead of blonds. She is sharp, smart, and has known refinement, heretofore. How did she 'smell the rat' concerning Dick! I sometimes wish I had not put myself under such a responsibility; but yet, I hardly know how I could get along without my pard. Such company as *hers* isn't bought cheap. If I were to choose for a wife between her and the madame—dash it! I scarcely know which I should take. The madame—but, bah! The idea of talking so spooney!"

And he laughed to himself at the idea of such a thing.

Near his shanty, at the bend in the canyon, he met Dusty Dick, whom he perceived to be pale and tremble.

"You overheard the woman, eh?" Sandy said, patting her upon the head in a fatherly way he sometimes indulged in.

"Oh! yes! yes! and I never experienced such a fright. Oh, am I discovered again, Sandy?"

"No! no! pard; the madame simply had an odd notion that I was giving these ites of Whoop-Up an unfair deal, but I soon persuaded her out of it."

"I don't like that woman, Sandy," Dusty Dick said, slowly. "She puts me in mind of a panther on the eve of springing upon its prey. I am afraid she will betray me to the town—and sacrifice your honor, which would be worse then all else."

"Don't fear, pard; she hadn't better play knaves against kings, if she knows when she is well off. Besides, should she betray us, one alternative is left."

"What is it, Sandy?"

"You could *marry me*, and be acknowledged as my wife, Dick!"

There was a start and a swift, sudden glance, then a trembling all over, as if in a spasm, on the part of the fair masquerader, then she shook her head, gravely, an unusual hoarseness in her voice.

"No! not that, Sandy—not that. The alternative would be a pistol-shot through my head, for I could never marry you—nor any one."

Sandy did not question her further; he had long been aware that she had a secret locked in her breast, but what it was he had not even dared to guess.

At the shanty, Sandy had partitioned off an apartment for Dusty Dick, with a lock and key to it, and this was Dick's bed-chamber, while Sandy bunked down in the kitchen—and parlor combined.

For a couple of days after the events just related, Dusty Dick was indisposed, and remained closely at the cabin, and having overworked himself, Sandy took a couple of days off for a hunt in the mountains, which was very successful, for he each day fetched home any amount of squirrels and smaller game. Elated with two days of success, he started out on the third morning, determined to put in a third day, as he had a good superintendent at the mine whom he could trust.

As he was passing the Mastodon on his way, who should hail him but Colonel Joe, from the doorway.

"Hey! hello, Sandy, you galoot! Hold up a bit. Durn et, w'at's gittin' inter ye, boy, they ye don't come around no more? Haven't forgot your old pard, I hope?"

"Oh no; far from that, colonel. I do not drop good friends so easily; but you see, I don't drink myself, and therefore don't find much occasion to visit saloons."

"Not unless there's a blonde siren behind ther counter, eh? Oh! ye needn't try ter stuff me, boyee! I saw ye a few nights ago buzzin' the madame. Sandy, an' I warn't the only one, nuther. 'Twixt you an' me, Sandy—an' ye seem sorter a son to me—I'd advise ye ter drap thet madame. She's tuk a shine ter that yaller mustache of yourn, and ye ken't tell w'at might happen. Sum o' these female critters ye ken't trust. Thar war my wife, Angelina, fer instance. All I hev left ter remember that dear woman, Sandy, ar' a bald spot atop o' my head, an' a dent in my left ear, whar she did some extra-fine tooth-carvin'."

Sandy smiled through his eyes at the colonel's attempt to be facetious.

"Don't worry that the blonde madame will ever be anything to me," he replied. "My inclinations don't run particularly in that direction. But you must excuse me now, colonel, for I'm off for one more day's recreation in the mountains. I'll come around and fetch along my new pard some of these evenings."

"All right, Sandy; I'd like ter see ther pilgrim, fer they say he's good-lookin' fer ther times. But I say, old boy, hold on a bit; I've got a new pard sence I see'd you last—a rich old galoot—a kind o' Senator, or the like, you see, who pays cash down, an' won't drink tarant'ler; kerries his own champagne in a big Sarytoga!"

"Some speculator, I presume, eh?"

"Wal, yes; I guess that's about ther caricature of ther matter—calls hisself Honorable Something-or-other—name's writ down on a copy-book inside—an' wants ter b'y out these hull mines. I told him I reckoned you wouldn't sell, but he sed he'd come around an' see you."

"Tell him he needn't put himself out of the way on account of me," replied Sandy, as he trudged away, "for I won't sell."

"Good fer ye, Sandy! Stick ter yer bed as long's thar's plenty o' feathers in et, an' ye'll eventually grow ter be a rich and influential citizen like myself. An' thet reminds me thet I heven't hed but six good snifters this whole blessed mornin'!"

Which recollection caused the colonel to hasten his footsteps toward the interior of his establishment, while Sandy continued on his way, accompanied by his faithful Buffalo, and was soon out of Canyon Gulch—far up among the wooded peaks of another range.

"No, I will not sell out," he muttered; "would you, Buffalo?" with a glance at the dog. "I am realizing a handsome thing out of the mine, and, better than all, am giving a gang of honest, industrious men of families employment at paying wages. No doubt there are capitalists who would like to step down into the little city of Whoop-Up, and grasp the tyrant's reins in their hands; but they'll be mightily disappointed when they find that very few poor men are so poor but what they can stand firm for their rights."

Sandy was an enthusiast on the labor question, and if the country to-day had more of his make and resolute mind, there would, undoubtedly, be a change for the better, when every man would, in a greater or lesser degree, have an independence, and not be ground down under the heel of the master of money.

Sandy was a good shot, and he rarely fired the second time at the same game. It took but one shot to settle the matter, as a general thing.

But, to-day, his luck must have forsaken him, for the day quickly passed and night was creeping on, when he came to the conclusion that he should have to return to town with only a pair of gray squirrels.

He was some distance away from Canyon Gulch, and rather than go by a roundabout way, he followed a short natural corridor or shelf that ran around the mountain to the side opposite Whoop-Up. In many places the ledge was very narrow and dangerous; in one instance his feet had just struck upon a sort of plateau, when the ledge he had left caved off, and went crashing down the dizzy mountain-side hundreds of feet.

It was a fortunate escape, but he found that it effectually cut off his retreat. There was no means of getting off the plateau except by dropping a couple of hundred feet into a dark defile below. And the vexatious part of the situation was not lessened when he discovered that he was not the only one on the plateau. For company he had a huge cinnamon bear, who was just crawling out from a hole in the rocks!

Chapter 5

A MUTINY—HON. CECIL AND THE FEMALE ROAD AGENT

Deep down in a dark mountain pocket, not three miles from Whoop-Up, where the light of the sun never penetrated because of the matting of tree-tops which almost met overhead, a camp-fire was brightly burning. The bottom of the pocket was level and of hard-pan rock, covered here and there by patches of moss, upon which a score or more of men in the wild, fantastic garb of rangers were sitting or reclining, as the case might be.

Others were engaged in playing upon musical instruments, such as the violin, guitar and flute, and the melody they made sounded weirdly beautiful as it rose and rolled away through the mountains. Now the men strike up in a grand chorus, in some favorite mountain song, the air purely rendered by a pair of tenor voices, and the alto, barytone and deep, thundering bass swelling out grandly with the melodious strains of the song.

Then there comes a lull, after which conversation takes the place of song.

"I tell you what, boys!" said one brawny fellow, who seemed to feel himself a sort of ruler among the others. "I tell ye, et ain't half w'at et's cracked up ter be. I'd ruther go back ter ther road again and play road-agent, instead o' regulator. I say it ain't half w'at et's cracked up ter be."

"You had better not 'spress them opinions afore Deadwood Dick, Barker, ef you don't want ter swing ter ther handiest limb," spoke up another.

"We'll all agree thet et ain't half ther fun a-layin' idle that there is a-dashin' about in the saddle, but ef we're goin' ter serve under Dick, we've got ter go and do as Dick sez; thar's no two ways about that; you hear me."

"Wal, then, I propose we quit Deadwood Dick an' go back ter ther road on our own hooks," proposed the man Barker, lighting his pipe with a brand from the fire. "Hayr we've bin playin' pins an' thet sort o' thing fer six months or over, an' I calcylate we've redeemed ourselves in ther eyes o' the world no more'n w'en we robbed ther stage an' made every pesky pilgrim pony up. Thar ain't enny o' us as hes got rich out o' bein' honest, I kin sw'ar, an' I propose thet we mutinize."

"'Sh! don't make so free wi' talk, Hen Barker. Ef Deadwood Dick shed be anywheres in sight—"

"Cuss Deadwood Dick!" was the growling, sullen response; "cuss him, I say. I ain't afeard o' him, fellers; why need you be? He don't owe us nothin', ner we him; so why shed we allus stick ter him? Now, fer instance, w'ile we're layin' heer idle, fat stages aire rollin' inter and out o' Whoop-Up—two or three o' 'em each way, daily; an' not a single galoot dares ter tackle ther trail. I say its a durned shame, an' I purpose thet we remedy ther defect. Them in favor o' slopin' back ter ther old bizness again will make it manifest by sayin' *I!*"

"*I!*" "*I!*" came in a chorus of voices, which embraced the entire crowd. "Hurrah fer ther road!"

"All right, fellers; then thet settles ther matter. Grab yer weepons an' git ter yer horses, fer thar's time to reach the Whoop-Up trail before the evening-stage comes along!"

Probably there would have been a general stampede, only for the step that sounded close by at this moment, and the words brought to hearing in a clear, ringing voice:

"Halt! you treacherous fools, halt! The first man that moves toward leaving camp risks death!" and into the firelight strode the noted outlaw leader, Deadwood Dick!

The old prince of the road who has figured in so many thrilling scenes and strange disguises; the dare-devil young captain who, of all men, had spread terror and alarm through the Black Hills country.

He was much the same as when we last left him in his village among the golden hills; (see BEADLE'S POCKET LIBRARY NO. 41, "Deadwood Dick's Eagles.") indeed, time used him lightly, and there were no perceptible changes in him. He was still the handsome knight of the hills, and under his new *regime* had done good, even if he had not freed himself from the bad reputation of having been a road-agent.

Now, he stood confronting the score of mutinous spirits who had long served under his orders, with a stern fire in his black eyes—those eyes which were so all-powerful in their peculiar magnetism—stood with folded arms and proudly haughty carriage.

"Oh! it's you, is it?" growled Barker, savagely. "Well, say your say in a hurry, an' be quick, fer we're goin' ter stop ther stage, ter-night, an' make our pile, you bet. We ain't a-goin' ter be held in under no one's heel, in purtick'ler, but lay fer luck, an' shar' ekal."

"You are a fool!" Deadwood Dick said in a contemptuous tone. "You deserve to be gibbeted, but you are not worth the trouble. Go! every one of you—I denounce you all as mutineers, and you no longer are pards of mine. But, look out for me! I have not done with you yet. Every one of you will pay the penalty meted out to deserters. Beware!"

Then with a strange laugh—his old, startling laugh, that had so much import in its meaning, the ex-road-agent chief turned on his heel and strode away into the darkness, leaving behind him a group of staring men.

"Ye heerd w't he sed, b'yees?" demanded Barker. "I motion thet we take the cuss an' hoist him to a limb!"

To this all agreed, and a general stampede was made in search of Deadwood Dick.

Which was fruitless, for the young chief was not to be found.

From that night, the Black Hills country of gold was once more thickly infested with outlaws and road-robbers; no stage drove through the canyon trail without receiving a visit, and it was dangerous for a man to be abroad at night if he was known to have an ounce of gold about him.

The cessation of road robbery that had followed the reign of Deadwood Dick and his Regulators, was now almost—in a day it seemed—superseded by a reign of crime and utter disregard of the law. Deadwood, Hayard, and Custer each established vigilance committees, and a reporter for the leading Deadwood City paper got up an editorial, something after this pattern:

INCREASE OF CRIME.—It has reached us that the once notorious road-agent, Deadwood Dick, who of late—with his men—has been playing Regulator and waging war against ruffianism is at last dead, and under the turf; and, now free from his control, his whole great band has again taken the trail as road-agents, all over the Hills, and pandemonium ensues. Peace to Dick's ashes; but we should have wished him a longer stay with us, as he seemed to hold the controlling power of legions in his hands.

On this same day that Sandy had gone a hunting, only to be caged by accident in with a huge cinnamon, the Honorable Cecil Grosvenor was riding along through Canyon Gulch in its northern course, beyond where settlement an Whoop-Up civilization had pitched its line of white tents, and beyond even where the miner's pick or the prospector's staff had yet reached.

On either side the canyon walls rose rugged and nearly perpendicular to a great height, and close to the western side the shallow waters of Canyon Creek gurgled noisily.

A trail ran along the eastern shore which had been made for the daily stage to Deadwood, and it was bounded on either side by thickets of various shrubs and chaparral.

"The-Man-from-Washington," as he had been immediately nicknamed by the Whoop-Up-ites, seemed in ill humor to-day, for he vented unnecessary spite upon his horse, and kept a sharp lookout on either side, as if expecting some one. A dark scowl hovered about his eyes and forehead, and he appeared to be unusually nervous.

"Curse the luck!" he growled, biting at the ends of his mustache, and glaring about as if he would like to annihilate some person. "Curse the luck, I say! Who could the woman be, if not *her?* I thought her dead and under ground long ago and here, in all probability, she has turned up to devil me again. Ha! I thought so," he concluded, drawing rein, as a female rider wheeled a large horse out of a sharp bend square across his path, and presented to his view an outstretched arm and hand containing a shining revolver.

"Halt! that's right!" exclaimed a clear female voice, which caused the Washingtonian to start in recognition, although the figure upon the horse was clad in black and deeply veiled. "I didn't hardly expect you would dare come out here and meet me, when I had the letter dropped in the Mastodon House post-office; but I thought it would be well enough to come and see. There! there! don't attempt to draw a weapon, for you know I'm reckless, and would just as lief shoot you as not."

"By Heaven! can this be you, Marie?" the Honorable Cecil managed to articulate, interrogatively. "Can it be possible, when I have all these years mourned you as dead?"

"I reckon it's I, old hypocrite!" was the cool assurance. "There! don't let me warn you of the danger of reaching toward your vest pocket again. It is I, or all that a matter of six years left of me, after roughing it in the world I was cast upon."

"Then, I thank God," said Honorable Cecil, with an attempt to do the devout. "Put down the pistol, Marie, and let me come forward and welcome you back."

"Bah! don't be a fool, old man!" replied the strange horsewoman, with a sneer which also resembled a chuckle. "I don't want any spooneying or foolish acting on your part. When but a young girl, I married you at my dying father's wish, because you were one of the leading stock and bond gamblers in Washington, worth your half a million or more. The first year, I found you out to be an ugly brute. The second year you developed into a first-class savage, and finding my life with you unendurable, I pocketed your loose change, and, in the vernacular of the mines, I *sloped!* I took pity on you; you never heard from me again until last night, when you received my note to meet me here. Your name remained spotless in Washington, for a horrible railroad accident occurred about this time, and a few mangled remains of your wife were brought home and quietly interred. Am I not detailing facts?"

"Ah! very true; and I mourned—"

"Bah! you old hypocrite; shut up your lying! It won't go down your humble servant's throat. What brings you out here, sir—some villainy, I'd almost swear."

"No, indeed, Marie. I am very poor of late years, and came out here to try and retrieve what I have lost in disastrous speculation."

"You lie, old man. You own two among the finest properties in Washington, besides having half a million's worth of secured bonds, and plenty of other wealth. I say you lie!"

"You speak plain, woman—shockingly plain for a woman who figured as a belle in London society."

"But oh! so true, Cecil Grosvenor. You know I never deviate from the blessed truth. I saw you the day you came here to Whoop-Up, and instantly it occurred to me that you would be perfectly overjoyed and willing to loan me some of your wealth—"

"Never! never! you she-devil!" the capitalist cried fiercely, now nearly beside himself with rage. "Not one penny of mine shall you ever touch."

"You forget, Cecil!" was the reply, in a provokingly cool tone. "Just gaze into this tool I hold, and realize the discomfort contained in the six loaded cells. These poor 'sells,' too, to encounter in the hands of Mad Marie, who is pretty widely known as a woman shootist."

"How much money do you want, curse you, to keep you quiet?"

"Oh! knowing that you never go empty-handed, I'll take what you have in your pocket-book, and that diamond pin you so proudly display upon your immaculate shirt-front. Come, don't be offish now, but put the pin in your wallet, and drop it on the plot of grass there by the roadside; then turn your face about and return to Whoop-Up!"

"You shall pay dearly for this, you virago!" the Honorable Cecil gritted, as he complied with her request. "I'll have my revenge—I'll hire some one to take your life."

"Of course, dear, I expect nothing else; but I shall not go to sleep with both eyes shut. I formed a habit of sleeping with one eye open ere I left you, lest you should try to murder me some night. That's right," as the man hurled the wallet upon the grass. "Ah! you have a watch and chain, too, I see; but I won't be so mean as to deprive you of *all* your gaudy adornments this time; so now, I guess you may go."

"Curse you!" The-Man-from-Washington fairly yelled, as he hesitated to go. "You shall die for this outrage, you—"

"There! there! you old loafer. Don't hurt your tongue in addressing me with the idea of frightening me, for I've heard men who could lay way over you at sw'aring. Go, now, and if any one tells you you've lost your pin and purse, tell them Deadwood Dick's men robbed you. Don't for the world let any one know that a weak woman played road-agent to you. Go, now, I say. If you want me drop a letter to Mad Marie, in the post-office at Joe Tubbs's Mastodon, and I'll seize my pen in a vise-like grasp to answer you. Adieu! My pistol covers you until you are out of sight."

With oaths breaking from his lips, the defeated speculator headed his horse back toward the mining town, and spurred away in hot haste, followed by a mocking laugh from his tormentor.

"A thousand devils overtake the she fury!" he gritted, in the white heat of his rage. "I'll hire some ruffian to hunt her up and cut her throat, even if it costs me a small fortune. She is getting cunning, but has triumphed over me for the last time!"

Chapter 6

A CONFLICT WITH BRUIN

Sandy's was a situation few men could wish to confront.

There he was safely imprisoned upon the plateau, with the positive assurance that he must enter into conflict with the huge cinnamon bear, who was crawling out of a sort of cave in the mountain-side, with growls that were anything but music to his ear.

Since coming West Sandy had never chanced upon anything of the bear kind, and knew as little about them as the school-boy at home.

After crawling out upon the plateau, the huge brute squatted upon its haunches for a few moments, and surveyed Sandy in evident contemplation of a fine feast, while Sandy stood still in his tracks, utterly at loss how to act. On reflection—for a man can reflect a great deal in a short space of time if occasion demands—he doubted if his forty-four caliber rifle would do any service in an attack against Bruin, for the reason that he used short cartridges with a small charge of powder, while it takes a heavy ball (77 grs. of powder and 350 grs. of lead) to successfully shoot either a grizzly or a cinnamon. Very few men can kill a grizzly or cinnamon bear in three running shots as it is, with the long 45 cartridge.

Sandy had learned this in conversation with old hunters, and consequently concluded that either his rifle or revolvers were useless, and, if used upon the brute, would act only to stimulate his fury, while they did no particular harm.

He accordingly drew his knife, and edged out into the center of the plateau, nearer to the ugly brute. He had no desire to be crowded off from the plateau into the abyss below.

As he advanced the cinnamon reared upon his hind legs, and came on, with a flaming desire expressed in his eye. Sandy braced himself, and stood upon his guard. He knew it must be a struggle between life and death, and he set his teeth together in a firm determination to sell his life as dearly as possible.

Buffalo, his huge Newfoundland, had been left behind, beyond where the ledge caved off. With his assistance in diverting the attention of the great brute, the attack might have been more equal.

On came the monster, with his frightful jaws distended, nearer and nearer, and then Sandy sprung forward, and struck a blow into the animal's breast which proved effective, inasmuch as it started a flow of blood. Unfortunately, before he could dodge, the miner received a tremendous slap from one of Bruin's paws, which sent him reeling halfway across the plateau.

He still was possessed of his senses, however, and turned to meet the maddened animal.

Instantly drawing one of his Smith and Wesson revolvers, Sandy fired, in rapid succession, six shots into the gaping wound which he had cut with his knife, then dodged and ran to the other end of the plateau, flushed and excited. Something in the fight had an enticement and charm for him, although he was confident that it was not the slap he had received on the side of his head. The bullets had staggered the huge brute, and the blood was spurting from the wound in a sickening stream; yet he came lumbering back again with a roar that seemed to jar the very plateau—came on with furious rage and frenzy depicted in the hairy countenance and in the pinkish eyes.

Sandy drew his other revolver and stood firm, a new light in his eyes. When the brute was but three yards off, he fired two shots, with unerring precision—one bullet into each eye of his ponderous enemy.

With a fiercer roar the bear rushed on, with blood streaming from his eyes and totally blinding him—rushed on, straight off of the plateau, and went crashing helplessly down into the gulch far below.

"Good enough! I couldn't have beat it myself. I was just getting ready to dispatch the brute myself with my Winchester rifle!" exclaimed a voice, and looking up, Sandy beheld a face peering down at him from a ledge far above. "Reckon you got rid of him just in time, for it would soon have been too dark for straight shooting."

"I suppose so. Anyhow, I am not sorry that I disposed of the brute. How's a fellow to get out of this—do you know?" Sandy asked.

"Maybe I can give you some assistance. I'll lower one end of my lasso, and if you are good at climbing, you can get up here, from where I can guide you safely down the mountain!" was the reply, and then the face withdrew from sight, and directly one end of a strong, but slim rope was lowered to the plateau where Sandy had fought and killed his cinnamon.

Slinging his rifle to his back and securing his revolvers in their places, Sandy seized the rope in his grasp, and up he went with the agility of a true Simian, soon pulling himself upon the ledge above, where stood his rescuer, and the dog, Buffalo.

"Calamity Jane!" he ejaculated involuntarily, for in the features of the stranger he recognized a description he had obtained of the noted young female dare-devil.

"At your service, sir!" was the reply, with a cool laugh. "You stare as if I were something quite different from the ordinary mortal."

"Yes, ahem! excuse me!" and the miner stammered and blushed in confusion. "You—you see, I'd heard so much concerning you, that I—I really was surprised. You will pardon me, and—"

"Oh, yes; you bet yer boots! But 'twixt you and me, pardner, you did remarkable execution in that b'ar fight. I don't b'lieve thar's another galoot in Whoop-Up as could do the job in quicker time, or more scientific manner. Didn't get nary a tear?"

"No! I had a remarkably lucky escape," Sandy replied, marveling, even while he spoke, at the wild beauty of the girl, of whom the men of Whoop-Up told so many strange yarns. "I escaped with only a cuff on the side of my head."

"Which did you more good than a pint of medicine. It aroused the fight in you. It's all the medicine a man wants to brace him up."

"You discriminate between the two sexes, eh?"

"Certainly; men need a slap and a woman a slight, to wake 'em up. Anyhow, that's my logic. Shall I conduct you down the mountain, or can you go it alone?"

"You can guide me if you will, and take the bear for your pay."

"Agreed. Give *me* a cinnamon to corn away for winter chawin'. What's your name, pard?"

"They call me Sandy, here in the mines!" the miner replied, following carefully in the steps of the girl, as she began to descend a zig-zag mountain path.

"What! ye ain't the chap w'at helped old Joe Tubbs find thes streak o' gold range, are ye?"

"If I remember correctly, I was the first one to find a nugget."

"Well, you're a brick. Joe was tellin' me about you. Got a pard, I believe?"

"Yes—Dusty Dick."

"Like myself, a girl in male attire!"

"What makes you think that, pray?"

"I know it!" Calamity Jane replied, with a chuckle.

"It doesn't matter how I found it out. I don't blame you for protecting the girl, nor her for accepting your protection, and all may go right until discovery becomes general. Then, come you unto me; I may point out to you a way out of the mire."

"*You?*" Sandy demanded, incredulously.

"Yes, I. By the way, let me warn you to look out for breakers ahead. You cannot see them. I do not know in just what shape they are going to come, but come they will, surely."

"How do you know? What have you discovered likely to endanger me?"

"That's my secret. If I were to tell you, like as not, by some blunder, you'd bring yourself into double peril. Now, you cannot comprehend my words, hereafter you will. I'll keep an eye out, and don't ye fergit it."

"I reckon I can look out for myself, ma'am," Sandy said, with a spice of independence. "Ah! Here we are at Canyon Gulch, now."

"Yes, and here I will leave you, as you can easily find your way now. Good-bye, and look sharp around you!" Then the girl dare-devil suddenly turned, and was lost in the gloom, while Sandy trudged wonderingly along into the wide-awake town of Whoop-Up.

"Exceedingly strange, and wonderfully beautiful," he muttered meditatively. "Hers is a magnetic beauty that *attracts*; the madame is fascinating, in a voluptuous sense; little Dusty Dick is the most quiet and womanly; yet around the trio there hangs a mystery in each case, and the long and short of it is, I'm getting interested with the whole. Well, well, if I can't take care of myself, I ought not to claim a right to the name of man. Dick I have with me; Madame Minnie will not bother me if I keep away from her, and Calamity Jane— Well, I can't determine much about her."

Neither could any one else in all the rough society in which the eccentric girl had for two years moved as a "bright, particular star."

Sandy went home, and found Dusty Dick sitting in the doorway of their unpretentious shanty, engaged in picking at a guitar, which had been one of the miner's gifts.

"Ah! is that you, Dick? How have things gone during my absence?"

"About in the usual channel, Sandy; a couple of duels above here in the street, I believe, and consequently work for an undertaker, had one been handy."

"Humph! it is strange that such a warfare must constantly rage between fellow humans, isn't it? If all got along as well together as you and I, Dick, I don't think there'd be many deaths and crimes to answer for."

"Very true, Sandy; but there's your supper awaiting, inside. I got hungry and ate mine."

"That's right, pard; never starve yourself in waiting for me, for there's no telling just what minute I may arrive. Ah! the odor from that antelope-steak is really like the smell of the promised land, after a fellow has been a-hunting and slain his maiden cinnamon b'ar."

"A bear, Sandy?" and the beautiful eyes of Dusty Dick gazed up inquiringly, calling a pleasurable flush to his brown cheek.

"Well, yes—that's what I said. You see, I and a big cinnamon got into a disagreement about our respective rights to a certain mountain plateau, and after his boxing me severely on the right ear, I tumbled him off into a gulch and teetotally smashed his bruinship. Being a somewhat larger load than I felt disposed to tote home, I surrendered his carcass to Calamity Jane, who chanced to be near."

"That strange girl, Sandy, whom the people talk so much about?"

"Yes, the same."

"Is she pretty, Sandy?"

"Well, yes, in one sense of the word; but life here in the Hills has—well, has ruined her prospects, one might say, for she has grown reckless in act and rough in language."

"Yet she may have a true woman's *heart* under her rough exterior, which is as susceptible to love or pain as a woman of careful behavior."

"Truly spoken, little one, but she could not ever arouse half the adoration for her in my breast, that I bear for you," the miner said, and honest light glowing in his eyes. But he regretted the words the next moment, for they brought such a pained expression over the features of Dusty Dick.

"You should not talk that way, Sandy. You forget that I am only your pard—more I can never be."

"Enough said, Dick; I did forget myself, but will curb myself in the future. But get ready, for I am going to take you around to-night, to see the sights; I must do it to throw off suspicion. Calamity Jane already knows your disguise."

"She! How, pray?"

"I give it up. She knows, nevertheless, and will keep mum, I take it. Do you feel like playing your part to-night, in good shape?"

"As well to-night, perhaps, as at any other time. I have mastered some of the vernacular and bravado of the mines, and will do as well as possible."

Sandy finished his supper, and fed Buffalo enough for any two men; then took his revolvers, cleaned and reloaded them, and thrust them into his belt. Usually, unless going on a hunt, he never wore them outwardly displayed, but something prompted him to have them handy to-night.

Dusty Dick always wore a single revolver at his waist, and despite the general feminine terror of fire-arms, he was no novice at a shot.

When all was in readiness the two left the cabin, accompanied by Sandy's inseparable companion, Buffalo, and debouched into the single, long, crowded street of the town. It was about half after eight in the evening, and all places of business, of a score of various natures, were brilliantly lit, and the street was a strange and wild sight of lights and surging humanity, from one end to the other.

Chapter 7

SANDY AND THE ''HONORABLE''

"Here! we will stop into this place where they play keno and faro. You can take a peep at the animals," said Sandy, and they accordingly entered a large room in one of the shanties that lined the street, and found themselves in a bar-room, gaming-parlor and dancing-hall, all combined in one thirty by forty apartment, under one roof. Here were a long bar and many tables, at which crowds of long-haired men were risking and losing; further on was a music-stand, beyond which a couple of sets, comprising burly miners and roughs and gaudily-dressed females, were dancing.

After loitering about for a while, Sandy signified his intention of departing. "But let's have a little something at the bar first, to say we've patronized the place. What'll you have, Dick?" in a louder tone.

"Let out ther sherry wine for me, ye galoot!" Dusty Dick replied, ranging himself along the bar, and addressing the barkeeper. "Hurry up yer stumps, or I'll get over thar an' grab a hold o' ther ribbons myself."

The bottle was quickly forthcoming, and Dick swallowed a few drops of the wine, which was a wonderfully pure article to be found in the mines. Sandy took soda for his. Then the twain left the place, and sauntered toward Colonel Joe Tubbs's "howtel," at the upper end of the street.

Here a motley crowd was collected in the great bar-room, for the mails from Deadwood and the East had just arrived, and many an eager, anxious miner was looking for a letter from the dear ones at home.

"I reckon there's no mail for me," Sandy said, with a grim smile, "for the simple reason that there are no dear absent ones in my case, you see."

"Nor need *I* look for letters, either," Dick replied, sadly, "for none of the friends of my childhood stood the test. Ah! who is that remarkable-looking personage at the other end of the room?"

"Why, that's the dare-devil, Calamity Jane. Don't be afraid of her, but act your part if she comes up."

Although Colonel Joe was busy at dealing out his "p'izen" to a long range of red-shirted miners, he found room at the bar for Sandy and Dusty Dick.

"Hello, Sandy, you hoss! range up alongside hayr, in ther stall. Got yer pard along, too, eh?"

"Yes, Joe, this is Dusty Dick, my pard. Dick, Colonel Tubbs, one of the oldest inhabitants."

The introduction was acknowledged by a hearty handshake, Tubbs failing to notice the smallness or softness of Dick's hand.

"You may give us a couple of sodas, Joe," Sandy said; "you know we don't take anything stronger. Will you join us, seeing this is the first time we've met since this morning?"

"Sandy, b'yee, ye bet yer boots I will! Why, it's a scandulous fac' thet I haven't hed only sixteen real *good*-sized snifters since dinner. Twenty is my reg'lar rations."

"You'll get the 'jims' if you don't stop drinking so much, Joe."

"Aha! Sandy, there's where ye are behind yer mark. I've got a cast-iron tank inside o' me, an' et'll take years ter fill up wi' p'izen. I'm good fer ter make a bar'l look sick any day, an' don't ye fergit it."

"I believe you, Joe. You seem to stand it pretty well, all except your nose—that is giving you away."

"Better polish it off, an' sell it for a colored meerschaum, old man!" put in Dusty Dick, as she turned away.

Not being in a hurry, they stood leaning against the wall at one side of the bar-room. Sandy puffing away at his cigar, and both idly watching the different faces around them. Miners came in and applied for mail, and woe be to the purse of him as was so fortunate as to get a letter, for he was calculated to call up all of his acquaintances, besides treating the "post-office," which embraced Colonel Joe and three assistants.

A man is conceded to have no honor in Whoop-Up if he cannot "respond," after being blessed with a letter from the "States."

"Do you see that villainous-looking rough, who is sitting over there, Sandy—the one looking this way?" Dusty Dick asked, pointing out not less an individual than the Danite Ghoul, Arkansas Alf Kennedy. "Oh! mercy, he has seen me motioning, and is coming this way. What shall we do?"

"Sh! or you will betray yourself. He won't do anybody harm, I reckon. Put on your 'cheek,' an' bluff him!"

It was evident that the Dakota-Danite was in high dudgeon, for he came striding up with a bluster and a swagger, his eyes bloodshot from the effects of the whisky which scented his breath.

"See, here, younker!" he cried, addressing Dusty Dick, with a fierce oath, "I wonter know who ye war p'intin' at, over that d'rection? Do I owe ye anything, or d'ye want ter make my acquaintance?"

"Get out, you galoot!" Dick replied, independently; "I reckon ye was lookin' this way first. What you blowin' yer b'liler-head off fer?"

"I'll show ye, mighty quick, ye little cuss," the Danite replied, reaching for a weapon; but before he could draw one, the muzzle of Sandy's revolver was shoved within an inch of his reddened nose.

"Hold up, pilgrim!" was the miner's calm advice; "I reckon ye better be sure o' yer game before ye raise your gun. If you ain't desirous of getting salted down for winter use, you'd better peg along in another direction, pretty lively."

"Who are *you?*" Arkansas Alf demanded, with a snarl.

"They call me Sandy, fer short, sir; for long, I measure five foot ten."

The Danite turned away with a frightful string of oaths, and then Sandy nodded to Dick.

"Keep watch of that fellow, pard, when he's near about, hereafter. He has a bad name here in the Hills."

"Who is he, Sandy?"

"Arkansas Alf, the Ghoul, they call him. He's about as bad as they make 'em, they say."

The two pards soon took their departure from the saloon and returned to their shanty. To their combined astonishment they found the door unlocked, and on entering, found a light burning in the kitchen and a man sitting before the bed of coals on the hearth, idly fingering the strings of the guitar—a man of medium height, with a handsome form and frank, pleasant face, and such eyes as neither Sandy nor Dick had ever gazed into before—dark, brilliant, magnetic.

He was attired in gray, fashionably-cut clothing, with a diamond pin upon his shirt-front, and a silk hat upon his head.

"I beg your pardon, pilgrim," he said, arising and bowing, as both Dusty Dick and Sandy stopped short near the door. "My intrusion here may seem unpardonably bold, but I have a paper here which I trust will explain all," and he extended an enveloped note.

Sandy took it and stepped to the light, at the same time tearing it open.

"Humph!" he muttered. "It is from Calamity Jane."

So it was, and written in a neat, womanly hand, with the following result:

> Mr. Sandy:—Please keep this gentleman in your ranch until he chooses to leave. He will pay you liberally, and you will confer a great favor on me. He is Deadwood Dick, the ex-road-agent, supposed by everybody to be dead. Yours, etc.,
> CALAMITY JANE.

"Well, well!" Sandy muttered, with rather a grim smile, "that girl certainly does not lack for assurance. So you are Deadwood Dick, eh?" turning to the stranger.

"At your service. Calamity let me in here, with the word that it would be all right, as I wanted lodging until morning. If, however, I am in your way, I'll seek elsewhere—"

"Perfectly welcome, sir, if you can accept of my accommodation. There's my cot yonder—I'll fix me up a bed on the floor."

"I beg your pardon, but you will let *me* lie on the floor, as I am perhaps more used to it than you, after a rough life of two years in the heart of the gold country. Please retain your own cot, the same as if I were not here."

It was accordingly so arranged, for Deadwood Dick would have it no other way, but rolled up in a blanket and lay down near the door. Dusty Dick retired to and locked himself in his own room, and Sandy stretched himself upon the cot without undressing. This was nothing unusual with him.

When he awoke in the morning, at sunrise on the mountain-tops, Dusty Dick had breakfast already on the table.

"Hello! where's the road-agent?" Sandy asked, sitting up and rubbing his eyes and staring about.

"Gone an hour ago," Dick replied, dishing up the meat and pouring out the coffee. "Sandy, he was a handsome fellow."

"Well, yes, I suppose some would call him handsome. I've read of him, and they say he's a wild customer."

"He didn't appear so. He was dressed more after a civilized fashion than any one I've seen here yet."

"Didn't fall in love with him, I hope?" The poor fellow has already been bored by love-sick maidens, and then, too, he's married."

"Ah! *is* he? Then I'm sorry," was the reply accompanied by a roguish little laugh. "Come; your breakfast will be getting cold."

So Sandy ate of the tempting repast, and betook himself off to the mines, whistling merrily in the course of his walk. In rounding the bend in the canyon, he almost ran against the Honorable Cecil Grosvenor, who was returning from an early morning walk for his health.

Both men came face to face—then each leaped back as if stung by an adder, their eyes bearing a light of recognition.

"*You*, Cecil Grosvenor!" Sandy exclaimed, growing a shade whiter than was his usual color.

"Yes, Sandy!" was the reply of the Washingtonian, who seemed to be the least surprised of the two. "You see I address you by your western title; in some respects it is better than your Eastern name!"

"How do you mean?" the miner demanded haughtily. "My name was never a reproach in my Eastern home. Indeed it was always spotless until—"

"Until certain complicated circumstances made it necessary for you to put a considerable distance between you and the place of your birth!" finished the speculator, with a bland smile, as he gazed triumphantly at the miner.

"You needn't jeer!" Sandy replied, with self-command, "for I do not fear you, nor the whole world. With the crime of that one act put upon my shoulders, I am no *murderer!*"

"What! You do not imply that *I* am one?" the Honorable Cecil demanded hotly. "Beware how you word your address to me."

"If you see yourself in my words you certainly must be guilty," was the calm reply of the miner. "Indeed, everybody said that you did in reality murder your first wife by ill treatment and abuse. Your second left you, I hear, doubtless fearing that she would follow the first to the grave."

"Oh!" the speculator said, with a sigh of relief, elated that the case was made out no stronger; "as to that you merely deal in idle supposition, with no positive proof. I hold a stronger hand against you, if you remember."

"I defy your power!" Sandy said, with set teeth.

"If you have come out here on purpose to fight me, we will see how the fight is to come out in the end. Remember, I shall not move to get out of your way this time—not a step."

"I suppose not, but I dare say you will be ready to pay liberally to be let off!"

"Not a cent, Cecil Grosvenor—not a copper will I give you; so go ahead, and do your worst."

"But listen, man; you have established yourself among these miners as an honest and reputable citizen, and have made your pile of money, from all that I can hear. How would it affect your financial or personal standing to know that you are a—"

"Stop, you old villain—never speak that word in my presence. I will kill you, if it is the last thing I do. Remember!" and stepping to one side the miner strode on along the route to the mine.

Grosvenor stood looking after him until he had gone from sight; then kept on toward his hotel, a devilish expression upon his face.

"That man must die!" he muttered, under his breath— "die and never come to life again. Curse him, he makes me feel uncomfortable when he gazes at me, and yet I know of no power he has over me. Few know that I came here out of pure spite against him—that I came to put him out of the way!"

He strode along, his brows knitted in a dark scowl, and his mind busied in a villainous scheme. Just as he came opposite Sandy's cabin, he stopped stock-still in his tracks, and gazed in through the open doorway, as if he was struck suddenly with paralysis, a curse breaking from his lips, in a gasp.

Dusty Dick was standing in the kitchen, busily engaged in washing up the dishes, and did not notice The-Man-from-Washington, who, after a moment's sharp survey, passed on up the gulch, a strange light upon his sinister face.

"Heavens! I can scarcely credit the sight of my eyes!" he gritted, seemingly to shake with a new emotion. "She *here* and in *Sandy's* cabin? It is the last place on God's footstool I should have looked to find her. Ha! ha! I have both the birds within my reach—yes, three of them, counting Marie. Curse the woman—she always was an enigma to me. I wonder how I shall play the hand all around and play it successfully. It may cost me hundreds, but I shall in the end gain thousands. Yes! yes! it was a lucky day, after all, that set me down right among the game I am hunting!"

Chapter 8

A NEW CANDIDATE—DEADWOOD
DICK AGAIN

>> <<

About this time, the depredations of the road-agents and outlaws of
the Hills became greater in rapidity and boldness of action. They
grew so bold as to dash into the very outskirts of the town and commit their robberies, and this so aroused the people of Whoop-Up's sin-
gle-streeted city, that they swore dire vengeance on the marauders.
But, they had done this before, and yet had not even killed an agent
in revenge for the spoils that had been taken from the town.

The chief gang that were troublesome around Whoop-Up were the
deserters of Deadwood Dick's band, now under the leadership of the
ruffian, Barker. The agents had given him the high-sounding title of
Eagle Claw, and by this he became known universally.

On the day which had seen the meeting between Sandy and the
Honorable Cecil Grosvenor of Washington, a gang of the outlaws had
dashed boldly into the town, and, after firing a score of shots, had
frightened off a crowd, then robbed a store, and got off, unmolested.

An hour afterward, a crowd of miners were collected in the street
outside of Joe Tubbs's saloon, eagerly discussing the outlook.

"I tell ye, feller-citizens!" Tubbs himself cried from the top of a
handy stump; "thar ain't no use o'talkin' about perseverance or prudence bein' a vartue. Hayer we peaceable an' undemonstrative citizens
o' Whoop-Up's sublime sphere hev bin outraged ag'in, right in broad
daylight! I say et's a shame—er gol-durned reproach onter our handles
as honest men. I propose thet we drop ther Vigilance movement, an'
resort ter Regulation—put some *man* at our he'ds, an' devote our hull
time ter wipin' out these dasted road-agents. Them's my sentiments,
an' I propose the crowd treat me for ther beauchiful suggestion so
timely brought before ther investigatin' committee."

But even though the worthy colonel proposed, the crowd were not
disposed; they were excited after "ther road-agents."

"I second old Joe's motion concerning ther Regulators!" cried another man, a miner, who had suffered several losses from these gentlemen of the road. "We're all ready, every one o'us, ter take up ther
trail o' vengeance, but we want a man ter lead us. Whar's ther a man
as sez he will?"

There was a momentary silence. Then a newcomer in the city of Whoop-Up steeped forward into the ring.

"Feller-citizens," he said with a glance around, "if you're agreeable, I'll accept o' ther offis!"

And as assurances that the crowd were agreeable, a shout of "hurra!" went up from a hundred throats, seemingly. Ready were the miners to go, with some one to head them.

The candidate for election was a man of but medium size, evidently, but a peculiarity of wearing more clothing then necessary upon his person, made him look broad and burly. At least four suits of serviceable woolen clothing wore this new chief of Regulators, with stoga knee-boots upon his feet, and a battered-up hat upon his head. His face, with the exception of the nose, was covered to the ears with a luxuriant growth of reddish beard, and a mass of hair of a like hue fell unkempt and matty upon his shoulders. He eyes were sharp and bead-like in their glances, and altogether he was a remarkable-looking personage. He stood leaning upon a rusty-looking rifle of large bore, and gazing calmy into the sea of faces around him.

"Hurra fer ther new Regulator!" yelled Colonel Joe from the top of his stump. "I say, you galoot, w'at mought yer name be?"

"It mought be 'most anything, I reckon, pilgrim," was the grim response; "but it ain't, ef ther old eclipse knows herself. I suppose it might be practicable to call me Bullwhacker, ef ye've no objections."

"Hurra! Bullwhacker it is then," replied Joe. "Now, then, capting, jest choose yer galoots, an' *lay* fer these road-agents—d'ye heer? You'll hev ter excuse me a few minutes from ther debate, gentlemen, ef ye please, for it's a scandulous fac', thet I heven't hed but six good solid snifters this hull blessed morning."

And Joe made for the Mastodon as if his life depended upon his getting to the bar in a stated number of seconds. He was an odd one on the ludicrous side of human nature, yet despite his love for stimulating drink, was a genial good fellow.

Old Bullwhacker, the newly-elected chief of the Regulators, soon became a popular light in the mining circles of Whoop-Up. He was jovial and eccentric, had plenty of cash with which to treat his men and was just the one fit to command. Where he had come from, or who he was, aside from this rude cognomen, no one knew; nor were they liable to find out by his telling.

He selected for his use ten men aside from himself, and armed them with Winchester's 45-caliber rifles, which were got from Deadwood, and the Regulators were in working order. But it was some days ere there was any occasion for them to exert themselves. The road-agents, under Eagle-Claw, had suddenly become quiet, and there were no new reports of marauds by them.

Bullwhacker, however, had his men ever near and under strict discipline; he never moved but they were near at hand as a sort of protective bodyguard. Although he had never manifested any particular disposition to being what the world of the country of gold calls "fast and tough," Bullwhacker was pretty generally regarded as a scaly customer to tackle, and, by a certain class, was feared. He had such a slow motion at one time, and was so rapid when the case demanded, that it gave him an aspect of being ever ready, no matter what the emergency.

The golden days of September rolled along in the town of Whoop-Up, as in a peculiar dream of exciting pleasure. People thronged the street and filled the places of business both by night and by day.

The mountain continued to yield rich productions of gold; and silver lodes too were found in places. Shafts and tunnels were being pierced into the mountain-side, all the way from the bottom up toward the misty tops, and ore was blasted out and lowered to the gulch-bottom in incline plane cars—or, as in one case, by large buckets from a mighty crane, managed by mule-power. Everywhere were sounds of busy industry in one Babel of noises—the crushing sound of ore-breakers, yells of mule-drivers, the shrieks of steam-whistles, and the ring of axes far up the dizzy mountain, all peculiar to their locality, yet distinct from the sights and sounds of the long street of the magic growing town.

Everybody had the fever; it was a poor cuss who couldn't reap a harvest now, thought the excited people. All along the stage routes to the town, eager, hopeful miners were prospecting; maybe where they would pass over, some speculator would stake off his claim, report gold in paying quantities, hoodwink some fresh arrival—generally known as a "tenderfoot"—and sell him for a big figure what was in reality but a barren rocky waste.

If you got cheated, you must put up with it with all the grace of a saint, unless you wanted to fight it out, and then, like as not, you'd get the worst of it; for it was all in the mines and among the mining element, where law, personal respect, and charity toward mankind, were literally a dead letter. No stage came in or went out without its load of either expectant or disgusted passengers, and thus the population was an ever-moving one, and the people that composed it a spice and variety of humanity.

And as one day rolled by only to merge into another, Sandy kept on working in the mines, the same as he had before he had met the Honorable Cecil Grosvenor in the gulch. He went armed, however, for he knew this Washingtonian well enough to suspect that some attempt would be made through his instrumentality upon his life.

Dusty Dick had not seen the speculator except at a distance; and since then had kept closely to Sandy's shanty, but never mentioning to the miner the cause of his sudden seclusion; for this strange creature whom Sandy was harboring was an enigma whose secret was closely locked in her own breast.

If she had recognized a foe in the Washingtonian, she spoke not of it. Evidently she had not recognized him.

Calamity Jane came much to the cabin, especially when Sandy had returned from his work at night. She was kind toward Dick, in a sisterly way, often dropping her a feminine offer of exchange of confidence, which the mysterious waif would not listen to. She was wholly up to her character—no longer a female even among her own sex.

With Calamity Jane it was different in that she could be equally sociable with male and female. She was witty, well-educated, when she chose to drop the rude vernacular of the mines, and altogether a pleasant companion.

At least she had a faculty of being able to cheer Sandy out of the blues, when he had them: and it came to the anxious notice of Dusty Dick that nothing but a dawning love could alter Calamity's rude bearing of old into the pleasing woman of now; she was learning to love Sandy!

Sandy!—well, Dick entertained no anxiety toward him in this respect, for she knew it would be useless. Sandy was one of those eccentric freaks of human nature that might love

And love o'er again,

without the world becoming wiser for it by studying him.

He held his emotions in a firm grasp, and controlled them—smothered them back as a general thing out of sight of human observance. Even Dick could not read the miner's feeling toward Calamity, but believed that he entertained a respectful admiration for her. Somehow, since they had been together, the young pard had grown to expect things, which all the time she knew would be impossible, of Sandy—to reserve him as hers alone; and a sensation of unrest and anxiety filled her heart at every visit of the girl dare-devil, although she knew she had no right to for one moment entertain a loving thought of the stalwart yellow-haired miner. Whether Calamity had a keen sense to perceive this it is impossible to say; but as the days rolled by, though the girl's admiration increased for the miner, she tried to screen it when in the presence of Dusty Dick.

Maybe her woman's instinct taught her that it was but natural for a woman to love a noble, handsome man, and that other hearts than her own could be so pierced by Cupid's shafts.

So Dick was finally spared some of the heart-pain and anxiety; but the sharp eyes of the young pard could not be blinded to the truth, for all that.

Honorable Cecil Grosvenor stopped Calamity one day as she was walking through the gulch.

"Hold up!" he said, approaching with a pompous strut; "I wish to speak with you, my dear young lady."

"Get out!" Calamity replied so sharply that Mr. Grosvenor leaped back a pace—"none o' your endearing epithets to me, you old buzzard. Say your say, and move on; my time amounts to business."

"Oh! it does," replied the speculator, reaching into his pocket for a well-filled wallet; "then let me pay you for answering a few words."

"Put back your money, ye fool. I ain't acceptin' hush-money."

"All right; then answer me what I want to know. Is Deadwood Dick, the noted outlaw, *dead* in reality?"

" 'Spect he is; leastwise that's what the Deadwood papers say."

"But are you sure? Is there not some place where I could leave a letter so that it would reach him?"

"Well, I don't just know about that, old man. I don't know w'ether they've got a stage line runnin' up ter whar Dick is, or not. Might give me yer word, an' I mebbe can strike on an angel who will kerry it up;" and the girl laughed coolly. "Reckon Dick won't do you any good though."

"Oh! that's to be found out," the Washingtonian replied grimly. "Here's my letter to him;" and he handed her a large business envelope, which had already been sealed. "Give that to Deadwood Dick, and I will pay you your price. Good-day to you." Then his honorship turned and strode on up the gulch.

The meeting had occurred in front of Madame Minnie Majilton's dance-house, and the blonde proprietress was standing in the door. When Grosvenor had departed, Calamity heard her name called, and looking around saw the madame motioning to her.

"Well, what is it?" she demanded, approaching the entrance to the dance-house, and regarding the madame sharply. "What d'ye want?"

"I want to advise you," Madame Minnie said familiarly. "You haven't got a very honorable name among the men; do not make it worse by associating yourself with such men as that 'blood' whom you were just talking with. He has no more scruples than a wolf, and should his eye fasten particularly on you, he'd brook no expense to accomplish his villainous aims. Look out for such as he."

"Why?—you you know him?" Calamity asked, gazing after the portly form of the Washingtonian, as it was receding from view up the street.

"Yes, slightly," Madame Minnie replied, with a cool laugh. "He came into my place here, and I showed him the door with the point of a bowie. He went!"

"I presume so," Calamity replied, and turned away, going up the gulch-canyon, as it ran north. "That blonde is either a deceitful traitress, or a respectable woman," she muttered; "I wonder which?"

She kept on up the gulch for a couple of miles, then paused by a ledge of rocks that formed the canyon walls. Here she slipped the letter she had received into crevice, and then retraced her steps toward town.

That same evening, while the Honorable Grosvenor was sitting in his room at the Mastodon Hotel, he received a visitor—a rough-looking old codger, bent in back, with a mass of hair upon his face and head, and a perceptible limp in his gait. He hobbled along with a cane, and presented rather a forlorn aspect.

"Hello! who the deuce are you?" the speculator growled, looking up from his paper. "What do you want?"

"'Sh!" was the reply: "not so loud, if you please. I am Deadwood Dick!"

Chapter 9

THE WASHINGTONIAN PLOTS
AND PROPOSES

➡➡   ◄◄

"Oh!" the Washingtonian said, rising with an instant change of countenance from displeasure to blandness; "I mistook you for some beggarly vagrant. All because of your shabby appearance, no doubt. Pray be seated."

The visitor accepted the invitation by dropping upon the sofa, and producing a cigar and lighting it.

"You wrote that you wished to see me on important business," he observed, gazing straight at his honor with his penetrating black eyes. "I got the letter out of my post-office a short time ago, and came to see what *you* could possibly want of me."

"Ah! yes; ahem! I am glad you came; but, pray, how am I to know that you are in reality Deadwood Dick, the road-agent?"

"By accepting my assurance. I don't generally unmask in such close quarters, or I might be able to prove my identity by revealing my face."

"In which case I should be as ignorant as ever, having never seen you to know you heretofore. But, let that drop. I accept you as Deadwood Dick, so let's come to business. You are in need of money?"

"Well, no, not particularly. I realize about five thousand a year from mining interests which I won, and that sum keeps one in loose pocket change."

"But, you would not hesitate to add to your wealth, if you could do so by doing a little work of an unpleasant nature—especially to a man of my stamp. You outlaws do not hold life in the same regard as we—well, we of the East, of the better class."

"Well, that depends somewhat on circumstances," Deadwood Dick replied, coolly. "If we owe a man anything we generally pay him in our kind of change; don't go into bankruptcy to cheat them out of their dues. So you call yourself one of the upper ten, do you?"

"Ahem! yes, I suppose that would be the proper name for it—am from Washington, you see, where a man must either be an aristocrat or a nobody. Grosvenor is my name, and I represent a large amount of bonded and other wealth, besides being the president of a leading bank."

"Exactly; but you see, this don't interest me, particularly. The objective point is, what do you want of me?"

"Listen and you shall learn. There is a young miner in this town of Whoop-Up, who is in my way, and I want quietly removed. His name is Sandy, and you can easily find him, as he is very popular—lives in a cabin a few rods around the bend. You care not for life, as long as you get money; a pistol bullet, rightly sent, will do the job, and you shall have—well, say fifty dollars."

Deadwood Dick, in his disguise, arose with a quiet laugh.

"No; thet ain't my lay-out, old rascal!" he said bowing his way toward the door. "Good-day to you; when you have any more such jobs to let out, just give 'em to some ruffian which I don't claim to be. The man Sandy shall be properly warned to be on his guard; again, good-day, sir!" and in a minute more the road-agent had glided from the room.

"Devils take the man!" the Honorable Cecil cried, springing after him, to find him gone. "It seems I have been misinformed concerning the fellow. He don't do that kind of business, eh, and will inform Sandy? Well, just let him, and—hello! who's this rough-looking customer coming up the stairs? Ha! an idea! Maybe he'll serve me!"

The individual he had reference to was the Danite Ghoul, Arkansas Alf, and he followed the speculator into his rooms, without a word, having evidently intended a visit.

Once inside, the two villains, so opposite in personal appearance, confronted and gazed at each other for a moment in silence.

"Well," Grosvenor said, interrogatively. "I calculate you must have intended paying me a visit, since you walked in without an invitation on my part?"

"Yas, I reckon thet's about ther size o' ther matter," Arkansas Alf replied, grimly, as he stretched himself into a comfortable seat upon the sofa. "Sit down, sit down; don't stand thar starin' like a ghoul. I want ter talk ter ye."

The speculator sat down, first, however, bringing out a bottle of champagne from a huge Saratoga, and setting it upon the center table with goblets.

"Now go on," he said.

"Precisely," Arkansas Alf replied, scratching his chin—a sharp, wolfish gleam in his eyes. "In the first place, I calkylate ye're a fellow from Washington, wi' a name suthin' like grosemeyer, or—"

"Grosvenor—Honorable Cecil Grosvenor, at your service, sir."

"Yes, I reckon thet's about it. Once upon a time ye hed a pard up whar ye lived who stole a haul o' money an' lit out fer parts unknown."

"Ah! yes—Jake McOmber, eh?"

"Thet's the galoot. Wal, Jake cum West, an' we met an' got ter be pals. Jake cuts a weazand now 'n' then; I am known as Arkansaw Alf, a Ghoul—a Danite o' this wicked land o' Dakota. You wrote ter Jake about comin' ter meet ye heer, eh?"

"Yes, and got no answer."

"Wal, that was because Jake war down sick, so he sent me and my boys over inter ther Hills, heer, ter look after yer case."

"Ah! capital. I was just trying to make a strike with a road-agent named Deadwood Dick, but he was too sanctimonious for my purpose.

"What! Deadwood Dick *alive* and in Whoop-Up?" the Danite exclaimed, his face growing tigerish in expression, and his eyes evilly gleaming.

"Yes, here, I reckon. A fellow in clever disguise, calling himself such, just left as you came up. So you are ready to serve in my behalf, eh?" and the speculator drummed musingly upon the table.

"Yas, I reckon so, providin' ye've got plenty o' tin, and will shell out liberal. I've got two pals ter help me, and we kin do 'most anything in the way of sendin' off sinners on a long pilgrimage, or knockin' over weemin, or—"

"Oh! you'll do, no doubt, if you are anything like the Danites I've read of. What would be your price—well, say to take a woman and strangle her, and let her be found in a conspicuous place, *dead?*"

"Wal, thet depends sumthin' on her size, weight, and fightin' capacity. We kin ginerally send off a female in furst rate style fer fifty dollars."

"Enough said; I'll give a hundred dollars to attend to the case properly. Then I have another woman for you to hunt up and annihilate. I'll double my offer on her when she is dead. Her name here, I believe, is Mad Marie. Then there is a man who I wish disposed of."

"Phew!" the Danite said, with a detonating whistle of surprise; "you're right in fer layin' up treasures, ain't you? Wal, name yer subjects, and I'll go ter work."

"Not just at present," the villainous speculator said; "I am not quite ready yet. When I am I will let you know. You can easily be found, I dare say."

"You bet, w'en thar's any sech a lay'out!" the ruffian replied, rubbing his hands together in devilish delight. "You'll generalely find me fer ther lookin' down below. Ain't ye goin' ter treat afore I go?"

"Yes, help yourself; it's the prime article, you'll find;" and the Danite evidently did find it so, for he drained the bottle before he arose to depart.

"Nothin' more ye wish, now?"

"No, nothing; you can go. When I need you I'll hunt you up;" and then the Dakota Danite took his departure.

"Ha! ha!" The-Man-from-Washington exclaimed, as he heard the outlaw descending the stairs; "things are at last working into my hands just as I wish. That fellow is a tool that can be used repeatedly without resharpening, so long as he is fed on whisky and money. Sandy's pard—curse her; she shall go first, and then he shall follow. I wonder—"

He did not finish the sentence, but pulled on his gloves, donned his hat, and descended to the street, cane in hand. Lighting a cigar, he sauntered down the busy street, and finally fetched up in Madame Majilton's establishment.

The madame was behind the bar, engaged in shaking dice with a dirty miner, and was looking most royally beautiful in a suit of silk and lace, with diamonds at her throat and pendent from her ears. Her blonde complexion made her ever fresh and lovely looking, and then her superb form greatly heightened her personal beauty.

She looked up with a slight frown as the Honorable Cecil entered and leaned against the counter.

"Well, what do you want now?" she demanded, in a tone that was not particularly inviting. "Have you come here to insult me again?"

"Hardly!" was the reply, with a bland smile; "I deserved your scorn then, no doubt, for I was in an excess of champagne. No doubt you've been there yourself. I will step into the next room and be seated; when you are at liberty, please join me."

Madame Minnie bowed, and the speculator passed on into the next room, where she soon joined him, after cheating a miner out of the drinks.

She seated herself, a deal table separating her from the Washingtonian, and supported her chin between the palms of her hands as she gazed at him keenly.

There were diamond rings of great value upon her fingers, and the loose sleeve falling back to the elbow revealed a round fair arm that was perfection in itself.

"You are the most beautiful woman I ever met!" Honorable Cecil exclaimed, involuntarily, carried away by the power of her charming presence. "And that leads me to what I was going to say. I am from Washington—Honorable Cecil Grosvenor, at your service. I represent a great deal of wealth, and I have no wife—no heirs to all my vast estates. My life is devoid of any sunshine whatever, not having a female companion on whom to lavish my boundless affection. You are a beauty and can be refined—would make a resplendent star in the Washington social world—a ringing belle among belles. How fancy you the picture; how would you like to marry me, and let me take you into a paradise of love, wealth, social distinction and luxury?" and the speculator stopped here, and gazed admiringly at the beautiful woman in front of him.

As for Madame Minnie, she leaned back in her chair and laughed so boisterously that the Honorable Cecil began to feel uneasy and got red in the face.

"You old fool!" she exclaimed, by an effort controlling her merriment, "do you suppose I'd give up this glorious life here for the sake of ingulfing myself in the social miseries you depict? No! a thousand times, no! I know of all the delights you picture, but they don't tempt me. In Washington you have well-clothed, gold-enamored dummies; here, in the mines, though of times rudely dressed, you can find *men*. The difference is, Washington is a refined hell, with nothing but imps and devils for inhabitants; Whoop-Up is a rough Paradise, with now and then a sprinkling of angels."

"Ah! you look on the wrong side, my dear madame. Cannot I prevail upon you to accept? I would give my thousands for such a glorious creature as you—"

"Enough! I would not bind myself to such a man as you for your whole weight in diamonds. I know something of life after 'roughing it' so long. There is only one man in all the world whom I would for a moment think of marrying."

"And he is—"

"It little matters to you who. He is handsome—a quality you cannot boast of—and is all that is noble and generous. Such a man I have it in my heart to love—no other, be he king or millionaire, sir."

"That man lives in Whoop-Up?"

"Since you are so inquisitive, yes."

"I think I know to whom you refer—he is called Sandy, here."

"You are a pretty straight guesser, old man!" Madame Minnie replied, lighting a cigarette and puffing away with the utmost composure. "The man *is* Sandy. But, for instance, how would you like to take a bride into your Washington *soirees* with a cigar in her mouth and a bottle of tarant'ler-juice under her arm for sickness? That's the way I always travel."

"Oh, that would never do; you'd have to be trained, of course. But this man Sandy—do you know what he is?

"No; and I care not what his past has been: his present is irreproachable. Anybody will tell you that."

"Probably, but present good behavior cannot blot out or atone for the past, you know. Between you and me, Madame Majilton, that man Sandy is a forger, and a felon—a *murderer!*"

"Sandy a murderer? I do not believe it, Cecil Grosvenor. He is no such man as would murder."

"But, there's where you mistake. He is outwardly a gentleman; inwardly, a demon."

"I would run my chances in taking him for all that."

"Humph! and find yourself in a tiger's nest. Besides, you could not get him—he has too exalted notions concerning woman!" the speculator said, rising to depart. "If, however, you think better of my proposal, you can address me at the so-called Mastodon Hotel."

"Very well, sir; but pray do not watch anxiously for any change in my decision, or you will surely be disappointed."

The Honorable Cecil bowed, with a bland, doubting smile, and took his departure, and Madame Minnie watched him down the street.

"Sandy a felon!" she mused, turning her gaze in the direction of the Lightning Lode mine: "I cannot believe it of him. This is news to me. And yonder schemer said I could not win him. Maybe not; but we shall see—we shall see. In the meantime"—and a strange gleam shot into her eye—"in the meantime, something else."

Chapter 10

THE BLOW FALLS AT LAST

Sandy was working away in the mine, when one of his men approached him with a note in his hand.

"An old cuss give it to me, sir!" he said, bowing, "and sed give it ter Sandy; so I reckon as et must be fer you."

Sandy took the note and retired to a niche where a light was burning, and there opened the note. It was written in a neat business hand, slightly feminine some of the letters were, and ran as follows:

SANDY:—Look out for the Washingtonian chap, Grosvenor, who stops at the Mastodon. He tried to hire Deadwood Dick to shoot you, but did not make a success of his intentions. He is a double-dyed villian, and will, no doubt, try some other villainous plan, as he seems desirous of getting rid of you.

This was all, there being no signature. A faint smile of contempt wreathed the miner's mustached mouth as he thrust the note into his vest pocket.

"So the old viper really means business, does he?" he muttered, as he went back to his work. "Well, let him proceed. Even if he kills me, the world wouldn't mourn my loss."

He worked the day out, and went home at early dusk. The cabin door was closed but unlocked, and he opened it and entered.

Dusty Dick was sitting at the table with his head bowed upon his arms, crying—as Sandy could see that the slight form was trembling with emotion. He put away his pick, pouch and rifle, and approached the table.

"What! crying, Dick? What's gone wrong?" he said, laying one browned hand upon the flossy curls of the youth. "Has any one molested you?"

There was no answer except a low moan from Dick, for several minutes; then he raised his face to Sandy, such a tearful, agonized expression upon it as the miner had never before seen.

"Oh! Sandy, I thought you were never coming, and got so frightened."

"At what, dear?" and the miner's tone was tender and sympathizing as he bent over this disguised pardner of his, whom he was growing unconsciously fonder of each day as the autumn days wore dreamily by. "Who or what could give you affright?"

"Oh! Sandy, it is the one man in all the world whom I most fear— my enemy! He has arrived, and found me. I was sitting in the door-way when he passed, and he shook his clinched hand at me. God knows how I ever got in here and shut the door—I do not. It seemed as if all objects were reeling round and around me."

"You poor child," and for the first time Sandy seated himself close beside her. "I pity you from the bottom of my heart, for it is a sin that one so young in life as you should know the meaning of the word trouble. It is coming to the point that you are to be found out, and I—"

"Dishonored," Dick replied, drying her eyes. "God forbid. I will fly, and then maybe my enemy will follow and murder me, and these peo-ple of Whoop-Up will never know that you were harboring a woman."

"No! no! You shall not think of leaving my protection. I have been your protector so far—I'll see you safe through. Who is the villain who is molesting you?"

"His name is Cecil Grosvenor!"

"What! that inhuman wretch? By Heaven! not he?"

"Yes, Cecil Grosvenor. Can it be possible that you, too, know him?"

"Know him? He is the bitterest foe I ever had or have to-day. It was to murder me that he hunted me up here in Whoop-Up."

"Then Heaven help you, for he will surely carry out his object un-less you fly. It was to escape death at his hands that I came off here into this wild country!"

"What are you to him, Dick," the miner asked, "that he should want to kill you?"

"I cannot tell you now—sometime, maybe, you shall hear my story. To tell you that the ever-ruling curse, money, is the main object is quite sufficient. What is the cause of his enmity against you."

"It is a bitter story, Dick; I would rather not tackle it now, for I get stormy when I tell it. But, as you say, you shall hear it sometime. I never try to think of it, for it makes me less than a man. It is enough that Cecil Grosvenor is an enemy to both of us, and enmity means evil. I shall make you a proposal: Marry me, and we will leave this place by the next stage for California, where we can bury ourselves out of the reach of this man. I am rich, and you shall never want for the comforts of a home, or the protection of a strong arm. It is useless for me to tell you I love you with a whole heart—you must have seen this in my past actions. Will you do it, Dick?"

"No, Sandy," was the sober reply, tinged with sadness; "*I cannot.* If you do not wish to hurt my feelings—if you do love me, as you say you do—please never allude to the subject again."

"All right, Dick!" and the miner turned away, lest he should betray his emotion and disappointment. "But you will at least let me be your protector as heretofore?"

"Unless I had best leave the place to escape my foe; then, how could you extend your kindness?"

"You shall not go; you must stay with me, and I will fight both our battles."

He stood before her a glorious love-light shining in his eyes, his arms folded across his massive chest—stood there looking so grand and noble before the woman he loved of all others—the woman whom he dared not speak to of love, or hold to his manly breast for one wild ecstatic moment.

"Well said and done, Sandy!" a cool, familiar voice exclaimed, and the startled pards looked aroud to behold Calamity Jane standing just within the room, leaning idly against her rifle, having evidently been a spectator for some time.

"You are a noble man, Sandy, and I respect you the more for this."

"*You* here, girl!" the miner exclaimed, almost harshly. "You come and go like a hovering spirit. How did you get in?"

"I came in close behind you, and one closing of the door answered for both of us!" Calamity replied with a chuckle.

"And why?"

"Because I wanted ter talk wi' ye. Didn't expect what I saw, or I should hev waited. You needn't feel confused, though, nor vexed for I reckon, I'm about the only friend you'll have in Whoop-'up, directly, 'less it's Deadwood Dick."

"Why so?"

"Because—well, you see, thet old chap from Washington, who ye was jest talkin' about, has got the report spread that ye're not doin' ther fair shake—that Dusty Dick, here, is a gal—that you're a wolf in sheep's clothin—that you are a runaway forger and felon—an' so forth, an' so forth. So et's going to pull down hard on the honor ye've built up here in Whoop-Up, you see."

Sandy walked around the room a couple of times, abstractedly; then threw himself into a chair and bowed his head in his hands. The blow had been struck—the very blow that he had been dreading ever since Dick came.

It had struck him in a spot more susceptible of being wounded than any other component part of hmself—his honor, as a man.

"You are sure of this?" he asked, looking up, after a painful silence.

"So sure that I accept the reports o' my ears. Every galoot on the street has got his mouth full o' it. I kinder trigged the result, while ago; to-day I traced the report ter ets source—the Honorable Cecil Grosvenor from Washington."

There was a short silence, then Sandy again spoke:

"Calamity, you have shown a friendly disposition toward us since we first met, and I believe you are a friend!"

"And you jest bet yer boots on et, Sandy!" was the reply in the girl's grim way. "First along, Sandy, I got some very foolish notions into my head about you but a leetle bit ago, while I war a witness ter thet scene, I crushed out them thoughts—ground 'em under my heel, an' ye can see ther print o' a number three in the floor, back yonder by the door. *Now*, I am your friend."

As she spoke, the wild girl stood gazing at the floor, as if thinking, even while speaking, and there was a strange mournful ring to her voice which Sandy could but interpret. The sudden bright look that mantled her countenance the next moment, however, was a relief to him and also to Dusty Dick, who stood leaning against the table watching her rival with burning gaze.

"It's all right now, Sandy," Calamity Jane said, with a smile, which her auditors knew was forced, "it's all right. You love your pard, and she loves you, though she may deny it; so ef ye kin hitch traces together, it's much better."

"You are a brave-hearted, good girl, Janie!" Sandy said, considerably affected, "and I scarcely know how to thank you for your self-sacrificing confidence. If ever I have an opportunity to repay you, I shall assuredly do so. Will you not tell us your story that we may know you the better?"

"No! no!" and a fierce expression for an instant made the girlish face grow savage. "Not now. Sometime I will. You may have heard the varying stories about me, and may wonder why I lead this wild life of mine. Before I let up with et, I've got a *man to kill*—one of the basest, vilest wretches upon God's fair earth. For years I have been waiting for him to come here, and at last he has come. It is only a matter of time, now, till I kill him."

"Surely you would not commit murder, girl?"

"No! not murder—I'll wait tel he tackles me, then I'll shoot him in self-defense, you see!" and a strange vengeful laugh escaped her lips. "You don't know the extent of my wrongs or you'd say shoot, too."

"Probably!" Sandy replied; then after a moment—"what would you advise me to do, in the event of what you have told us? Whoop-Up will evidently be too hot for us."

"Don't mind anything about it, but go along at your work just the same as before. If you are quizzed or pointed out, don't give 'em enny satisfaction, 'less et comes ter insult; then use yer revolver in earnest. Stay and fight it out by all means. To leave, now, would be an acknowledgment of shame and guilt."

"Very well, I will stay then, and fight it out. If they get me roused—"

"They'll find a tiger, you bet," Calamity replied, enthusiastically. "Good for you! If they work too cluss, keep 'em at a distance, and remember that you have friends near. You, Dusty Dick, can show your hand ter help your pard, an' you wanter do it. Good-bye; you can look for me again, at most any time."

She then took her rifle and left the cabin, as quickly as she had come, leaving Sandy and Dusty Dick alone.

Outside, in the long, brilliantly lit street of the town, the surging restless crowd had divided more into groups, and were eagerly discussing this bit of news with which the town had become afflicted.

All believed Sandy to be a scamp and hypocrite, for Cecil Grosvenor had spread his seed wide and thick, so that it should take root.

No one ventured to stop or broach the subject to Calamity Jane; they knew her too well of old, to think of laying her against one she liked.

She met Cecil Grosvenor near the Mastodon, and stopped him in his evening walk, by stepping directly in his path.

"See here!" she said, pulling a revolver from her belt, and showing it under the astonished Washingtonian's nose—"you old wretch, do you know what I've a mind to do?"

"Don't! don't! put down the weapon—what do you mean, girl?" he gasped, changing from red to white in a twinkling. "Do you hear? put down the weapon!"

"No! I won't do anything of the kind, you coward!" Jane declared, coolly.

"Ain't ye a sweet specimen o' a hypocritical nuisance, ter call yourself *Honorable* So-an'-So? I've a notion ter put a bullet clear through your head. Old man, do you know that you played a sham deal against Sandy?"

An expression of devilish satisfaction came onto the speculator's countenance, and he chuckled grimly.

"It was my trump card, you see!" he replied. "It struck home well, I see, judging by the discussion in the streets. I did the town a favor by exposing a disgraceful nuisance!"

"Look out, you imp o' Satan," and the hammer of one of Calamity's No. 32's came back one notch; "ef ye go ter braggin', I'll make further breathin' on your part a thing o' the past. I stopped ter tell ye that you're an old villain, an' if you try any more of your games you're a dead man. Do you hear?"

"What business is it to you that you interfere?" Grosvenor sneered, eying the dare-devil girl savagely.

"You'll find out ef ye play another trick against that man, Sandy. He's my partic'lar friend, an' 'twixt me an' Deadwood Dick, he'll be taken keer of, an' don't ye forgit it."

Then the girl passed on.

Chapter 11

IN THE STREET—SANDYS'S DEFENSE— DUSTY DICK GONE!

Calamity Jane had not been gone half an hour, when there was a sharp Indian-like whoop, and a band of horsemen dashed out of the blackness of Canyon Gulch into Whoop-Up's single street. There were upward of seventy-five of the outlaws, all well-mounted and armed, and masked—a great crowd they appeared, as they rode yelling and hooting into the town, firing, and with deadly effect, right and left.

"Road-agents! road agents!" rung the yell of the surprised towns-people and miners; "hurrah! to arms! sweep the dogs out of existence!"

This cry was spread universally from one end to the other of the long street—was caught up by nearly every tongue, and everything that was to be had in the shape of a weapon was seized by the crowd that sprung to the place of battle. And a battle in earnest it was to be.

The road-agents had evidently come into the town with the intention of cleaning it out, small, comparatively, though they were in numbers; they made a stand near the center of the town, and fought fiercely with carbines and revolvers.

Every shot they fired told disastrously upon the ranks of the resolute defenders for a time: but encouraged by the fearless fighting of old Bullwhacker and his Regulators, the crowd pressed fiercely in upon the road-agents, determinedly, firing a terrible volley of bullets into their ranks. Of all the defenders in that desperate conflict, none did more excellent service than the much-clothed leader of the Regulators, old Bullwhacker. He stood at the front with a large pair of army revolvers in his clutch, firing continually, until they were emptied; then his Evans repeater came into hand, and sent forth a deadly stream of fire wreathed lead. The man was wonderfully cool while others were yelling and excited around him, and many a poor fellow dropped dead, while he stood calmly in the midst of the affray, his garments seeming to turn aside the deadly bullets that hissed like lightning-hail through the air.

On—on waged the battle, the road-agents fighting like devils for victory, the defenders imitating their example, to save their property and emulate their bravery. It was warfare in dead earnest—bullet for bullet, blood for blood.

Sandy left his cabin when he heard the cry, and stood for a moment outside of the door, listening and watching the crowds that went past.

"What is it, Sandy?" Dusty Dick asked, coming to the door; "why are all the men rushing up the gulch?"

"There's an attack from the road-agents," Sandy replied, drawing his pair of revolvers, and revolving the cylinder to see that all the cartridges were right. "I reckon it's my duty to take a hand, too, if there's fighting to be done. Those ruffianly out-laws need to be killed, and now's the proper chance. Go back in the shanty, and don't admit any one except they give a cough and a rap."

"But, you may get wounded or killed!" Dick gasped, in alarm.

"How much could you care if I did get toppled over!" the miner demanded, almost fiercely, as he wheeled and confronted her, gazing strangely into the disguised face and beautiful eyes.

"Very, very much!" was the reply; "but go; you may be needed."

Sandy obeyed and strode rapidly up the gulch. The fighting was just around the bend, but when he got there the last shot had been fired; the road-agents had broken from the wall of humanity, and were dashing down the canyon at mad speed, mountain-ward.

It would have been next to useless to have pursued them, for ere the pursuers could have got to their horses, the desperadoes were out of sight in the night's gloom, which reigned beyond where the lights of the town reflected. And, besides, there was enough to attend to on the scene of battle, where full three-score lay bleeding, either dead, dying, or wounded. Among this number, two-thirds were townspeople or miners; of the road-agents only one man was found alive, and by Old Bullwhacker's order he was immediately strung up to a limb and paid the earthly penalty of his crimes.

Fifteen were killed outright of the defenders, but, as it turned out, they were men without families. Of the rest who were more or less wounded, only three afterward died.

Was such a disastrous battle with road-agents reported here in the East? Probably not; for the Associated Press dispatches have never yet been known to report one-third of the crimes or casualties that occur in the wild land west of the Missouri. Yet the above battle did occur, with the result we have chronicled.

It was rather a doubtful victory on the part of the Whoop-Upites; yet they were in a measure jubilant over it.

Every care was offered the suffering and wounded; Sandy himself made bold to step forward and propose a purse for burying those who did not have sufficient money, liberally offering to donate fifty dollars.

The men looked at each other, and then at the handsome miner, who had within the day been dishonored in their eyes. One then stepped forward, a grim expression upon his face.

"I ruther calcylate we don't none o' us want none o' yer money, Mr. Sandy!" he said, with a glance to see that the crowd approved of his words. "We kin accept o' yer proposal an' do the liftin' among us. You'd better keep yer money fer thet leetle critter ye've got corraled down at yer shanty; it'll take all yer spare cash ter keep sech as her a-goin'!"

"Look out!" and the yellow-haired miner advanced a pace nearer, his face and eyes flaming. "Hint if you dare that anything is wrong between me and my pard, and I'll break every bone in your accursed body!"

"I reckon we don't chaw back what we say, pilgrim. My name is Bulldog Brown, at yer sarvice, an' ef ye want anything o' me, jest sail in. We do presume ter say thet yer pard, Dusty Dick is a woman, an' a rusty hypocrite you be to—"

The fellow didn't finish the sentence, for the miner fiercely leaped upon him, and with a tremendous blow, which would have staggered an ox, felled the brute to the earth. Then he bounded back, one of his revolvers cocked and ready in either hand.

"Now, then, where's the wretch who wants to repeat the insult? I'll lay him out in stiller shape than I did this fool!" he cried, glaring around, for he was terribly angered.

There was an angry murmur in the crowd, and a general motion toward rushing upon the miner; but it was not to come to battle, for at this juncture a man stepped forward with a pair of revolvers in hand, and stood alongside Sandy. It was none other than the Regulator, Old Bullwhacker. He waved back the crowd, and they stopped at his beckon, for no man had ever won such a popularity in Whoop-Up in so short a time as the much-clothed unknown.

"Hold! stop!" he cried, in a clear, ringing voice; "the first galoot who moves a step ag'in' this miner will directly after be a dead man. Let there be no more bloodshed. There's been enough, God knows. Sandy did perfectly right in knocking yonder nasty-tongued brute down fer insultin' him as he did.

"As ter ther pard, I'll stake my pile she's all square, ef Dusty Dick be a woman."

"An' I, too; an' I'll lick thunder out o' any chap in the crowd as says she ain't!" cried a ringing voice; then came a Comanche-like whoop, and Calamity Jane bounded into the scene.

Immediately the five men left out of Bullwhacker's band, and several others stepped over to the Regulator's side. This was the straw that broke the camel's back, and the crowd broke up and dispersed.

Calamity went over to where Sandy was restoring his revolvers to his belt.

"One card in your favor," she said, with a low laugh. "You did handsome, but you should have shot a couple of the cusses to show them ye warn't afraid. That's ther only way to git along out hayr. See what a change my comin' made; they knowd I'm business clean through. Look out fer 'em, for they'll try you a lick again. Now, go home and go to bed."

"Not until I have thanked you and these who have defended me!" Sandy said, warmly grasping her hand. "I already owe you so much— how can I ever repay you?"

"Once I might have been unmaidenly enough to have named a reward, but that is past. I don't expect to get any—never!"

She turned away abruptly, but not before Sandy had caught a glisten in her eyes which he knew to be tears. He was tempted to follow her—then came the picture of Dusty Dick in his imagination, and he resisted.

He kindly expressed his thanks to Old Bullwhacker and the others who had so bravely stepped over to his defense; then strode up the street toward his cabin with a carriage as haughty as any king.

Madame Minnie Majilton had seen him go up to join in the affray, and stood in her doorway watching, as he came along with free, elastic strides.

"I was so afraid that you would get hurt, Sandy," she said, in an anxious tone. "I just heard that they made an attack upon you—how was it?"

"They cast insulting slurs, and I retaliated by knocking one down. Reckon I should have got the worst of it, but for the intervention of Calamity Jane and Bullwhacker;" and the miner laughed as if he shouldn't have cared.

"I wish I had been able to have come to your rescue, Sandy. Come inside a few moments."

"What for?"

"I wish to give you counsel."

"I have had plenty, thanks."

"No—but come in; I wish to speak to you concerning—well something of vital importance."

Sandy hesitated a moment, then followed the beautiful blonde into a little room which she used as a parlor, adjoining the dance-house. Here he accepted a seat, and she also seated herself directly opposite him, across the little deal table.

A flood of light from a lamp chandelier, falling upon her fair head and features and bared white whoulders—for she was in a magnificent costume—had an additional effect of increasing her wondrous beauty; she knew it perhaps full as well as the man before her and put on one of the fascinating smiles she knew so well how to manage. After a moment of hesitation, she turned to Sandy:

"Did it ever come under your notice, Sandy, that a woman has not that control over her feelings, which is peculiar to men?" she asked, looking shyly into his eyes. "If so, you will not think bad of me for what I am to say to you. Sandy, I love you!"

"What! you, whom I have not met a dozen times—you love me!" the miner exclaimed, starting violently, astonishment depicted upon his face.

"Yes, I. You are astonished—nearly dumfounded;—yet, still you survive between the siege of three madly idolatrous loves."

"Eh? how do you mean?"

"I mean that three women in this very town adore you—worship you as the only perfect man in the mines. First of all is Dusty Dick, who has got you into all this trouble in the eyes of your friends; secondly, ranks that eccentric dare-devil girl, Calamity Jane. She probably loves you in the fiercest, most intense manner. I fill the third place myself. I am beautiful, and of a generous, impulsive nature—the very woman suited to you. I have money, independent of yours. I have brought you in here to ask you to marry me. Earlier to-day Cecil Grosvenor proposed and I refused him. I want you, Sandy—will you take me?"

"No," the miner said, with emphasis, as he arose to depart. "When I want a wife I shall do the picking and proposing, myself."

"Very well. If you don't want me, I shall not be offended. Maybe you'll change your mind, you know."

"Yes, maybe," Sandy replied, with a low, sarcastic laugh, as he left the saloon. Somehow he was out of sorts to-night—especially with such as the bewitching Madame Minnie.

But he was not prepared for the discovery that awaited him on his return to "head-quarters," as he called his shanty. The door was open —the candle was burning upon the table, but Dusty Dick was *gone!*

Yes, gone; but where?

In some alarm the miner began to search around the shanty. Nothing which had been Dick's was missing except his rifle and ammunition.

Had he gone purposely, or had he been abducted for murderous purpose by the instrumentality of Cecil Grosvenor?

For a moment he stood in the center of the cabin, and tried to determine in his mind which, but a lonely feeling crept over him, and stepping out into the open air, he locked the door after him.

The crowds in the street were the same as at the brightest hour of day, only a little noisier, if anything. The music from the neighboring dance-houses, the shouts of drunken roughs, the jolting rumble of incoming stages, were a few of the sounds that served to make the night hideous.

In vain Sandy glanced around in hope of catching some glimpse of Dusty Dick. Nowhere was the youthful pard to be seen among the throngs that surged by.

He was still standing, undecided what to do, when he heard a well-known whistle, and Calamity Jane came up, with a flourish.

"Hello! what are you looking so down in the mouth about, Sandy?" was the salutation. "You look as if you'd lost your best friend?"

"So I have, girl—one of them. Dusty Dick is gone!"

"Gone? the deuce, you say!"

"Yes, gone. I just returned, to find the shanty empty."

"She's around town somewhere, no doubt, and'll be back directly."

"No, I think not. Her rifle and ammunition are both gone. Either she has left because of the discovery and talk, or has been abducted; which, I cannot determine."

"Et's the former," Calamity said, instantly. "To spare you further trouble, she has pulled out. I wouldn't hev done it if it had been me, but she hasn't had the experience, you know."

"Has any stage left town within the last hour?"

"No, Why? Will you hunt after her?"

"Most assuredly."

"Don't do it. Give the matter into my hands. I know the mountains and places best. Go on at your work: don't worry if you don't see me in three days!"

Chapter 12

A DIABOLICAL PLOT—AN ADVENTURE

So Sandy went back to his shanty and passed a sleepless night, for he was much troubled concerning the strange disappearance of Dick.

On the following morning he arose late, and after breakfasting on some cold meat, went to the mine known in Whoop-Up as the Lightning Lode.

It was a huge intermountain cavern, which had entrance through a narrow tunnel, only large enough for the passage of a mule and a single car. Inside there were many sections of the cavern where the rock was pierced with dark shafts and long passages, huge pillars supporting the ceiling of rock here and there. All this great work had been accomplished by drilling and giant powder, and the rich quartz rock was drawn by dump loads out to the breaker and crusher in the gulch.

At the entrance to the mine Sandy met his superintendent, a man of forty years, named Bronson.

"Well, has everything gone right?" he asked, pausing a moment.

"No; on the contrary, everything has gone wrong," Bronson replied, dubiously. "The men, all but three or four, came and got their wages an hour ago, declining to work in your employ any longer."

"Humph! I expected it," Sandy replied, with a faint smile. "Let the fools go if they choose. Do you share their views of the matter?"

"Well, n—no; but I'd kind o' like to see it cleared up, you know," Bronson replied. "Don't know as et makes so much difference, but then—"

"You shall know all in time. I was simply protecting a woman I found in distress from the brutal villainy of a wretch who is in this very town to-day. The disguise she had adopted when I found her—I only added a few finishing touches."

"Very well, Sandy, I accept the explanation and believe you. I'll tell the few men remaining. It would be better if you were to make this explanation general."

"I don't choose. Let it be found out without any interference. I crave no man's friendship."

"What shall we do about more men to work at the mine?"

"Stick out a placard: 'More miners wanted at $2.50 per day.' That will fetch 'em. I was thinking of raising their wages the other day. Be sure to hire none of the old gang, as new hands will answer better, I think."

And accordingly Bronson stuck out a placard in a conspicuous place:

WANTED—Twelve or fifteen new miners to replace deserters at the Lightning Lode. $2.50 per day. Apply at once to the Super-intendent.

This card caught the eye of Honorable Cecil Grosvenor, as he was returning on his handsome bay mare from a morning gallop down the canyon.

"The very opportunity for ending the game!" and a cruel, malignant smile came upon the sinister countenance of the speculator as he grasped the thought. "I have the very plan in my mind, too. My first work is to hunt up the Danite, and instruct him."

He galloped on to the livery, dismounted and hurried on to the Mastodon, a few doors away. On search, he found Arkansas Alf in a rear room drinking wine and fleecing a Texan herder at cards. At Grosvenor's motion, he threw up the game, and they went to the bar-room where they were soon the occupants of a stall, which was one of a dozen which flanked a side of the apartment.

"Waal?" the Danite interrogated, leaning his arms upon the table, and gazing grimly at the Washingtonian. "What's the rip?"

"Nothing in particular, except that I am ready to have you go to work. You know where the Lightning Lode mine is?"

"Reckon I do."

"And the man, Sandy?"

"Sart'in sure."

"Well, *he* is the man I want put out of my way. Here is my plan. He has advertised for new workmen. You must go and make an appli-cation for a job, for you and your pards. Work cheap, and ask to be allowed to sleep at night in the mine. At night you must work silently and cautiously. Charge every available place heavily with giant pow-der, all to be connected with one long main fuse. This you must run around the base of the hill to where you can hide in the bushes. Be at your stand to-morrow, just before noon. When the hands of your watch point to ten minutes of twelve, listen and you will hear a gun report—then light the fuse, mount your horse, and get safely into the mountains. I will be at the junction of the Deadwood and Gosslin trails, when you get there, and you shall have a round hundred for your work."

"Keerect! I'm your huckleberry, you bet. Shall I go now?"

"Yes, make haste, and secure a job if possible. You'll find powder enough for your purpose in the mine. Make everything sure—and remember I am not to be mentioned in the matter."

"Very well, boss. What about ther two feminines ye spoke of?"

"One of them I hear has escaped. I shall make no effort to secure her, as she will probably be brought back by curiosity. The other woman, Mad Marie, I know nothing about, further than that she is in this vicinity. You will have to rely upon your detective abilities to find her."

"I'll keep an eye out. Thet chap, Deadwood Dick, is a-goin' ter take my eye, fer thar's five hundred dollars or more on his head, which I'd love ter finger."

The ruffian then took his departure. He went to the mine, accompanied by two ruffianly-looking associates named Fletcher and Kengrove, and hired out to Superintendent Bronson, with permission to lodge in the mine, and protect it from being robbed during the night by outside parties.

———

Calamity Jane, later that day, left the town, and riding up the gulch, turned off among the mountains, through a dark, lonesome ravine, through the bottom of which a small creek dashed noisily, and where but little of the light of day ever penetrated.

She was mounted upon her thoroughbred cayuse, which had few rivals in the Hills, and well armed with a sixteen-shot Winchester rifle, and a brace of holster revolvers, besides those she wore in her belt. Every bit of a mountain knight she looked, as she rode along, scanning everything around her with a sharp gaze.

The further she went the route continued in the ascending, and winding up into the heart of the mountain wilderness. Suddenly she drew rein and listened intently.

Ahead of her, around an abrupt bend, came clear and sharp the ringing thud of hoof-strokes—then a fierce shout that echoed around the hills, with clinging reverberations.

"Hello! some one coming this way, I reckon!" Calamity muttered, wheeling her horse to one side, just behind a clump of manzanita bushes. "Either red-skins or road-agents, I predict, after some lone pilgrim."

She had not long to wait to learn that her prophecy was correct.

A single horseman came dashing around the bend, with his horse running at full speed, while sitting with face backward, he was grasping a rifle in his hands, ready for use.

He managed to retain his seat with as much ease as though he occupied a fronting position, which evinced superior horsemanship.

From her position, Calamity could do no more in the way of a glance than to make him out as a young man—his face she could not see. Nearer and nearer he came; then a band of five mounted horsemen burst into view around the bend, yelling like so many Comanche red-skins.

They were road-agents and some of Deadwood Dick's band, all armed with carbines of Winchester pattern, and were in hot pursuit of the lone fugitive, whose easy riding so attracted Calamity's admiration, that she wheeled her cayuse out into the ravine with a ringing shout.

"Let 'em have, pilgrim—plug et to 'em like blazes, an' I'll back ye! Hurra! Whoa up thar, you imps o' Satan, fer ef ye buck ag'in' Calamity Jane yer bound ter get snagged ag'in' an earthquake!"

The words were loud enough to be heard by pursuers and pursued; then the girl dare-devil raised her rifle to her shoulder, and sent a leaden death-dispatch with unerring aim into the road-agents, killing one outright, and wounding a horse.

Seeing that he was reinforced, the fugitive opened fire, also dropping one of the desperadoes from the saddle, although the wretch was only wounded. Three others were left, and they came on with furious oaths and curses, beating their animals with the carbines to increase their speed, and then firing wildly.

One chance bullet struck the fugitive's animal in the ear, and penetrated to the brain. Instantly the poor brute began to stagger, then stumbled and dropped dead a few feet from where Calamity had taken her stand. Luckily the rider was prepared, and he leaped lightly from the saddle, and escaped injury.

At the same instant Calamity's rifle again cracked twice in succession and each unerring bullet dropped its man, either dead or wounded, from the saddle. Seeing that he now had no chance, the remaining outlaw turned his horse abruptly around and took the back trail, urging his animal in mad desperation, with both spur and voice. Bound to finish the victory, Calamity fired the remaining thirteen cartridges in her repeater, but only succeeded in wounding him, as he disappeared from view.

Then she turned to the rescued fugitive, who was standing by his dead horse, and gazing at her in admiration and wonder.

He was a man of some five-and-twenty years, with supple, handsome form, and a light, jovial face, which, while it possessed no particular beauty, was a good-naturedly good-looking face, with perfect features, dark brown eyes and hair, and a slight dark mustache. He was attired in citizen's garb, and armed with a rifle and a pair of revolvers.

Clearly, he was astonished at his sudden rescue, for he stood gazing at Calamity as if she were something more than mortal.

And she laughed in her cool way, as she crossed one shapely limb upon the neck of her horse, and returned the stare in genuine Black Hills fashion.

"Guess you war purty nigh about glad to get away frum them agents, pilgrim, warn't ye?" she demanded, at length, while she lit a cigarette.

"Indeed I was!" the man replied, with enthusiasm. "I've had all the road-agent experience I care for, since I've been fighting the devils for the last half hour. There were twelve of the fellows when they commenced the chase, a couple of miles back."

"An' ye dropped 'em all, eh?"

"All but the three you fetched down and the fellow that escaped.

"Wal, then, you're a brick—thet's all! Couldn't a-done better myself. Reckon you're a fresh 'un in these diggin's, eh?"

"I am. I only arrived at Deadwood yesterday, and, purchasing a horse, set out for a ride to Whoop-Up, wherever that may be, having no idea that the distance was so great. But excuse me, please, you're a woman, are you not?"

"Well, yes, I reckon I am in flesh, but not in spirit o' late years. Ye see, they kind o' got matters discomfuddled w'en I was created, an' I turned out to be a gal instead of a man, which I ought to hev been."

"Indeed? There is something in your face which reminds me of a girl I used to know six years ago, before I went East, from Denver. What is your name, ma-am?"

"Calamity Jane, at yer service."

"What? Janie was my little sweetheart's name!" the stranger exclaimed, drawing nearer. "It cannot be that *you* are indeed Jennie Forrest—the same I once knew. She left Denver for Virginia City a couple of years after, since when I have never heard a word from her."

"Yes, I am Jennie—she that was Jennie Forrest," Calamity replied, slowly. "But who can you be?"

"I am Charley Davis—don't you remember me? Six years ago, on your sixteenth birthday, you promised to wait for me and become my wife!"

"*You* Charley Davis?" the girl exclaimed, delightedly; "then thar's my paw—grab it! I'm glad to see you as a b'ar is to hug a human."

The stranger eagerly accepted the proffered hand and shook it warmly, while he gazed admiringly into the face of the girl-scout.

"You have greatly changed, Jennie, but it is for the better, excepting your attire. Why dress thus, when the attire of your own sex is more becoming?"

"I don't allow ye ken beat men's togs much fer handy locomotion an' so forth, an' then, ye see, I'm as big a gun among the men as any of 'em. An' ef ye're going' to Whoop-Up let me advise ye in one respect: snatch off thet b'iled shirt, an' put on a flannel or caliker. Reckon they'd set you up as a swell ef ye war ter go in thet way."

"Oh, I'll run all the risks. But, Janie, isn't your attire rather unmaidenly, considering your sex?"

"Maidenly—unmaidenly?" Calamity muttered, staring hard at him. "Charley Davis, when you left me, with a betrothal kiss clinging to my lips, I was a maiden, and as modest as they make 'em. But terrible changes have come since then. I am now a world's dare-devil, people say. Ask me nothing, for I shall tell you the same measure—nothing. In Whoop-Up—this trail takes you there, by turning to your left at the canyon below—in Whoop-Up you may by chance hear all that the world knows of the story. Go—hear, and then you will not be surprised."

She spoke with a fierce earnestness that was thrilling, and then drew up her bridle reins as if to go.

"Hold on! shall we not meet again, Jennie?" Davis exclaimed, anxiously—"very soon, I hope?"

"Probably, as I'm generally around. What brought you here, sir?"

"To hunt up a man whom the Government wants. I am a special police-detective, you know."

"Oh, you are! Well, in Whoop-Up you kin take your pick out of all the worst devils in the West; so go ahead, and success to you."

Saying which the girl dare-devil rode on up the ravine, leaving the stranger to pursue his way on to Whoop-Up afoot.

Chapter 13

DICK RETURNS—THE MINE
A MAGAZINE

Calamity kept on her course through the mountains, penetrating many ravines and dark defiles, and scouring the adjacent timbers sharply. She was in search of the girl who stood between her and

Sandy's love—Dusty Dick, unknown to either, who had fled from Sandy's protection. Why she had taken upon herself the mission, Calamity never could have told exactly. She was interested in Sandy's welfare and happiness; perhaps this was what prompted her.

But the day wore away, and she found no traces of the runaway, and then headed her tired animal back in the direction of the mines.

It was growing dark in the pine-crested hills, and she urged her steed along at a sharp gallop, the sharp clattering of the animal's shod feet upon the rocky trail causing long, detonating echoes to fill the night with weird sound.

"Go along, Jacko!" she urged, applying the spur when the animal lagged. "We must hurry and get back to town, for there is work there for me. By this time that wretch, Arkansas Alf, is up to his deviltry, and I'm going to thwart the game."

A couple of hours of swift ride brought her back into the bustling flash city.

Sandy sat in the door of his shanty, smoking an evening cigar, when Calamity rode up, and slipped from the saddle to the ground.

"Any news?" the miner interrogated, eagerly, a hopeful light shining in his eyes.

"None at all concerning Dusty Dick. Guess she's hid whar she ain't goin' to be found so soon. Don't be discouraged, tho'; I hain't looked the whole mountains through. She may have gone to Deadwood."

"Probably we shall never see her again," Sandy replied, slowly. "She may have killed herself."

"No! nary a time! Thet warn't her lay-out, and don't ye fergit et. I'll find her before long, Sandy. Did you know of a man in Washington named Charley Davis?"

"I think not. The name does not sound familiar. Why?"

"Oh, I don't ask for any partic'lar reason. Thar's a man here by that name—didn't know but he might be an acquaintance of yours."

"No, I guess not. Going?" for she had remounted with a nimble leap.

"Yes, I must be going. Did you get new men at the mine?"

"Yes, twelve or thirteen, to replace the deserters."

After Calamity had gone, Sandy knocked the ashes from his pipe, and entered the shanty, locking the door after him. To him the place now had a desolate, lonely look, since Dusty Dick was not there; he could scarcely do less than feel sad, for with his whole manly heart he had loved the beautiful girl-woman, who had played her *role* so well as his pard, and her absence seemed like that vacancy left by a sudden death.

All the trinkets he had bought her, even to a handsome gold watch, had been left behind, and with a careful fondness, he marked the way she had left everything, and preserved the order, accordingly.

Sitting down by the table, he bowed his head upon it, and closed his eyes wearily, for despite his prosperity and success gaining worldly wealth, his life lacked much of the essential light which makes living even endurable.

For a long time he rested thus with his head bowed; the room was in silence, only the faint hum from the bustling street broke the monotone stillness.

How long he knew not, for when he imagined himself to be awake, he was in reality asleep and in dreamland. The first knowledge he had of his having been asleep, was when he was slowly awakened by the sound of a stealthy footstep. He knew then that he was awake—assured himself of the fact by unclosing one of his eyes sufficiently to catch a ray of light from one of the candles that was burning in the room. He then immediately closed his eye again and by harder breathing, feigned sleep. Something told him to do so; yet what? For the world he could not have told. Some one was in the shanty, but he knew not who. He felt a draught of air from the door, and knew that it must be open a trifle; besides, the noises of the street came in plainer. At length he heard the stealthy step again, and intuition, rather than sound of movement, taught him that some one was approaching him. The next moment he felt a hot breath fan his cheek, and a pair of soft lips touch his forehead; then there was a swift, silent effort at retreating. With a cry he opened his eyes and sprung to his feet—reached out and caught the flying figure by the shoulder, even as it would have darted out into the night.

A moment later the two were face to face—the miner greatly astonished, and Dusty Dick—for it was no one else—crestfallen and confused.

"*Dick?*" Sandy ejaculated, in wonderment. "By Heaven, this is beyond my comprehension!"

"Let me go, Sandy," was the faint, choked reply. "Release me, and let me depart."

"No, not by any means," and the miner crossed the room and shut the door. "How did you get in?—ah! I forgot; you had a key. Dick, tell me, why did you run away from me?" and Sandy's tones were reproachful, yet tender. "You cannot imagine how I missed you."

"It was to save you from further annoyance, Sandy—"

"Pooh! you were foolish enough to suppose you could help the matter in that way. Where did you hide?"

"In the mountains."

"And why did you return?"

"Because I couldn't stay away. I wanted one more glimpse of your kind face before I forever left this place. Besides, I had a frightful dream, last night, that you were in imminent danger, and I could not go without coming to assure myself that it was untrue."

"Dick you must not leave me. I shall not permit it. What could you do wandering about the world?—and then, too, Grosvenor might again hunt you down, and ten to one you would not have as willing a friend to fight your battles as I. Promise to stay with me till I get ready to pull out. It won't be long, as I shall sell the mine soon at a sacrifice in order to get out. In the mean time, let the fools talk who wish to."

"And when you go you do not think me unwomanly enough to follow you around wherever you might choose to lead?" Dusty Dick exclaimed, with a spice of anger.

"Certainly not, unless we can before that time effect some compromise. Perhaps you would allow me to send you back East."

"No, no! not while my enemy lives. He would quickly follow, for he has sworn to murder me, if it costs him a life's devoted labor."

"Don't worry about him. I think his race is about run—am positive it is. If he gives me further molestation, I'll shoot him, and done with it. Will you promise to stay, and—and await developments, let them come as they may?"

"Y-e-s, on one condition."

"Name it, and I promise to grant it beforehand."

"It is that you will not mention the love for me you profess, until—well, until I give you permission."

"I promise. Now, then, we will resume the old life. It will be best for you to remain as strictly in the shanty as possible, and never part company with your revolver. Admit no one, unless it be Calamity Jane, Deadwood Dick, or the Regulator chief I pointed out to you once, who calls himself Old Bullwhacker. These three I believe to be warm friends, who can be trusted implicitly."

And so it was, at the midnight hour, that Dusty Dick was reinstated in Sandy's home.

About this same time, the man, Arkansas Alf, stood in a black shadow which enveloped the rear part of the Mastodon Hotel and yard, conversing in a low tone with Cecil Grosvenor, who had come out.

"Yas, pilgrim," the Danite was saying, in a careful whisper, "everything is ready for the explosion, as you d'rected, you bet. Me an' ther b'yees jest finished a bit ago. The mine ar' heavily charged wi' giant powder, an' thar is sum thirty or more 'leads' runnin' ter ther main fuse, w'ich is so neatly hidden, that they won't be discovered."

"Good! you are a brick," the villainous schemer said, his tones expressing his satisfaction. "I want it to work right, you know."

"Et will, you bet! An' I've arranged it better. Jed Fletcher will touch off ther fuse in place of me, ter 'void suspicion, ye see, w'ile I'm playin' off drunk heer at the Mastodon; then he an' my other pard'll slope fer Deadwood, whar they ken lay low 'til I git ready ter jine 'em. D'ye see?"

"Certainly. Your plan is excellent, inasmuch as I have noticed that Calamity Jane has been watching you rather sharp. She might suspect somethin', you know, but your plan prevents danger."

"Curse Calamity Jane!" the Danite Ghoul exclaimed, fiercely; "I haven't been able to get a straight bead on her since I came here, or she'd 'a' bin a stiff afore this. I've got a grudge ag'in' her—I hev, you bet! What time d'ye say!"

"Fifteen minutes to twelve. I'll be up here at the Mastodon, and shoot off my revolver at some object, as a signal for the fuse to be lighted."

"Very well—ther fuse shall be lighted, an' them in ther mine'll be blowed ter Kingdom Come," the Danite replied, as he strode away out of the darkness into the brilliantly illuminated street of the town. As he left the shadow of the building, his sharp eyes detected a form skulking along ahead of him, and he at once recognized it as the same person whom the Honorable Cecil had pointed out as being the ex-road-agent, Deadwood Dick, in disguise.

With an oath Arkansas Alf bounded in pursuit, and overtook the rusty-looking codger in the middle of the street.

"Hold up, you old rip!" he cried, slapping him on the shoulder, and whipping out a formidable revolver. "Jest hold yer hosses, ef yer please, till we settle this matter!"

The old man wheeled around in evident surprise.

"What mought ye be wantin'?" he asked, in a voice which had a perceptible tremor in it.

"I'll show ye, d'rectly, ye ornery cuss. I reckon yer road-agent days are about over. I say, Bullwhacker," and the Ghoul hailed the Regulator, who chanced to be passing along, "come over heer an' see if this ain't about ther size uv a galoot ye want."

"Who've ye got?" the much clothed road Regulator demanded, eying the old man and his captor in surprise. "What right have you got to arrest a man right here in the street?"

"The right o' a citizen," the Danite replied grimly. "Besides, I want sum reward-money. This man is no one else than Deadwood Dick, in disguise."

"What? *this* Deadwood Dick? I heard he was dead, in reality; anyhow, you've had your trouble for your pains, Mr. Kennedy, for the Gov'yment hes withdrawn all offers of reward lately, beacuse ov Dick's late valuable sarvice as Regulator. Ther stage fetched in the news not an hour ago."

"I don't keer a tinker's cuss!" the Danite replied, sullenly. "Jerk off this disguise, and ef the galoot's Deadwood Dick, I fer one'll lend a hand ter boost him up ter ther nearest limb. Hurray! a road-agent raisin'!"

A crowd of miners had by this time collected, and as all were enemies of Deadwood Dick, it looked pretty skittish for the old man.

"Well, I guess you'll have to pull off them false whiskers, old chap!" the Regulator said; "seein' as how these men calkylate you're their game. If you're Deadwood Dick, I ken't do ye much ov any good, bein' a Regulator. Reckon you'll have to swing!"

"Reckon I won't!" was the cool reply, which somehow sounded familiar to the crowd. "Et ain't quite my forte ter perform gymnastics in ther atmosphere, ef ther old p'onnygraff knows etself." Then the old man stepped back a pace, touched a spring in his clothing, and his ragged garb fell to the ground, revealing a well-fitting buckskin suit beneath. Off then came the wig and false beard, and there, before the astonished crowd, stood—not Deadwood Dick, but the dare-devil, Calamity Jane!

"A cute cuss, warn't ye Alf Kennedy!" she chuckled, grimly. "Didn't know that ye war snaggin' ag'in' death itself, did ye, you villain? Ha! ha! all you bloodthirsty galoots—how d'ye like my style, fer Deadwood Dick?"

"You! Jane Forrest?" the Danite exclaimed, reeling back at the sudden apparition. "Curse you!"

"Don't curse me, Alf Kennedy! It is I who should curse *you*, my *destroyer!* There! there! put up your pistol; I ain't o-going' to kill ye *yet.* I'm reservin' ye til sum time when I shall have time to attend yer funeral."

And, turning on her heel, she strode fearlessly away, while Arkansas Alf made his way toward the Lightning Lode, to advise his pards.

———

Honorable Cecil Grosvenor's apartment at the Mastodon consisted of a room which overlooked the dark side of the gulch, and was lighted by a single window in daytime. At night his only light consisted of a dingy lamp.

After leaving Arkansas Alf, he entered the hotel which was flourishing under Colonel Joe's supervision, and ascended to his room in an excellent frame of mind, for him.

"In a short time more the man who stands between me and a big fortune will be dead!" he muttered, exultantly. "Then I will go back East and—keep well away from Washington. The rest of my days can be spent in wealth and luxury. Ha!"

He uttered the latter exclamation as there was a crashing of glass, and a stone came hurtling into the room.

On picking it up the speculator found it it to be wrapped in white letter-paper, on which was writing. Examination disclosed the following, which had been penned in a woman's chirography:

CECIL GROSVENOR:—You are playing a dangerous game against a man who will in the end crush you. I, for one, will help him do it. Your wife,

MAD MARIE.

P.S. Your plots and schemes will avail you little—*Sandy* will triumph.

Chapter 14

THE EXPLOSION AT THE MINE

On the following morning Sandy went to the mine as usual, and found the gang already at work, with the exception of three men, whom Superintendent Bronson announced as having left without claiming their wages.

"The same three, by the way, who wanted to lodge in the mine," he said.

"Probably they made the best of their night's stay by picketing what gold they could get," Sandy said, with a smile. "After this we'll get a trusty guard—my dog Buffalo, for instance. Very few would attempt to pass him, I reckon."

All unsuspecting of danger, or the diabolical plot of Cecil Grosvenor to blow up the mine, Sandy went in to work along with the rest of the miners. The work of getting at the rich rock was prosecuted generally by blasting with that strong explosive, "giant" powder. One blast often was sufficient to dislodge enough rock to fill a car, which was then drawn out into the crushing mill, near the mouth of the mine.

Sandy worked away this morning with renewed energy, for the return of Dusty Dick had acted upon him like a rejuvenator; he felt twice the ambition to labor that he had before, while she was away.

Somehow, he felt that his whole existence was bound up in her keeping—she, little more than a stranger to him, whose real name he did not know.

About twenty minutes before the steam-whistles were to blow for twelve o'clock, Sandy was arrested in his work by directing a heavy blast, by a quick touch upon his arm. Wheeling about he confronted Calamity Jane.

The dare-devil girl's face was flushed with excitement, and her eyes had a dusky, scared expression.

"Hello! You!" Sandy said, with a nod. "What can I do for you—"

"Quick! get out of the mine—there is no time for words. Fly! every mother's son of you, for the mine'll be blown to flinders lessn'n five jiffies!"

She spoke in a swift loud tone; then turned and hurried toward the mouth of the mine. It did not take Sandy but an instant to comprehend, and he ordered every man to fly, for his own life's sake, from the danger.

Bronson and himself were the last to leave the doomed mine, and hurry out upon the stream shore, where the other miners and Calamity Jane were standing. A small crowd was gradually collecting, making wondering inquiries in regard to the hasty stampede from the mine.

And they had but a moment to wait before they were answered.

Simultaneously, almost, with the echo of a pistol report in the upper part of the town, there appeared, in the mouth of the mine, a hissing, vivid glare of flame, which expired in a second, to be followed the next minute by one of the most frightful explosions that ever jarred the pine-crested mountain in the vicinity of Whoop-Up's flash city.

Nothing, of course, was seen of the explosion, but the thundering roar of the concussion echoed far and wide, over hill and valley, and the jar made the earth tremble as if shaken by an earthquake. Sandy, Calamity, and the others standing in the immediate vicinity, were thrown violently to the ground, but luckily sustained no serious injuries. The glass in the neighboring shanty windows was badly broken, and the whole town pretty badly shaken up and startled.

Several gangs of men, who had at the moment of the explosion been working in the mountain-side, above the town, were precipitated promiscuously down the sheer declivity, doing more or less injury to flesh and bones.

A crowd hastily assembled from the upper part of the street, and began to press inquiries as to the nature and cause of the explosion; a general excitement prevailed, and many were the questions that were leveled at Sandy.

"I don't know anything about the matter!" the miner replied, standing proudly erect, with folded arms, and gazing around into the grim faces of men who only yesterday had regarded him with suspicion; "cannot tell you anything, except that at the peril of her own life this heroic girl"—with a nod toward Calamity—"came into the mine and warned us to quickly abandon it, as an explosion was about to occur. We barely got out, and then she went off."

"I reckon it's a snide game ter dislodge us fellers up above!" one miner growled, who had come down to the gulch, end over end. "Et's a darned nasty joke at the best of et, I say!"

"That's me!" chimed in half a dozen others, grimly. "Et ain't ther kind o' work we'd take ye to do, Sandy; but considerin' what's been said lately, ye really don't seem ter be ther man we tuk ye fer."

"Hold up, hayr—don't git up no row over a few spilled oats!" cried Calamity, stepping fearlessly forward. "Ef ye're going' ter intimate, thet Sandy hed anything ter do wi' thet explosion, yer durned liars, every mother's son o' ye. I happen ter know all about ther matter."

"Bully fer ther gal! Hip hooray fer their heerine o' ther gulch!" cried a voice, and old Colonel Joe cavorted forward into the scene, red nose and all. "Hooray, I say fer C'lamity. A boss gal ar' she, ye galoots, an' don't fergit it."

"Shet your cellar door, you old whisky-sucker!" a miner cried, authoritatively pushing Tubbs aside. "Now, then, heave ahead, girl, and let's heer you say, fer I move thet we investigate this matter."

"Hooray!" so do I!" put in Colonel Joe, polishing off the end of his sorry nose with a kerchief, "an' I'll lubricate ther investigatin' committee as cheap as ary galoot in this fragrant city of Whoop-Up, dog my cats ef I won't."

"Yas, I'll say my say!" replied Calamity, with a contemptuous glance over the crowd. "Ef ye think I'm lyin', w'en I git thru, spit her out, an' I'll guarantee to lick the cuss as sez so, I warn you. Sandy hedn't nothin' ter do wi' ther explosion as I sed before. I an' four others war the only ones as knowed et war ter come off. I only got inter ther secrit by overhearin', on two occasions, the plan o' the cussed business. Shouldn't 'a' overheard that only I war keepin a watch o' ther ruffian Arkansas Alf—who are the notorious Dakota Danite, by the way—who I hed some business ter settle wi'. A feller hired him an' his two pards ter go hire out at ther mine yesterday, when hands war skeerce, an' last night ter charge the mine wi' giant powder, wi' a lead-fuse up the gulch yonder. The business was ter be set off at fifteen minutes o' twelve to-day, an' blow Sandy hayr ter atoms. That's how the thing stands, pilgrims. I only hed about time ter get Sandy word a bit ago, on returnin' from a scout, then she went off!"

"Hurra! hip! hip!" yelled Colonel Joe Tubbs, enthusiastically, and his proposition was followed by a cheer from a portion of the crowd. "Ye're a clear quill angel, C'lamity, an' don't ye fergit et. Ef I war legally unhitched from my Angelina Aramintha Tubbs, dog my cats ef I wouldn't propose."

"Yer yarn is all very well, gal!" said the miner who had previously proposed an investigation; "but he ken't expect us ter take yer word for et wi'out proof. Yer character don't consist altergether o' truth and —"

His sentence was finished in a ringing shriek, for Calamity had drawn a revolver and shot him, even while his sarcastic words left his lips, and he fell to the ground, wounded through the breast.

"So much fer your lyin', you miserable whelp!" the girl cried, wrought suddenly to a high pitch of anger. "If I was dishonored once, by one such as you, no man's defiling touch has reached me since. That villain still lives who foully robbed Jane Forrest of her maiden name, but *never* of her honor; that same man has dared to come to this very town, and do menial work for the wretch who planned Sandy's destruction; but as there is a God to hear my oath, he shall never live to ruin any others. I have already set the day."

When she ceased speaking, there were several minutes of silence, not a word being uttered. The crowd had swollen greatly in numbers— Cecil Grosvenor came with it, but the moment he caught a glimpse of Sandy, he wheeled suddenly and retraced his steps toward the Mastodon, a fierce but smothered oath breaking from his lips.

"Then the game still lives, eh?" he gritted, a malignant expression on his face, as he hurried along, which caused more than one man to glance at him curiously the second time.

"Ten thousand devils take that Danite! He has either betrayed me, or else has worked so clumsily that our game was discovered and balked. The girl, Calamity Jane, is mixed up in the affair. Curse the luck, anyhow! What shall I do? Will it be dangerous for me to remain here? I will run the risk. If it comes to the worst I can buy my way out of town with *money* which these groveling idiots worship."

The silence after Calamity's oath was finally broken by the miner Gorgon, who had acted as spokesman for the people.

"You claim to know this man who plotted for Sandy's destruction— why don't ye give the name?" he said, eying the dare-devil sharply, as he lay upon the ground, unable to rise, because of his wounds.

"Certainly. The man's name is Honorable Cecil Grosvenor, from Washington; he who stops at the Mastodon. He is Sandy's enemy; come heer on purpose to murder him, an' also to kill the woman Sandy hes under his protection, whom ye hev known as Dusty Dick."

"Gentlemen, ye've all heerd the gal's word, an' I'll vouch fer ets truth; so cl'ar away, an' hev no more argyment!" cried the Regulator, Old Bullwhacker, riding into the crowd authoritatively. "What if Sandy did blow up his own mine, w'ich I'll allow he didn't; et's none o' yer bizness, as I ken see. Cl'ar away now, an' no more o' yer quarrelin' wi' a man as haint done ye no injury."

And as the much-clothed Regulator was pretty generally accepted as the law of the town since his arrival, there was a lively scattering of the crowd back to the heart of the street, or to such work as had been abandoned for the purpose of visiting the scene of the explosion.

Soon Sandy, Calamity, and the miners belonging to the Lightning Lode were the only ones left on the spot, and they endeavored to make a discovery of the damage done the interior of the mine. But they were disappointed in finding the entrance utterly choked up with huge rocks and bowlders, which had been dislodged by the explosion.

"Set the men to work, Bronson," Sandy said, "and get a passage cleared into the mine. You may find some valuable quartz rock dislodged by the explosion, and can mine it and send it to the crusher. I leave matters in your charge, to-day, as I have some business to attend to elsewhere."

Bronson bowed, and with the miners went off to attack their labor.

Sandy then turned to Calamity Jane with extended hand and glistening eyes.

"Calamity, my dear girl, how can I ever repay you for your heroic efforts in my behalf? But name the way, and gladly I will go to work to repay my debt."

"Don't talk o' pay, Sandy; you're friendliness toward me is sufficient remuneration for all that I have been able to do for you. There is only one thing—"

"Name it, Jennie, name it."

"It is this: if you ever kneel to pray to the All-wise Ruler above, just give me a favorable mention."

"Bless you, of course I will!" Sandy replied, as the eccentric girl strode away, and he took an opposite course in going toward his cabin. "I wonder if Dusty Dick has heard and become alarmed at the explosion?"

A few minutes later he approached his cabin, to behold Cecil Grosvenor standing at the door, pounding upon it with his heavy cane, and at the same time cursing Dusty Dick, who was inside.

"Let me in, woman, or durn my eyes I'll butcher you, directly!" Sandy heard the Washingtonian cry, fiercely; then the miner stole silently up, and a moment later the villainous speculator found himself lying sprawling in the middle of the street. When he discovered who had been his assailant, he hastily scrambled to his feet and made a move toward drawing a revolver, but the click! click! of Sandy's weapon caused him to desist.

"Put up your shooting-iron!" the miner said, grimly, "and get yourself out of town on the quick-step if you desire to save your hide. Remember, that I give you only this chance: the next time we meet, you'll get used rougher yet."

"Will I?" the Honorable Cecil exclaimed, in blind fury, as he limped away. "I'll have that woman in there, Sandy, if I have to buy the whole town to help me get her. I promise you that—I swear it!"

Calamity Jane after leaving Sandy, met Charley Davis further up the gulch, returning from a view of the town.

"Ah!" he exclaimed, shaking hands in delight, "I never was so glad to see you, Jennie. What was that bu'st-up a bit ago? It nearly jarred the senses out of me."

"Sandy's mine blew up," Calamity replied.

"Yes? By the way, Jennie, I saw this man, Sandy, this morning—he is one of the men I particularly wish to see. His name used to be Earl Beverly, out in Washington. My other victim, Honorable Cecil Grosvenor, I have not found yet—probably I shall have to hunt elsewhere for him."

"Cecil Grosvenor? Why he is here in Whoop-Up—the same man who tried to blow Sandy up, in the mine."

"Ha! then I'm in luck. I have both of the birds in one grasp!" the detective exclaimed, with a triumphant chuckle. "So Grosvenor is up to deviltry out here then? Well, I'll have to attend to his case directly. Good-day, Jennie, if you call that going," for the girl was hurrying away. "A strange creature, that—not much like the little Janie Forrest I knew years ago."

Chapter 15

A NEW ATTACK WITH DISCLOSURES

Sandy watched his enemy until he had disappeared around the bend; then turned and gave the signal and was admitted by Dusty Dick, whose face was very pale, and form trembling with excitement.

"The old villain frightened you, eh?" the handsome miner said, throwing down his mining implements in one corner, and sinking into a chair.

"Oh! yes!" Dick replied, with a shiver. "He used such terrible threats, that I could do no less than get scared. He is a very bold, wicked man, Sandy."

"Yes; I've recently had an illustration of that fact," Sandy replied, with a grim smile. "You heard the explosion? Well, the wretch hired some ruffians to blow up the mine, with me in it. We got out, however, by the warning of Calamity Jane, and balked the schemer. I'm going to have a settlement with him presently."

He meant it, too. He had come to the conclusion that discretion in this case was gradually ceasing to be the better part of valor. He foresaw that if he remained silent and let his enemy plot and scheme without question, he would be the loser in the end.

All the rest of the day he kept closely inside of his shanty, and was in a brown study.

Dusty Dick went carefully about the duties of the house, with womanly gentleness, using caution not to disturb the miner in his reflection.

Just at dark she discovered that a large crowd of miners and townspeople were gathering on the street, in front of the shanty, and in terror she aroused Sandy, to call his attention to the fact.

He glanced out of the window; then crossed the room to his ammunition corner, where he buckled on his belt of revolvers.

"I can't quite imagine what the fools mean, now!" he said, his face flushing angrily. "I suppose it's something more concerning the mine explosion. You remain in here out of sight, Dick; if you're wanted I will call, and you can come out. Don't be afraid, for they shall not hurt you while I live."

Then the miner opened the door, stepped outside upon the little threshold veranda, closing the door behind him quickly.

A series of screeches, groans and hisses greeted his appearance; it seemed to him that the whole town had turned out in one mass, for a sea of grim faces and forms filled the width of the street—faces that were of every type of expression.

Several men fronted the assemblage, on horseback, among whom were Cecil Grosvenor, Arkansas Alf, the Danite Ghoul, and the new Regulator chief, Old Bullwhacker.

As the miner came out, the Regulator motioned for the crowd to be silent, and when the desired silence was established, he rode a little nearer, and drew rein.

"I suppose you don't exactly understand the meaning of all this as-

semblage, eh?" he said, good-naturedly. "If not, I will explain. These
people have seen fit to put me ahead of 'em in thet matter, as a sort o'
police, tho' et's much ag'in' my grain. They've ordered me ter come
here and enforce the rights o' this man at my left, an' make yer give
up ther woman as ye've got inside. They've got sum leetle proofs ter
display, they say, an' ef et's all as they allow, I reckon we'll hev ter
take the gal, an' mebbe lock ye up fer trial on charge o' abductin' another man's wife."

"What's this you say?" Sandy cried, sternly—"*another man's wife?*
Whose wife have I been keeping, pray?"

"*My* wife!" Cecil Grosvenor cried, an expression of gloating triumph
upon his bloated face, which was purely devilish.

"My wife, Earl Beverly, *alias* Sandy Whatever-you-call-yourself.
The woman inside your cabin was legally married to me in the city of
Richmond, Virginia, less than seven months ago. For some unaccountable reason she fled from my board, and I have been searching for her
ever since, as last to find her living here with you. I have enlisted all
these people in my cause and I demand that you deliver up the
woman whom you have harbored and palmed off as a boy."

While the speculator was speaking, Sandy stood like one struck
dumb. It had never occurred to him that Dusty Dick had been married—he had believed her a maiden whom some villain was trying to
coerce or wrong in some way.

"Perhaps you have proofs of all that you say, Cecil Grosvenor," he
replied, calmly, as he surveyed with composure each face in the
crowd.

"I have proof enough in this!" the Washingtonian declared victo-
riously, as he waved a sheet of paper in the air. "Mr. Regulator,
please read it for the edification of the crowd and yonder gentleman
on the steps, if you will be so kind."

Old Bullwhacker received the paper, and glanced it over a moment
before speaking.

"It is a marriage certificate," he said, finally, "of the union of Cecil
Grosvenor, of Washington, to Miss Edna Sutton, of Richmond, Virginia, by the Reverend Jackson Dalley, in the presence of several wit-
nesses."

"Very well," Sandy replied—"that is your say. I'll now see what my
pard knows about it."

He turned to the door, opened it, and at a beckon Dusty Dick came
out on the veranda, trembling in spite of an effort to be brave.

"Dick," Sandy said, in a tone loud enough to be heard in any part
of the crowd, "Cecil Grosvenor claims that you are his wife, and
shows a certificate of his marriage with you. Tell us what about it."

"It is true, so far as the marriage is concerned!" Dick replied, speaking in a clear tone. "At the wish of a dying uncle and guardian I married that man, believing him to be a gentleman. I speedily found him out to be a brute. In my father's will which came to light six years ago, after his death, I was willed the whole of his fortune, with the proviso that it should be mine at the age of eighteen, and if I should then marry, my husband was to have control of my property. It was only at my dying guardian's advice that I married Cecil Grosvenor. He knew of the provisions in my father's will, and hoping to get entire possession of my fortune, attempted on several occasions to murder me. To save my life I fled and came West, preferring that he should have the money rather than my life. But he pursued me, and hoping to escape him, I donned this male attire and entered the mountains.

"This gentleman, whom you call Sandy, was the first to come upon and recognize me as a woman. In terror I begged him to keep my secret, and on learning that I was trying to escape an enemy, he promised—more, volunteered, out of pity for my plight, to make me his pard, trusting that he could do so without impairing his position as a man of honor, which he is. Fool that I was, I came here a lone, helpless woman, only to bring trouble upon my protector and sacred friend. I am *not* Cecil Grosvenor's legal wife, for since leaving him I have learned that he has a former wife living, from whom he never obtained a divorce!"

" 'Tis a lie—a base, malicious falsehood!" the Honorable Cecil cried, vehemently. "I never was married previous to my union with Edna Sutton, of Richmond."

"I can swear to the contrary!" cried a voice, and then the crowd separated, and a strange, deeply-vailed woman, clad in black, and well mounted upon a powerful steed, rode into the scene at a gallop.

"Cecil Grosvenor is a liar and a black-hearted bigamist. *I am Marie Grosvenor*, his only legally-wedded wife, and here, Mr. Regulator, is *my* marriage certificate," and she handed Old Bullwhacker a document.

"'Tis a black, infamous lie—an ungodly cheat!" cried Cecil Grosvenor, red with furious rage, while he attempted to draw a revolver; but a couple of Bullwhacker's men quickly stepped forward and relieved him of his weapon, and also served the Danite Ghoul in the same way.

"It is true!" replied Bullwhacker, quietly. "This document records the marriage of Cecil Grosvenor and Marie Lydia Galton, in Washington, several years ago. You will please raise your vail, ma'am."

The vail was raised—then all the crowd gave a murmur of surprise, for the woman on the horse was one they had seen repeatedly, and admired, too—the keeper of the dance-house of Whoop-Up, whose beauty stood unequaled—Madame Minnie Majilton.

"*You*, Marie!" Cecil Grosvenor gasped, in a hoarse tone. "By Heaven! I believe you are telling the truth! Why was it I failed to recognize you before? Your face seemed familiar; but your hair—"

"Has been cleverly bleached from its original color," Madame Minnie replied, with a low laugh. "Cecil Grosvenor, I'd advise you to go back to Washington, and not attempt any more nefarious games. Gentlemen, to give you an idea of the villain as he is, let me tell you that since coming here to Whoop-Up he *proposed* to me, his own wife, even while searching for yonder girl, whom it seems he has inveigled into a wholly illegal match. His brutality caused me to quit him years ago; no woman could live with such a beast as he is, for a beast he is in all his nature."

Then the beautiful blonde wheeled her horse and galloped away, leaving behind her an astonished audience.

"Gentlemen!" cried Old Bullwhacker, mounting the steps alongside Sandy and Edna, "ye've all heard about ther matter. I calkylate et's been made clear enough that Sandy heer has as much right ter purtect the gal as you or I, ain't et? Them as thinks my way will make et manifest by sayin' *I!* Contrary, *no!*"

There was a tremendous yell of "I," without a single dissenting voice, and then the crowd dispersed, leaving only Cecil Grosvenor and Calamity Jane behind.

"Look out for me, Earl Beverly!" the Washingtonian cried, as he shook one clinched fist toward the shanty—"look out for me, for this matter has not yet reached its climax. *You*, a forger and a murderer, shall pay the penalty ere I leave the Hills. Both of you shall die, as my daughter Elise died!"

Then he strode away, with oaths upon his burning lips.

"All that is evil is in that man," Sandy mused, as he watched the retreating form. "Hello! is that you, Calamity?" as the girl came up. "What is it?"

"I wished to speak with you a moment, for I think that you are in greater peril than before. You see the man standing over there on the bank of the creek? Well, he is the Charley Davis, of whom I spoke. He has come here to Whoop-Up on an important mission, and, moreover, he knows you, as Earl Beverly. Sandy, were you ever guilty of any criminal act in the East?"

The miner's face became tinged with a grayish pallor, and his eyes looked wild at the question.

"Crime!" he gasped, a sudden tremor passing over his frame—"guilty? My God, I had hoped never to be asked that question again. Yes—

in the eyes of the law I am a criminal—a forger, and an accused murderer. You heard Cecil Grosvenor throw it up in my face; it is the only weapon he has to brand me with. If he were in the States, where law reigns supreme, he would have me more in his power. Of the murder part I am innocent—the other; but, bah! why tell you? I know what you would say, Calamity Jane—that man, Davis, is a detective, and has come to arrest me!"

"Alas! Sandy, I have every reason to believe so, for he knows you, and has come here to find two men—you and Cecil Grosvenor!"

"Then, go tell him to come here and do his duty. If he wants me, I shall not refuse to go, for after fleeing from the States once to evade arrest, I am not eager to become a fugitive again. I may as well submit, and stand my trial now as in the hereafter; I shall have to have it, some time."

"But not now!" Calamity said, solemnly. "Listen to, and obey me, and you will afterwards thank me for my counsel. That man was once my lover, and is still, for that matter, and I can influence him. I will get him out of the way; then you are to get a couple of mules and two saddle-horses, pack up your worldly effects, and slide out of town with Edna during the night. It is your best move, for the present. Before you come back—but never mind. Just out of town you will meet an Indian boy, who will take you to a deserted cabin in Picayune Gulch, where you are to remain until I come. Promise me you will do this."

"I promise. You are a genius, Calamity, and I will trust you."

"Very well. Get ready and go at once. It won't be long ere I shall be with you."

Then, with a hand-shake, the eccentric girl was off down the street, whistling gayly a mountain melody.

With a cloudy brow, Sandy watched her until she had disappeared in the gloom; then turned and rejoined Dusty Dick in the shanty.

"Dick!" the miner said huskily, "are you going to live this life further with me—me, a felon? Had you not better take the next stage for other parts, instead of thinking of going with me?"

"No! a thousand times no! You befriended me once, and do you think I would desert you in your dark hour? No, indeed! That would not be womanly. I will go with you wherever you go, until you are freed from Cecil Grosvenor's scheming; then—"

She did not finish the sentence, but went on packing up. With the cloud still on his brow, Sandy assisted.

The property to be moved did not amount to much of a load when it was all gathered. Sandy owned several horses and mules, and he soon had a couple of saddle-horses and pack-animals at the door.

The Danite Ghoul in passing took notice of the fact, and hunted

Cecil Grosvenor up, in a saloon, where he had taken lodgings, after being promptly kicked out of the Mastodon by Colonel Joe Tubbs, immediately after the mine explosion.

"Sandy an' the gal's pullin' out o' town," the Danite said. "Shall I foller 'em?"

"Yes, do so by all means!" Grosvenor replied, fiercely. "They think to escape me, but will find their mistake. Find out where they go, and then report to me. Here are fifty dollars; see that you serve me well."

Arkansas Alf bowed civilly, and, after drinking at the bar, hurried out into the night, and hired himself a horse, preparatory to following the fugitives.

Chapter 16

DEVELOPMENTS EXTRAORDINARY— CONCLUSION

After everything was in readiness, Sandy and Dusty Dick mounted their horses, and leading the pack-mules behind, stole quietly out of town, taking the northern course of the gulch. Fortunately, there were few men on the street along the route, since all the saloons and gaming-hells and dance-houses were located further south, and the fugitives got safely beyond where civilization had pitched its canvas in the gulch.

Here they were met by an Indian lad, as Calamity had prophesied, who offered to conduct them to the deserted cabin in Picayune Gulch, an abandoned claim on the trail to Deadwood.

So they followed his lead, and by early day-dawn were established in an old, tumbledown mass of logs in a dismal ravine between the mountains.

The mules were unpacked and turned out to graze, and things were arranged about the cabin as comfortably as possible, the Indian lad assisting to bring wood and build a fire upon the broad hearth. He also fetched in a haunch of mountain deer, which he had killed, and helped Edna—still personating Dusty Dick—to prepare a savory meal.

"This seems like being banished to some isolated portion of the earth," Sandy said.

He was sitting in the doorway, gazing around discontentedly upon the impressive wilderness spread out before him.

"I haven't the least idea I shall stay here long, unless civilization follows me here."

"You won't go back to Whoop-Up?" Edna interrogated, pausing in her work of roasting the meat.

"Probably. If Calamity compromises with, or sends that detective off the track, I shall go back and attend to my interests for a while. First, however, I shall take unto me a wife."

"You speak with a great deal of assurance, sir."

"And *know* whereof I speak," Sandy replied, with a triumphant smile.

The breakfast was prepared and dispatched; then leaving the Indian boy at the cabin, Sandy called to Buffalo, shouldered his rifle, and started off in search of game. This time he kept his eye out in search of bears, lest he should have another unwelcome adventure with one of the fierce tribe. About noon he returned to the cabin with a fine brace of game. He found his pard alone, and in great agitation.

"The enemy!" she gasped, in answer to Sandy's interrogative look. "They are coming to attack us!"

"Eh? They are? How do you know?"

"The Indian boy has discovered them entering the gulch, and has gone to watch them. Ah! here he comes now," as the young redskin came trotting leisurely up the bluff on which the cabin stood.

"Well, what is this about intruders, boy?" the miner demanded; "where are they?"

"There!" the youth replied, pointing down the gulch to where several horsemen were rounding a bend. As they were still at too great a distance to be recognized by the naked eye. Sandy procured a field-glass from among his effects, and leveled it at them inquiringly.

"Ha!" he muttered, with a visible start; "What can this mean? Can it be possible that we have been betrayed and decoyed off to this place for foul purposes?"

"Why? what is it?—who are they?" Dusty Dick demanded anxiously.

"Who?" the miner gritted, with flashing eyes—"who, indeed, but those I have counted friends, now in company with my enemy. It is our combined enemy, Cecil Grosvenor, accompanied by Calamity Jane, the detective, Davis, and Old Bullwhacker with four of his Regulators."

"Do you think they are coming for you?" Dick asked, her voice trembling, and one hand clutching the miner's arm convulsively. "Oh! Sandy, what if they should be coming to murder us—or part us!"

"Don't worry, little one; we'll wait and see. If I find out that there's any treachery afoot, I'll blow the brains out of Cecil Grosvenor and Calamity Jane, and then fight the others. I can't quite make it seem, though, that the girl is so false and treacherous as would seem by a glance at yonder crowd."

With anxiously-beating hearts the trio at the cabin waited outside the cabin door, each armed with a rifle—for the Indian youth had taken a decided liking to Sandy, and signified his willingness to fight, should it be necessary.

Nearer and nearer the cavalcade came, and at last Calamity Jane held up a white rag on the muzzle of her gun, as a flag of truce, and Sandy, half doubtful what to do, waved his hat, for them to approach.

"We'll give 'em a show anyhow!" he muttered. "Watch 'em sharp, and if you see a treacherous move, let 'em have the contents of your revolvers, for they shan't take us without a struggle!"

Nearer and nearer the cavalcade approached, and finally halted upon the plot in front of the cabin, and at a word from Calamity Jane dismounted.

Sandy and his two companions had retreated a few paces, and put their backs against the cabin wall—each held a pair of cocked revolvers, leveled upon the new-comers, ready for instant emergency.

After dismounting, Cecil Grosvenor turned toward his foe, with a bland smile of triumph.

"You may as well put up your weapons, Sandy!" he declared, "For you see that we are over two to your one. You also see that I came prepared to take you and hang you up and I'm going to do it. Money is the root of all evil, and with some of the root I bought over these present to assist me in putting an end to you. So, you may as well surrender, instead of putting us to the touble of shooting you down where you stand!"

"No!" Sandy thundered; "I will *never* surrender, and he is a dead man who tries to take me! Calamity Jane, what am I to understand—have you joined with this villain and betrayed us?"

"Waal, et ruther luks that way, don't et?" the dare-devil replied, with a grim smile; "but, ye see, such ain't the case. When Calamity Jane goes back on a pard, ye can calkylate on ther world's comin' ter an end. Mr. Davis, you'll be kind enough to do yer duty, an' put Sandy's doubts at rest."

"Very well. My duty, ladies and gentlemen, lies in arresting this man, Cecil Grosvenor, of Washington, for bank robbery in said city, May last. Regulators, seize him."

With alacrity the men obeyed, and even before the villainous speculator could gasp out his surprise he was handcuffed securely.

"Curses and furies! what means this outrageous insult to a law-abiding citizen?" he roared, livid with rage. "Release me!"

"Sorry for you, Mr. Grosvenor, but that ain't in the line of my duty!" Davis replied, with a smile. "I've been laying for you ever since you left Washington, and when we all accepted of your offer of money this morning, the matter was arranged between myself and these gentlemen and Calamity. You are my prisoner, and must go back to Washington and stand your trial as a defaulter and robber."

"And, I dare say, you calculate to take me along at the same time, eh?" Sandy said, with sarcasm.

"On the contrary, no, Mr. Beverly. It is a part of my business here, to implicate Cecil Grosvenor, and *free* you from guilt. If you will listen, I will relate you a little story:

"Several years ago—it does not matter about dates—you were a clerk in a banking-office, of which Cecil Grosvenor was the president. You had a small fortune of your own, and knowing this, this man, Grosvenor, made friends with you—invited you to his grand home, which was graced by a beautiful and aristocratic daughter. Here you were tempted by as fair and scheming a siren as ever reigned in the Capital, and led into dissipation. Once started you had no control over yourself, and soon lost your position and sunk deeper and deeper into the sloughs of drunkenness. Nor did you stop until you were suddenly awakened to the fact that you had squandered all your own available cash, and forged your employer's name to the tune of five thousand dollars.

"Elise Grosvenor hurled this gross charge in your face one day while you were riding along a steep highway on the shore of the Potomac.

"At the time you were, as usual, full of liquor, and the taunt maddened you. In an excess of rage, you drew a pistol and fired at her, and just at this moment, Cecil Grosvenor came riding after you in hot pursuit. You saw him—saw the frightened steed of Elise Grosvenor plunge over the dizzy height with its rider; then you put spurs to your horse, and escaped. You were never afterward seen in the East. Is this not true?"

"All true!" Sandy replied, his head bowed and face pale.

"Well, it chanced that at this time an old uncle had died, and deposited with Cecil Grosvenor, for you, a fortune of some fifteen thousand dollars. Of this you never knew, and, as the world was as ignorant as you, it all went in to increase the Grosvenor millions. Since then, Cecil Grosvenor has made and lost money—is now worth millions, but it is all in under his brother's name. His latest crime has been to leave Washington, after robbing several banks of large sums, he having official connection with such banks."

"Exactly!" Cecil Grosvenor said, triumphantly; "but, even allowing that all you have said be true, you have not yet cleared Earl Beverly of murder and forgery."

"We will get to that presently," Davis said, with a smile. "Little less than six months ago, while searching for you, I assisted in a raid on a faro-bank and dance-house in Kansas City. Among the creatures there we found one at the point of death, and, from her lips, I copied down her dying confession. She was *Elise Grosvenor*, once the Washington belle. She had not been killed on that day when her horse leaped into the Potomac, as supposed, but had been rescued, and, with her own consent, was carried in a yacht to New Orleans, to pursue a career which ended in death in a gambling den. In her confession, Earl Beverly, she declared you to be innocent of the crime of forgery. One night, when you were stupefied by drink, she and an accomplice had forged the checks, and given them to you to get cashed, which you did, without knowing of her sin. So, I have referred the confession to the Washington authorities, and to-day, Earl Beverly, you stand before the world an innocent man!"

"Thank God!" was all that Sandy could find voice to utter; then he staggered and fell in a swoon, strong, self-controlled man though he was. The news of his innocence was too much for him to bear.

Carefully he was raised and borne into the cabin, by Davis, the detective, and Old Bullwhacker, and anxious hands worked swiftly over him until he was restored to consciousness. He awoke from his insensibility with a start; then when he comprehended all, he bowed his head in silent prayer. He had scarcely finished, when there was a rifle-shot, and Cecil Grosvenor, who had been left outside in charge of a Regulator, was seen to throw up his arms and fall to the ground. Before those inside the cabin could reach him, his last spark of life had gone out—he had played his last game-card, and died. A bullet from some unseen avenger had done the deadly work!

At Sandy's request, a hasty search was made, but no one could be found in the vicinity on whom to lay the charge of the assassination.

"In my opinion, the blow has been dealt by that woman, Madame Majilton, who claimed to be his wife!" said Charley Davis. "Leaving you here, I will hasten to Whoop-Up, and learn if she has been seen to leave the town."

And hastily mounting his horse, the detective took his departure.

The body of Cecil Grosvenor was lifted and borne into the cabin.

The clothing was carefully searched by Calamity and Sandy, and as a result some six thousand dollars were found, in bank-notes, sewed in the lining of the coat.

This money was retained by Bullwhacker, to give over to the detective. At sunset that night, all that was of the flesh of the murdered villain, was consigned to the grave, after being placed in a rude coffin which the Regulators had fashioned out of some timbers.

Shortly after, Detective Davis returned from Whoop-Up, accompanied by a delegation of citizens who came in behalf of the townspeople, with the request that Sandy should return to Whoop-Up.

This the miner consented to do, after a time, during which he proposed to make the cabin his home.

So all returned to the town, except five, these being Sandy, Detective Davis, Calamity, Dusty Dick, and the Regulator chief, Old Bullwhacker. They remained at the cabin.

Several days were spent pleasantly in the wilderness; then, one night, a reverend gentleman came over from Deadwood, and there was a wedding in the little cabin, and Sandy, or Earl Beverly, and his pard, Dusty Dick—whose real name was Edna Sutton—were made man and wife.

There was a general handshaking, and Sandy pressed the hand of the Regulator, Old Bullwhacker so hard, that to the surprise of all, a false beard dropped from his face, and there stood revealed, *the ex-road-agent, Deadwood Dick!*

There was no use now of trying to play his part any longer, and so the young man removed all of his disguise. He stated that he had assumed it, in order to better fight against the sway of despotism, which had followed the desertion of *his* Regulators, and now that the trouble had in a measure subsided, he had intended to resign and return to his home in the hills.

A couple of days after the wedding at Sandy's cabin, all hands returned to Whoop-Up, except the bride and groom and Deadwood Dick. The latter, after a kindly parting with all who had been his friends, set out to join his wife, Leone, who, after the sudden disbanding of Deadwood Dick's Eagles, had gone to Haywood City to live.

Sandy and Dusty Dick (as they are still universally known in their home in the mines), went first to Deadwood, and then on a sight-seeing tour through the Hills, after which they returned to Whoop-Up, and were received with a rousing ovation by the crowd.

They are now living there in Whoop-Up's flash city, surrounded by hosts of ardent friends—who some day will have Sandy to represent them in the great Capitol at Washington—returning in honor to the city he had quitted in dishonor.

The murder of Cecil Grosvenor could not be traced to any authentic source, but Madame Minnie was suspected, and shortly after left the mines.

Davis still lingers around in the mines, and it's the gossip that he and Calamity will soon start East on a bridal tour. As to the truth of this, I cannot say; I doubt much if Calamity will ever marry, especially since Sandy is gone. She has been cheated out of her vengeance upon the Danite, Arkansas Alf, for the Vigilantes of Deadwood recently strung him up for road-agentry.

Joe Tubbs is still the proprietor of the Mastodon in Whoop-Up, and each day seems to add a brighter tinge to his nose; "yet, it's a scandulous fac' that he don't imbibe but twenty times in a whole blessed day."

Whoop-Up's chief Regulator suddenly disappeared, never to return as Old Bullwhacker; but occasionally there is some new and odd character created in the mines, under which Deadwood Dick generally manages to keep On Deck.